Praise for Alexa Riley

"Alexa Riley delivers their signature steamy, alpha feel-good romance with addictive helpings of secrets, suspense, and revenge!"
—*The Rock Stars of Romance* on *Everything for Her*

"Alexa Riley delivers big time in this first full length scorching romance! Addicting, fun, over the top, and utterly delectable, *Everything for Her* is a guaranteed delight from start to stop. I couldn't put it down!"
—Angie, *Angie and Jessica's Dreamy Reads*

"Alexa Riley has _____ more. Sizzling passion _____ safe love story that _____ the end."
—Nicho _____ for Her

"Just when you _____ get any better with their over the top romance, they go on and deliver a sizzling romance in their debut full-length novel, *Everything for Her*. Charismatic characters, palpable chemistry, blazing hot sex scenes, and raw emotions make this book an easy one to devour. Alexa Riley packs a one-two punch of entertainment that will have readers begging for their next Alexa Riley fix."
—Michelle, *Four Chicks Flipping Pages*

"Alexa Riley sucks you in like a vortex and grips your heart from the start like only she can do. No one else can give you an insta-love and make it 100% believable. Be prepared to go on a journey of love, uncertainty, devotion, and passion. This is the sexiest book I've read all year. You will be on the edge of your seat trying to figure out what will happen next. Prepare for your heart to pound rapidly in your chest and for Miles and Mallory to steal your soul."
—Tina, *Bookalicious Babes Blog* on *Everything for Her*

ALEXA RILEY

His ALONE

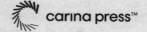

carina press™

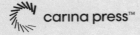 carina press™

Recycling programs for this product may not exist in your area.

ISBN-13: 978-0-373-00453-9

His Alone

Copyright © 2017 by Author Alexa Riley LLC

Photo by: Sara Eirew Photography

www.CarinaPress.com

Printed in U.S.A.

To strong women...
Dare a man to love you exactly as you are.

His
ALONE

**Also Available from Alexa Riley
and Carina Press**

Everything for Her

To learn more about Alexa's upcoming releases,
visit her website, AlexaRiley.com.

PROLOGUE

Ryan

Six years ago...

I SIT IN the metal chair feeling uncomfortable. I do better on my feet. I wish I could at least have my back to a wall, but this isn't my place, so I do as I'm told. I sit calmly and keep my breathing even, glancing around the room casually, making sure I show nothing. I have one goal here today and it's to get as close as possible to the man I'm about to meet. Going deeper underground than I ever have before— something I'm not sure I want. This might take me further down than I'm prepared to go.

We're in a back room of a restaurant in uptown Manhattan, and it's clearly used for privacy. There are two men at the far wall, standing next to an exit, and two men behind me guarding the way I came in. They both look like muscle; they'd be easy to handle. Too dumb to see what's coming. Directly in front of me is a small metal table and chair. I hear a click behind me. The door opens, and someone walks through. I wish for the hundredth time that I had my gun on me. I feel naked without it. I know I can defend myself without it, but I like feeling the weight of it against me. And often, someone seeing the hint of it can de-escalate a situation. But they took it from me when I walked through the door, so now I have to deal with it.

The man who walked in takes a seat at the table and leans forward. He's in an expensive suit that looks custom-made. The men around him are dressed similarly, myself included. When you're in this line of work, looks are everything. Even more so for a man like this. Money means everything to him. Money and power.

He sets a large manila envelope on the table between us and places his hand on top of it. He holds it there as he looks at me, his sapphire-blue eyes boring into mine as if trying to read me. *Good luck, asshole.*

"I've been told good things about you, Ryan. That you're one to keep cool and one we can trust. Is that true?"

"Yes, sir."

The first rule in business is keeping your mouth shut. The second rule is when you talk, say as little as possible. I've mastered both of these, and it's the reason I'm here today.

"You've worked for me for some time now, and I'd like to give you something of a—" He stops as if to consider what word to use. His smile is wide as he lands on it. "Promotion."

I sit and wait, breathing evenly and staying calm. It's what I do best. I'm rewarded when he takes his hand off the envelope and pushes it toward me, then leans back in his chair, watching my movements. I don't flinch, just wait for instructions like a loyal dog.

"I need information, and I need you to get it for me. You're a face that's not known around here, not associated with me directly. According to what I've been able to dig up, you were born in Ukraine and brought to America as a baby. You were raised in Chicago but ended up in New York a few years ago and made your way into my employment. Is that close enough?"

"Yes, sir." Rule number three, always speak with respect. It's close, but not all of it. Just the parts I want him to know. The most important thing to remember about lying is to keep your lies as close to the truth as possible, only blurring some things. That way, you never forget.

He looks me over again, eyes assessing and reassessing. I relax and wait like he wants me to. Just like I know I need to in order to get on his good side. As if getting what he wants, he nods down to the envelope, and I finally reach out, taking it. I hold it in my hands but don't make a move to open it. I know him. He wants people to follow his every word, and if he wants me to open it, he'll tell me.

"Once this meeting is over, we won't meet face-to-face again. You'll have my direct number and communicate with me weekly, giving me any information you can. All that you need to know is in there."

He stands, buttoning his suit jacket, and I stand with him, holding the envelope. He stretches out his hand, and as much as I don't want to take it, I remember rule number three. When he grips my palm, he pulls me forward a slight inch, but it's a power play. He wants to be the one in control, and though I'm much larger than him and far more skilled at killing a man, I allow him this move. Men like him need to keep the ego. It's all they have.

"I think you're going to be exactly right for this job, Ryan. You look like a Boy Scout."

His evil grin makes my stomach clench as he releases my hand. He walks out of the room, and three of the bodyguards follow him. The fourth stops and hands me my gun, and I tuck it back into my holster as I watch him leave. Once I'm alone, I clutch the envelope and walk out the back exit. I walk two blocks up to a park and look for an empty bench. When I sit down, I open the envelope and flip through the contents.

The first few pages are exactly what I expected. There are instructions to get as much information as possible on one particular person. There are pictures of locations, property, known assets and people of interest. I know who this is. It's his estranged son, Miles Osbourne. Everyone knows of the rift. But no one knows why. It was so bad Miles even changed his name back to his mother's maiden name, Osbourne. That had to really piss off a man like Alexander Owens. I'm guessing the rift is because Miles knows all about his dear old dad and wants nothing to do with him, but it doesn't look like Alexander feels the same. He wants Miles as close as possible, and he's going to use me to get that.

The last piece of paper contains one sentence. The

words make a chill run down my spine, and I stare at them for a long moment. There's an accompanying photo stapled to the page.

If she shows up, you alert me immediately.

The police suspect Alexander has had a hand in the deaths of three women, and I wonder if this one is another of his mistresses. Flipping the note over, I see the picture and my chest tightens as my breath catches. I reach out, touching the photo with the tip of my index finger. It's a little blurry and taken from the side, but there's no mistaking the beauty of the red-head in the photograph. Something about her touches a place inside me, and all my plans change. My blood pumps through my veins and I can feel my adrena-line rising. I will do what I need to do to make this plan work, but there's no way I'm handing this girl over to him. I look at the picture and I see it. This isn't a mistress. The same blue eyes I was staring at across the table look at me from the photo. I pull out the photo of Miles. There it is. She's his daughter, and I'm guessing she has all kinds of little secrets on her father. Ones he doesn't want anyone to know.

I've been hired by Alexander Owens to get close to his son, and that's what I'll do. I'll be best fuck-ing friends with Miles Osbourne before the week is over, but I won't ever harm the redhead.

Ever.

I need her.

PREFACE

Ryan

SHE THINKS I'M PERFECT. She thinks I look like Captain America. That I play by the rules. But she has no idea who I truly am. Or why I'm really here.

She thinks Miles was obsessed.

She has no idea what obsession is. What a man like me will do to get what he wants.

I'm dirtier than she knows. She thinks I'm good to the core, but she doesn't know the things I've done. The things I would do for her.

Only her.

ONE

Paige

I DIDN'T KNOW you could actually feel someone's eyes on you. I don't mean that creeping feeling when you think someone is staring at you and all the hairs on the back of your neck stand up. No, this is different. I can feel his eyes on every part of my skin. They make my body warm, in places I didn't even know existed. A part of me I'd buried long ago. Other girls probably feel this all the time, but not me. It's like he has intimate knowledge of my body, and somehow it belongs to him. His eyes, roaming my body, fascinate me. I remember every detail about them, and it's both a blessing and a curse.

When I look at him, I never know what eyes I'll receive. Sometimes they're bright green like a fresh shamrock. Other times, when the light hits just right, little blue specks shine through, making them appear almost cerulean. But my favorite is when they turn a dark green. They're the color of a morning forest, soft and crisp, and I know he's playing it cool. I often wonder if I'm the only one who can see the difference. He's always so calm and cool, but his eyes probably show me more than he wants. Or maybe I'm the one doing a little too much staring. It makes me wonder if there's more to this man who always seems so perfect. He's too good and clean. If he knew everything about me, I probably wouldn't get those eyes on me like I do now. The ones I secretly love.

At first I thought Ryan Justice didn't like me, but over the years I've noticed it isn't dislike, no matter how hard I try to annoy him. The annoyance I once read in his eyes has turned out to be hunger. The more I poke at him and push him away, the more that hunger grows. Or maybe that's my own I'm feeling. I should stay as far away from him as possible, because he could break me. I've already had one man almost shatter me, and I don't think I could survive another, no matter how bad I want it.

I turn my head and look across the crowded ballroom to find him leaning up against the wall with his eyes on me. Just like I knew they would be. Like they always are. He looks casual in his suit as he tries to appear nonthreatening, which is impossible when you're built like him. His size is intimidating, and even more so when he's got well over a foot and a half on you, like he does me. I know he hates the suits, because when we're at work he always ditches the jacket and rolls up his sleeves, revealing the tattoos that coat his thick arms. It's the one thing that always seemed off about him. The tattoos never matched the good ol' boy attitude.

It's as if everyone in the room knows not to block his line of sight on me, because even in this crowded room no one has stepped in his way. If I want out of

his view, I'll have to leave and find somewhere else
to stand. That's where the real inner battle begins. To
move or not to move. As much as I hate the staring, I
want it. I've been pushing for it, no matter how much I
try to lie to myself that I haven't. I've come to crave it.

This dress is exhibit A of that fact. I picked it out
with him in mind. I asked myself what would Ryan—
or Captain America, as Mallory and I call him—think
of this dress. Would it piss him off like it does when
I wear a sports bra and skintight shorts to our training exercises? At first I didn't do it on purpose, but
when I saw it bothered him, I did it more.

It's a head game I'm playing. No matter how much
I tell myself Captain isn't for me, I can't stop trying
to get his attention. I guess it's more like provoking
him, because his attention is always on me. I like it
when I get the rise, even though I push him away
when he gets too close. God, what is wrong with
me? I've become one of those girls who play games.
That isn't me, but I find I'm not always me when it
comes to him. I'm different. Or maybe it's not *different*, exactly. He draws out a part of me that I don't
want coming out.

I pull my eyes away from him and turn, giving him
a side view. The black strapless dress reaches all the
way to the floor, fitting snugly against me. It looks
conservative...until I move. There's a slit that runs
up one side, all the way from the floor to the top of
my hip. It bares my leg, my thigh, my hip, making it
impossible to wear underwear. Top that off with the
killer heels I have on and for once I feel tall. My legs

seem longer with the tall heels and cut of the dress. I
feel sexy, which is something I'm not used to. However, over the past few weeks I've found myself wanting to be more than just plain Paige.

I move through the room, cataloging everything,
even though we aren't officially on the clock tonight.
We're here only as light security, but the need to know
my surroundings is always there. Tonight, as always,
Captain and I are to protect my boss and half brother,
Miles Osbourne, and his girlfriend, Mallory. Mallory is my best friend, so I've always got her back,
and tonight is no different. We're meant to blend in,
but if something catches our eye, we're to point it
out to the security on call. The charity event is auc-
tioning off millions of dollars in different pieces, so
there's plenty of staff to handle this. Miles just likes
to take extra precautions. There are art pieces, jewelry
and God knows what else here that cost more than
one person makes in a lifetime. So you can't blame
the heightened awareness that's buzzing through the
room.

Moving through the crowd, I try to see if I can
lose Captain in the shuffle. I can feel him following
me, and I want to shake him. Nothing is happening at
the event and I'm getting bored as each second ticks
by. The space is locked up tight, and no one looks
out of place. I don't foresee anything happening and
I might as well have a little fun. I turn, trying to see
how close he is, but I've lost him in the crowd. He's
normally easy to spot, towering over everyone in the
room, but now he's the one hiding.

It's one thing I've learned about Captain over the past few weeks—he moves like a fucking cat. I didn't know it was possible for someone as big as he is to be able to move without making a sound. It's unnatural and sexy as hell. We both work security at Osbourne Corporation, and technically he's my boss, has been for years, but most of everything we've done together has been on calls or emails. Now I'm here working face-to-face with him every day. So all this is a very bad idea, yet I can't help pushing for it. Just a little more every day. We work so close together, and it would be awkward if something happened, but that still isn't enough to shake some sense into me, to stop this game I keep playing with us. Though I'm starting to question if I'm really leading the game at all.

Looking around the room, I still don't see him, and I wonder with a pang in my heart if he's left. He wouldn't leave the event and go home without checking in, but I didn't think he'd let me slip away from him so easily. Maybe all my pushing is working, and I get angry with myself.

Suddenly he's on me. His big hands cup my biceps as he pulls me down a hallway. He presses me up against the wall, and his palms come down on either side of my face, caging me in, his giant body in front of me as he leans in and stares. His dark green eyes take the breath right out of my lungs.

"What are you doing?" I manage to whisper.

I look up at him. Even though I'm in these ridiculous heels, he still towers over me. His face is set and completely unreadable, but there isn't a speck of blue in his eyes right now. Nothing but the dark green, and my stomach tightens as all his intensity is fixed on me. It's intoxicating to have someone so focused on you. No one has ever cared to watch me like he does.

Except I know why he's pissed. I might have poked a little too hard before we came here tonight. I let something, a lie, take hold and didn't try to stop it. We were both on Miles's and Mallory's details today, but I'd sneaked out and gotten Mallory a pregnancy test. Of course Captain caught me, because he catches everything. He never misses a beat and I wonder if he has a photographic memory like I do.

When he'd seen what I'd purchased, his whole body locked up. He assumed it was for me, and I didn't correct him. I let him believe I was the one who needed the pregnancy test. I did it to piss him off. It was the one and only time I'd gotten a real reaction out of him—something that wasn't a mannerly gesture. I'm sure his mom taught him to be polite when he was growing up, in a perfect house with his parents and three point two kids and a dog named Spike that stayed inside his white picket fence. I should have said something, but instead I let him believe that I was fucking someone and may or may not have gotten pregnant. Seeing the emotion all over his face should have been worth it, but a knot in the pit of my stomach told me maybe I'd taken it too far.

He pulls one of his hands from the wall, dropping it to my hip. I should push it away, but instead I stand there frozen, waiting to see what happens. His big palm rests on my hip, and he wraps his fingers around me. He's touched me before, but not like this. At work when he touches me, it's with a little too much ease. He started out only brushing past me, but then it progressed to tucking my hair behind my ear. No one touches me, except for Mallory from time to time. But the more time Ryan and I spend together, the more he does it. Like he's been doing it forever. Like we're lovers. As if it's his right to do so.

Normally I push him away or brush off his touch, and I hate when I do it. This time, though, I can't seem to find the will. I want his affection. I'm needy for it. I've been so starved for it lately. I need this moment. I need this one time, and then I'll be okay. I'll snatch it up and replay it over and over in my head when I need another taste of him. It has to be enough.

I'm going to blame it on my best friend falling in love with a man who looks at her as if she hangs the moon. Watching them together has been bittersweet. I love that she found it, but I know I'm losing her a little. Seeing her this happy makes me crave something I didn't want to crave. Love isn't in the cards for me. Even if deep down I know it's the one thing I want most. I have other plans in life, and falling in love isn't part of that. I've got a score to settle—avenging the one person who ever loved me. My mother. Well, loved me as much as she could.

Ryan moves his hand from my hip to my stomach and stops there. His eyes search my face, and I don't know what he's looking for. Maybe he's waiting for me to push him away, but I can't seem to breathe right as I wait for him to speak. I know he wants me, but

I've been such a brat, and I tricked him into thinking I was pregnant to make him mad. It's ridiculous because it's physically impossible for me to be pregnant; unless by immaculate conception. Maybe I thought it would make him back off, and that all the things he makes me feel would go away. If he wasn't watching me or touching me, then my feelings would stop. But now he's more in my space than he's ever been.

"You shouldn't be on fieldwork. It isn't safe." His deep voice rumbles from his chest and washes over me. I narrow my eyes on him, loving his concern but hating that he thinks he can tell me what to do. Before I can snap at him, he cuts me off. "I don't know who he is." Captain leans down a little more. His words are hard and filled with something I can't make out, an edge I've never heard from him before. "But apparently he's nobody important, because I haven't seen a man sniffing around you."

I want to tell him he has no idea what I do, but that would be a lie. I live in the same building as my brother, and it's one Captain monitors the security on. Along with us working security in the same building together, he pretty much knows every one of my moves.

"This baby is mine now. I'll take care of you."

His words hit me hard, shocking me. He did not say what I think he did. He wants to be the father of my baby? A baby that isn't his? He wants to step up and offer to care for me and my unborn child. Never mind that there is no baby, it's the fact that he wants to do this in spite of my pushing. In spite of all that I've done to hurt him, trying to keep him at a distance, he still won't give up. It's a reminder of how perfect he is. Too perfect for me. He always wants to do the right thing. I seem to always want to do the wrong thing.

Suddenly our mouths are on each other. Our lips connect and there's no softness to the kiss. It's fueled by everything I've been bottling up for him since the moment we met. The need and want I've been hiding, and all the fear of what could happen, is released in this kiss. The desire I've been hiding bleeds out as I cling to him, wrapping myself around his giant body. He easily picks me up, and my back once again presses against the wall. I want to close all the space I've been putting between us.

His mouth moves against mine, his tongue pushing its way into my mouth. He takes over the kiss, dominating it, and I let go. I allow myself to enjoy the closeness of him and soak it all up. I want every last drop I can get out of this.

He growls into my mouth, and I find myself moaning in response. I move against him as my dress slips to the side and I'm bare against his suit. He's moved one of his hands under me and he's holding my bare ass, his fingers digging into my flesh in a possessive, unbreakable hold. Something about the way he has me pinned to him so tightly is making me come undone.

Then he's gone.

I'm on my feet and he's turned around, his back to me. I'm in a daze, and it takes me a moment to realize he's talking to someone. Another man in a suit is telling him something, but I was too far gone to realize it. I'm lost in the moment we just had, stunned at how quickly all that perfection was ripped away. In the blink of an eye, everything can be gone. I've learned that lesson before, and it's not a pain I want to relive. It's not where my head should be, and I take a step to the side to steady myself. Captain turns and reaches for me, but I back up another step. Then another.

His eyes narrow on me as the guy continues to talk to him, and I hold up my hands in defense. I can tell he's going to make a grab for me, whether the guy is talking to him or not. I'd probably melt against him if he touched me, and I can't do that.

"Paige." He says my name in warning, but I shake my head. His hand clenches into a fist, but I don't give in. I need space, so I turn and I take off across the ballroom.

TWO

Ryan

I CATCH SIGHT of Miles as I watch Paige and Mallory enter a room next to the women's restroom. He looks me over and raises an eyebrow.

"Don't ask," I say, and walk toward the door. We stand there for a moment in silence. Things pass between us that we don't need to say, and I nod at his unspoken request.

I was hired by Alexander Owens six years ago to get close to his only son, Miles Osbourne. I was prepared to do that and a lot more, until I saw the picture of Paige. I knew what needed to happen, and I made my way to Miles to strike a deal. It turned out that we needed each other, and so our plan began to take shape.

He'd seen Mallory and fallen in love at first sight. He didn't want to expose her to Alexander and his corruption. He wanted to make sure she stayed safe. Miles's past had come back to haunt him before and he wasn't going to allow Mallory to be harmed. When I met with him the first time, I laid all my cards on the table. One of those cards was his half sister, Paige. Miles had no idea she existed, and I was able to bring that to light, showing Miles I was on his side. I then brought her into the fold. Paige became a part of the plan after that, even if she didn't know the whole story.

Miles and I formed a pact, and he's held up his end of the bargain. I've done everything I could to keep Mallory safe, to keep Alexander from touching what's important to Miles and to keep Paige as close to me as possible. When our deal was made, I chose my side, and I'll live with the consequences. Nothing is as important to me as Paige, and nothing will ever change that. Even if in the end she wants nothing to do with me.

I nod at Miles, and we take a step forward into the room our women entered. Neither of us is patient enough to give them more than a few minutes alone. When he opens the door, they both turn with surprised looks on their faces. My focus goes straight to Paige.

Mallory walks over to Miles and says something to him that I don't hear. I'm not paying attention to anything other than the beauty in front of me, the one I'd like to maul. The kiss in the hallway had been unexpected to say the least. One moment I was picturing her with another man and getting angry as hell. Then I was thinking about her having a baby and how I could somehow work my way into that life with her. I was fantasizing about us having a family and being together, and then the next thing I knew our lips were connecting and I was losing all my senses, wanting to make all those thoughts a reality.

I don't know who could have knocked Paige up, but

the bastard isn't anywhere to be found. I will find out
who it was and when I do… I cut myself off from that
line of thinking. I'll deal with that when I find him.
That someone could put his hands on what's mine
makes me sick to my stomach, but I'm not angry at
her for it. Maybe I should have staked my claim on
her years ago.

I'm so jealous I'm nauseated, and I can't stand the
feeling. If she'd have me, I'd never let her go, but she
doesn't know who I truly am. If she did, she wouldn't
want me. Playing with the one man she hates most in
the world would make her hate me. To know that I'd
worked for him for years, before I even knew about
her, and hadn't done anything to stop him in all that
time… Maybe her life would have been different if
I'd found a way to rid the world of him back then.
God knows what it was like to be raised by that man.

But I can be good to her and to her baby. I can
make her mine and raise her baby like it's my own.
I could love our child enough that it would belong to
me, and then we'd never be apart. My mind clears and
suddenly my path is obvious. If I make Paige fall in
love with me, then she won't care what my past is. If
she could feel even a fraction of what I feel for her,
then she'll understand and accept me before she finds
out the truth. I can do that. I can convince her that I'm
the right choice and that being with me isn't a risk.

"Got a little something," Mallory says, pointing
to her mouth and looking at me.

I reach up and wipe away the red lipstick that Paige
left on me after the kiss. As I clean it off, Paige pushes

past me and walks in front, trying to keep her distance. It's probably a good idea, because I know every time I get my hands on her she seems to melt. No matter how hard she struggles, one touch and she's mine. I'll make sure to get her alone, because we need to talk.

I nod to Miles as he and Mallory make their way over to the auction tables. I follow Paige and take a few long strides to catch up to her. I grab her arm, turning her to face me. The surprise on her face is clear, but so is the desire.

"You can't run out on me like that." I try to keep the pleading tone out of my voice.

"You can't tell me what to do." Her voice is low, and she's looking around the crowd.

I don't want to cause a scene, so I soften my hold and walk her over to the side and away from prying eyes. I rub her arms and feel her relax under my touch. I want everyone in the room to know she's with me. Her dress is going to be the death of someone if they don't. As I look down at her and see how fucking beautiful she is, my body aches to pick her up and hold her against me.

"Come home with me." It's not a question, though it probably should be.

"What?" She looks away, like I could possibly be speaking to someone else, then looks at me. "We can't. You're my boss."

The excuse is weak and makes me smile. Like she's ever acted like I was her boss before. She never listens to a thing I tell her to do. "If that's all you've got, then I'll quit."

"Good, maybe I can take your job. I could do it better than you, anyway." She raises her eyebrows, challenging me.

She's trying to get under my skin, but it just makes her more adorable. I love her spirit and the way she tries to act tough. But I know deep down she's a kitten with little claws who thinks she's a tiger. I laugh, thinking that's exactly what she is, and she cuts her eyes at me.

"What are you laughing at?" She pops her hip and puts her hand on it, and I can't help but picture a little ginger kitten growling and trying to catch a piece of string.

Reaching up, I cup her neck and run my thumb along the bottom of her jaw. "Nothing, kitten," I say softly. I like the nickname for her. If she could purr, she would, given the way she leans into my touch. Fuck, why can't she see she belongs to me? Her body knows it, but she can't let go. *That's okay, kitten. I'll fight for us, and I won't stop until I win.*

As if she realizes what she's doing, she takes a step back from me. As I'm about to make a grab for her, someone comes up behind me and puts a hand on my shoulder.

"Mr. Justice. We've got a situation. I tried to speak with you a moment ago." I turn to see the security guard who tried to talk to me earlier, when I was kissing Paige, and again I turn away, ignoring him.

I catch sight of Paige making her way to the entrance of the building, and I think maybe she's getting ready to leave. But I know her well enough to know she wouldn't walk out on a job, and even though we're extra tonight, she would still check in before she left. I catch a glimpse of her auburn hair and black dress as she exits the double doors and they close behind her.

"Sir, I wanted to let you know—"

"In a moment," I say, cutting him off and trying to go after her.

I speed up my steps, not wanting to miss where she goes next, so I can catch up with her. After I've made it to the doors and opened them, I stop dead in my tracks. Paige is across the room, standing in front of a man I've tried to keep her away from all these years.

Alexander looks up, and his blue eyes—just like Paige's—lock on me, and before I know it Miles and Mallory walk into the foyer, and the four of us are alone with him.

THREE

Paige

I WAS ABLE to walk away from Captain again, so I guess I have superhuman strength after all. All I wanted to do was to melt into him, but he doesn't know about my past. He doesn't know that deep down I don't think I'm good enough for someone like him. Maybe one day I could be. Maybe if I took charge of my destiny and got the revenge I really want, then I could focus on myself. Hide what I'd done. But the way my life is right now, I've got one focus and that's to pay back the son of a bitch who killed my mother. But that revenge could make me lose him. Lose everything. Captain always plays by the rules, and I'm on a path to break every one I come against if it gets me what I want.

When I step through the double doors, I keep walking, thinking I'll go outside and get some fresh air. Cool down a little. I'll take a moment alone and then go back in to tell Mallory I'm leaving for the night. There's plenty of security here, and Ryan can more than handle things without me. I often wonder if Ryan would even want me on his team if it hadn't been for Miles making him hire me. Sure, he wants to fuck me—he may even want something more—but I'm not certain he thinks I can do my job. He's often looking over me. He's even put a guard on me a time or two.

I'm lost in thought as I'm walking, not paying attention to where I'm going. Before I realize what I'm doing, I bump into someone and ice-cold hands wrap around my arms. They steady me and keep me from falling over, and I look up to apologize. But the words stick in my throat as I look into the cold blue eyes that mirror my own.

"Hello, Paige."

My father's voice sends a chill down my spine and I shiver involuntarily. They're the first words I've heard him speak to me since he killed my mother. Back then he told me if I ever spoke a word I'd end up like her. I manage to swallow the scream building in my throat, and he smiles at me, enjoying my terror. He always liked when people flinched away from him. It gave him some sick high. He'd almost savor it. His hands give me a squeeze and then let go. I think he's going to walk away, but he leans down and whispers in my ear.

"My, my, you've grown to look exactly like your mother. Such a beauty, sweet Paige. It was such a shame to end her life. What a waste. She looked magnificent every time I had her under me. Especially when she cried."

He leans back a little and looks down at me, a soft smile on his face. He reaches up, and his glacial finger wipes away a tear I didn't know I'd shed. The fear inside me leaches out in the only way possible. A single tear formed of my shame and my hate, and he derives joy from it.

"Just like her." His voice is full of reverence, maybe even desire. How my mother loved him, I'll never know.

This time when he smiles, it's wide and sinister, and I want to run. I want to leave this place and get as far away from him, and the memory, as possible. He looks past me, and I see his gaze lock on someone over my shoulder, but I don't turn to see who it is. I'm frozen, fear crippling me into stone.

"Look at our little family reunion," Alexander says, and I'm shaken out of my trance.

I take a few steps away from him, off to the side, and watch as he speaks to Miles. I look over and see Mallory partially behind him, with Captain nearby, staring at me. Understanding passes between us. He knows Miles and I hate our father. Miles has been working for years to tear Alexander's world apart.

My mind is churning as I look at Ryan. I want him to run over and hold me, catch me before I crumple to the ground. Sink into all that protective strength I know he has. But then I want him to stay where he is and not come near me. I don't want the evil that my father gave me to touch him. Or for my father to see another weakness I have. He's great at using anything he can against you.

I hear raised voices, and out of the corner of my eye I see a scuffle. Before I know it Miles has Alexander pinned to the wall beside me. Still I don't move.

Just like all those years ago, I'm standing here doing nothing. Still as weak, no matter how hard I try to fight it. To pretend otherwise. I watch as Miles chokes Alexander and Captain stands by, letting it take place. The two of us do nothing to stop what's happening, but allow it to continue.

Good, I think to myself. *Let it happen. Let it finally be over.* My mind wills it to happen.

But Mallory walks over and places her hand on Miles's, ending it. Miles lets Alexander go, and I can tell in the moment he's let everything go, as our father falls to the floor. I look down at the weakened monster at my feet and I want to spit on him. The man who's haunted me for years, who has never been far from my thoughts. I want to make him pay for what he did to my mother, and keep him from ever doing it again. To finally stand up for her. Miles might be finished. It's the end of the road for him. Maybe for Miles it's over, but not for me. It's only just begun. It won't be over until he's six feet under. I can't let go.

I look up and lock eyes with Mallory, trying to clear away the pain, and I take a breath to help it pass. She knows what I'm thinking. She's the only person I've ever told about that night.

"Your driver is out front, sir," Captain says, breaking through the silence in the room.

I feel Captain beside me, and his hand slips into mine, fingers lacing with mine and locking his hold on me. His strength flows through me, and it gives me what I need. In this moment, I need to feel safe and I need to get the hell out of here. I have to face the shame at how I was once again paralyzed by my father. How can I possibly think that I can get my revenge on him when I can't even face him?

Miles and Mallory walk out and slip into their limo. Captain looks down at Alexander and then pulls me toward the exit. I expected someone to call the police, but it looks like this happened so fast no one had a chance to see it. So instead, Alexander will lie unconscious on the ground until someone finds him and gets him out of there.

I follow Captain, letting him lead. Letting him take me wherever he wants to take me and not putting up a fight. Now is not the time for pushing away. When I feel myself being buckled up in the passenger seat of a car, I blink a few times. Captain shuts the passenger-side door and goes around the car and gets in the driver's seat.

There's so much I'm feeling at the moment, but when he reaches over and places his hand in my lap, I grasp it eagerly.

"I'm not pregnant, Ryan. That test was for Mallory. I didn't mean to lead you on about it—I liked winding you up. I'm sorry. I shouldn't have done that." He's making me feel so safe in this moment, and I want to give him something, even if it isn't much. It's all I really have to give him.

His fingers flex, and then he squeezes my hand. There's a small pause after the words leave my mouth, and I start to worry that he's angry with me.

"Thank you for telling me. It didn't matter, though. I want you however I can have you."

I look over and study his profile. His short blond hair, his hard chiseled jaw, his perfect nose and straight teeth. He's so handsome, it makes my chest ache. Picking up his hand, I bring it to my lips and place a kiss on it. He smells like rosewood and fresh cotton, and I want to curl into it.

I watch the streetlights of New York City pass by as he drives away from my personal hell. I picture leaving all of it behind and starting over someplace new, where Captain is with me and we have no past, no history, just each other. But that isn't reality. Life never seems to give me what I want.

FOUR

Paige

"Thank you for taking me home." I look up at Captain, feeling a little unsteady. Even more unsure of myself. We didn't speak another word on the car ride home. He'd followed me up to my apartment, one hand still locked with mine. I don't want to let it go. It feels like the only thing holding me together right now and keeping other thoughts at bay, things I don't want to think about right now. I want to focus on his hand in mine before it's gone and I'm alone again.

He reaches into his pocket, leaning forward, and I think he's going to kiss me, but I hear the lock behind me pop, and my front door swings open.

I'm not surprised he has a key. Probably has one to every door in the whole building. "I'm staying." He pockets his keys and waits. My mouth falls open a little as I think about him coming inside. He's being so forward, and a smile pulls at the corner of his mouth. "I don't mean like that, kitten. Keep those claws in."

The comment would normally make me snap back at him, but the smile on his lips and the softness in his eyes have me returning the small smile. As much as I try to say I dislike Captain for how perfect he can be,

it's one of the things that draws me to him. I know he
likes me, but he's never been crude about it. That's
not something I'm used to. Not with how I grew up,
and not even in college. I'm pretty; I know that. But
for some reason I've always attracted the assholes.
Maybe it's my attitude, but they seem to flock to me.
The good ones never seemed to pay me much attention. Until him. And now, for the first time, a man
has my attention.

"You really don't have to do that. I kind of want
to be alone," I lie. I don't want to be alone at all. The
apartment feels so empty now with Mallory gone. It's
been the two of us since college, but now she spends
her nights a few floors up, with Miles, and I don't
foresee her coming back. He's not letting her out of
that apartment. I'd grown used to having someone
around. Probably clung to it more than was healthy,
but when you spend years alone and then you get to
experience the joy of having someone so close, it's
hard to let go. She's all I've ever really had.

The silence in the apartment has been driving me
crazy. The walls feel like they're closing in.

Captain cups my face, his thumb rubbing along my
jaw, and I tilt my head into his touch. I don't want him
to stay because he thinks it's the right thing to do. I
want him to stay because he wants to.

"You can let me in, or I'll stand in this hallway
all night."

"You'd stand here all night?"

"I'd probably break in at some point," he admits.

"Until I think you're really all right and not just feeding me a line."

His confession pulls at my heart, because I don't think I'll ever be all right. I don't tell him that. Instead, I motion for him to enter. He locks the door behind us, letting go of my hand, and I see him release a breath. The relief is clear on his face.

"Didn't think I was going to let you in?" I ask over my shoulder as I make my way to the kitchen. I open the freezer and pull out a bottle of vodka. I grab a glass and pour myself a drink, shooting it back before pouring myself another.

"I never know what you're going to do." Captain takes off his jacket, tossing it over the back of the sofa as he rolls up his sleeves, revealing all those tattoos I love. I could close my eyes and trace them perfectly.

"That must drive you crazy." I make my way back toward the sofa and sit down. I slip my shoes off, and the motion causes the slit of my dress to fall open. I look up to see Captain's eyes zero in on my thighs before they quickly move to my face. Forever the gentleman. Until tonight, when I kissed him. Or did he kiss me? It was hard to know in that moment. I couldn't tell where he began and I ended. I'd never felt so connected with someone, and I wondered if sex was like that.

"No, I'm just always speculating which Paige I'll get." He comes around to sit on the other end of the sofa. I'm disappointed he doesn't sit next to me. Right now I could use more of his touches. But disappointment turns into pleasure as he pulls my feet into his lap and rubs them. The ache from the heels I'd been wearing all night fades away as his big hands engulf my feet and ease the pain.

I take another sip of the vodka, enjoying the massage. I lie there and let him rub me, and a comfortable silence falls on us. I shoot back the rest of the alcohol and set down the empty glass on the table next to me. With only that little bit of vodka, I feel warmth flowing through me. It relaxes me and helps me to forget.

I want to forget seeing my father. To forget how easily I'd frozen up when I was around him. It only further shows me how unprepared I am to see him. How can I seek revenge on a man I can't even speak two words to?

"How many of me are there?" I tease, trying to make light of Ryan's words.

"The one you pretend to be and the one you really are."

I lean back, folding my arms over my chest. His words sink home. I wonder if everyone can see through me so easily. Maybe it's the vodka, or maybe I want to know, but I ignore his words and go for something else.

"You think you want me." It's not a question, because I already know the answer. The kiss we shared said it all.

"Think?" His fingers dig deeper into my foot, making me moan at the pleasure. His hands still for a second, and I look at his face. He takes a deep breath, like he's trying to get himself under control, before he goes back to rubbing. Jesus, he's good at that.

I want to tell him all the reasons we'd never work. That he's too good for me. That there is too much of my father inside me. I can feel it. Where else did I get these dark thoughts from? What kind of girl wants to kill her own father? What kind of girl stands by and watches her mother die?

He would never do those things. Captain would have saved the day. Maybe he could save me. The warm buzz of the alcohol pushes me on. I slip my feet from his lap, and he reluctantly lets them go. I start to crawl toward him, and he doesn't move as I work my way to him and into his lap. I press my face against his neck, breathing in his scent of rosewood, and his arms wrap around me. Only holding me. I can't remember anyone doing this, not even my own mother.

"Did you know I remember everything?" I tell him a secret few people know about me.

"What do you mean by everything?" His hand on my back moves in slow circles. It's a lazy rhythm that makes my eyes fall closed, and I melt into him.

"Everything." I feel him pause for a moment before he starts rubbing again. "The first time I saw you, you had on dark blue slacks, a white button-up shirt. Your tie was long gone and the top two buttons were undone. When you'd turn a certain way, those damn muscles of yours would flex and strain under your shirt. I would get a glimpse of the tattoos trying to peek out your sleeves. I spent so many nights wondering what they looked like after that first day. How they would trace up your arms." My fingers are tracing them on his right arm now. I don't have to look to know I'm tracing them perfectly. I keep my eyes closed, my face buried in his neck, breathing him in. I want to smell his scent forever. It's somehow comforting. "It took time before I got to see them all, but I only needed one look. Now I'll always know their exact pattern. Sometimes late at night I trace them on my own arm."

"Paige." He says my name softly, but it vibrates through his body and into mine, making me smile. I brush my nose against his neck, then place a soft kiss there. He stills once again. I love how I can do that to him with one little touch.

It feels empowering, and after what happened tonight, I revel in it. I felt so powerless in front of my father. I thought after all these years I'd have been better prepared. No longer that scared little girl.

"That's one of the good things about remembering everything," I tell him, placing another kiss on his neck. "The bad part is sometimes you want to forget something you've seen, but time can't lessen the pain because you keep seeing it. The memory never fades."

"Oh, kitten." He squeezes me hard, like he's trying to take some of those bad things away. I wonder if he knows what he's doing. If he hadn't come in here tonight, I'd probably be in my bed replaying memory after memory of things I didn't want to recall, but right now all I can think about is his arms wrapped around me. The smell of him invading me. And the little taste I have of him on my lips.

Then, without warning, he's standing with me still in his arms and carrying me down the hallway into my room. He places me on my feet next to my bed, and then he untucks his dress shirt and unbuttons it. I can't help but watch each button pop, revealing more of his skin. His broad, hard chest comes into view, and I can only stare, stunned at the perfection. As I'm frozen in place, he goes for my dress, unzipping the side and easily slipping it off over my head. Never taking his eyes from my face, he drops the dress to the floor and opens his own shirt, then puts it on me. He covers my naked body and does up all the buttons, while the whole time I watch as he cares for me.

"Always the gentleman."

"If you only knew," he says, masking the words with a deep breath, and I almost don't catch them.

After he's finished buttoning me up, he pulls back the covers and picks me up again, placing me in the center of the bed.

"You'll never fit on the sofa." I reach out to him, wanting him to lie down with me. "Or were you…" I can't even finish my sentence, I'm so afraid that he's leaving. He saw me home, made sure I was okay and tucked me into bed. My hand drops, because I don't want this to end. I know when morning comes things will be different. I want to hold on to this for a moment longer before everything comes flooding in. Soon the memories will start pressing down on me, demanding to be heard.

"I'm not leaving." His voice is soft, and it settles the rising panic.

A sense of calm washes over me, and I reach my hand out to him again. "Then lie down with me."

He groans and kicks off his shoes. I flip the covers back, inviting him into the bed, making no move to go to the other side. My bed isn't gigantic, and with me lying in the center he'll have to touch me to fit his big frame.

He turns off the lamp and surprises me when the bed dips on his side. I think he's going to lie there, but instead he molds his body against mine, throwing his big leg over me, pinning me beneath him, wrapping around me completely. I settle into him and wonder if he can keep the nightmares at bay. When I'm with him, he keeps the memories from coming, and tonight, that's all I want. Peace, sleep and comfort.

FIVE

Paige

I WAKE RIGHT before the sun rises, and the darkness of my room begins to lift. It's not the sun shining in; it's more of a light gray. It's dawn and I've slept a dreamless night in the arms of a man I shouldn't want.

Stretching, I notice that he's not in bed, but his warmth is all around me. I sit up, thinking that he must have left, but see him sitting in a chair beside the bed, looking at me. His stare makes me feel shy, and I grab the blankets that have fallen in my lap. I don't use them to cover me; I twist them in my hands, giving them something to do.

"Good morning, kitten."

His voice is like caramel, and it slides across the room and coats my skin. I feel the stir of something low in my belly, and I want him to come lie down with me. I want him to stand up and climb on top of my body and wordlessly take me. Right here. Right now.

As the fantasy plays out in my mind, I twist the blankets between my fingers. Captain notices and looks down at my hands and then back to my eyes. It's like he can read my mind when his dark green eyes give me a sad smile. His scent of rosewood is all around me, and though I've convinced myself he's too good for me, I find that I'm desperate for him.

Maybe it's because I was vulnerable with him last night. Maybe it's because I'm really turned on by his naked chest and I want to get laid. Or maybe it's that I trust him. It's been a long time since I let my guard down, and the last time that happened was with Mallory. Giving my trust to someone is as intimate as giving someone my body, and yet here he is. In my room and in my space, and I want to throw all my apprehensions to the side and fall for him.

It would be so easy to love a man like Ryan Justice. He's good to the core, sweet, kind, and would never hurt me. Going to him and allowing him into my heart would feel like coming home. I know all these things like I know the sun is moments from coming up, and yet I remain motionless on the bed. All my past fears and insecurities bubble up as the first light breaks through the curtain and shatters our precious connection. The brilliance of the day caresses the space between us, and as if Captain knew it would happen, he nods and stands.

"I'm going to go home."

I feel so many emotions at one time. I'm sad he's leaving and relieved at the same time. I don't know that I'm powerful enough to ask him to go, and yet I'm not strong enough to let him stay. My heart was broken a long time ago, and I don't have room to love someone so perfect. Someone who could break me beyond the point of return and leave me with the wreckage. I know my past is dark, and I know what my plans are. Last night was a setback, and I need to push it away. I need to push Captain away.

I feel him move to the side of the bed, and his rough hand reaches up and cups my cheek. I'm forced to look up into his beautiful green eyes and see the little flecks of blue as the light touches them.

"This isn't the end, Paige." He rubs his thumb across my bottom lip, and my heart beats hopefully. "This is how our story begins."

He leans down slowly and brushes his lips gently against mine. My eyes flutter closed and I take in his scent and his presence and the warm sugary feel of him once again. And just as I think about how I want more, he's taking a step back. With one final look, he leaves my bedroom, closing the door behind him.

I fall back against the pillow and lie there trying to find the earth again. What in the hell just happened? I've kept him at a distance for so long, and one night I finally give in and suddenly I'm a mess. For most of my life I've pushed people from me emotionally, and until Mallory came along no one had made a dent. Sure, I loved my mother, and she loved me, but we weren't very expressive about it.

When my mom met Alexander, she'd been young. Too young. That seemed to be his type. Get them young and take advantage. Make it so they depended on him. He wanted his women to think he was God. When she was fifteen, he'd found her on the streets and brought her to work in some restaurant he owned. It was all a cover for laundering money and running drugs, but she'd been head over heels for the guy and went willingly. She never told me the whole story, but after she died, an old lady who worked in the restaurant told me everything.

Alexander had forced himself on her the first chance he got. My mother convinced herself that it was payment for all he provided for her. And the fact that he didn't let his men touch her. She did what he said and worked in the restaurant, but was always there when he came calling. Servicing him. It went on like that for a while, and unsurprisingly, she got pregnant. The first time, she was almost sixteen, and he wouldn't let her keep it. He had someone come in and give her an abortion against her will. After that, he put her on birth control and told her not to let it happen again. She knew about his real family, the wife and his baby boy, and he didn't want her messing that up. Dirtying his name, as if it wasn't already. But she got pregnant again not long after, claiming the birth control didn't work. He made her get a second abortion and told her if she got pregnant again, she'd regret it.

By the time she was twenty she was madly in love with him. Even though he treated her like trash and started hitting her, she still loved him. I'll never understand it. I think she had Stockholm syndrome or something. I'd always wondered if he had hit her too hard a few times and she wasn't all there. Reality wasn't something my mother dealt in.

She got pregnant and begged him to let her keep it—because she knew he would never leave his family and she wanted a piece of him. I don't know how she convinced him, but he let her, and I came along. She named me after her grandmother and gave me her last name. I was brought into this world as Paige Marie Turner, and my father never wanted anything to do with me. I think my mother thought she could love me enough that it wouldn't matter, but I believe she had only enough room in her heart for him. Alexander had consumed her soul and she wouldn't let him go.

I grew up in the restaurant and was shuffled back and forth to school by the old Italian ladies who worked there. One would think they would have shown me some kindness, but they mostly made sure I had enough to eat and left me alone. I can only assume no one wanted to get in the way of Alexander and his crazy lover.

I'd watch my father come and go, listening to all the things he said, never forgetting any of them. Maybe he thought I was too young to recall some of what I'd seen or heard, but I remembered everything.

As time went on, I learned to live with my mother's shortcomings and took care of myself and oftentimes her. But everything changed when she found out he'd left his family. When she heard that he'd walked out and let them go, she had the moment she'd been waiting for since she was fifteen.

In my heart, I believe she thought he would finally make her his wife and pull her out of the dump he'd thrown her in. That this was her moment to shine and be recognized as a woman of worth. Instead, everything went to shit.

I roll on my side and close my eyes, not wanting

to remember the rest. Not wanting to have the images of what happened flash through my mind. As the sun hits my face, I lie there and let it warm me while I try to push away the dark thoughts and all the hate that boils inside me. I wish Captain was back in bed with me. I wish I was wrapped in his arms so he would be all I could think about.

Then I hear a knock on the door.

Slipping out of bed, I realize I've still got on Captain's dress shirt and snuggle into it. His smell clings to it, and I inhale deeply, wanting to breathe him in. I walk to the door with my nose buried in the fabric and look through the peephole. When I can't see anyone there, I flip the lock Captain must have set when he left and open the door an inch. Looking down at the floor, I see a small brown bag there and open the door a little more. Looking up and down the hallway, I don't see anyone, and I reach for the bag, thinking maybe the doorman from downstairs brought it up.

I take it inside and close and lock the door behind me. When I catch the aroma of coffee and sugar, my mouth starts to water. Opening the bag, I peer inside to see a small to-go cup and something that looks like a Danish wrapped in waxed paper. On top there's a note, and I bite my lip to keep from smiling.

I'll have you know that getting you breakfast without a shirt on was interesting. But you're worth a few stares. I'm running home to change clothes and I expect you to put on your workout gear and meet me downstairs in an hour.
X Ryan

I blush and put my hand over my mouth, though I don't know why I'm trying to hide my smile. On Sundays Captain and a few of the guys I work with train together. I've gotten to go to only one session since I started at Osbourne Corp because of my schedule, and looking after Mallory. I was always in charge of her personal security, and now that she and Miles are always together, I'm able to go. It's a normal routine, sparring or working out, going over new security procedures and preparing for the next week, so I don't know why I'm giddy from the note.

But then I realize it's because this is different. Him waking up in my room and bringing me breakfast is not routine, and it's making me react to him like never before. I try not to read too much into the kind gesture, thinking that this is just Captain. Good to the core and perfect in every way. Even if he has to leave a lady unsatisfied in bed, the least he can do is bring her coffee.

I eat my breakfast, because like always, I'm starving. Once the Danish is gone, I make some eggs. After that, I grab a banana and take it to my room to snack on while I get dressed. Mallory always jokes with me about how much I eat and how small I am, but I shrug, not knowing how to respond. I guess being small takes a lot of energy.

Reluctantly, I unbutton the dress shirt and give it one last smell before I hang it on the end of my bed. The polite thing to do would be to return it to Captain, but I've never been good with manners. It's mine now, end of discussion. I might not be able to have him, but I'm keeping the shirt.

After pulling on some workout shorts and a sports bra, I grab my sneakers and lace them up. Captain hates when I wear so little to group exercises, but why would I stop poking at him now? After last night it feels as if there's even more reason to maintain the tone of our relationship. Knowing that I'm going to make him growly only spurs me on.

I didn't wash off the layers of stuff I had put on for the charity event, and it feels like I have a face on top of my face, so I brush my teeth and scrub off the makeup now. Pulling my auburn locks in a high ponytail, I think for half a second about putting on some lipstick, but then don't bother. He's seen me without makeup so often, why should I worry now? Things are going to be exactly the same as they were before the kiss.

The kiss.

The replay in my mind doesn't do it justice as I remember the feel of his big body pushing me against the wall. His warm tongue forcing its way into my mouth and how he commanded me to obey. His big palm squeezing my bare ass and the scorching heat that sizzled and crackled between us.

Gripping the edge of the sink, I try to shake off the memory. He's technically my boss, and we don't need this to happen. He's a perfect guy who needs to find his Miss America and settle down. That thought makes a nasty jealous monster stir inside me, and I shake that off, too. *Simmer down, Paige.* It was one

and mats around it. One wall is lined with mirrors, and workout equipment is scattered throughout. We usually rotate around the gym until the end of the day, when we enter the ring.

When I got here today, I'd nodded to the guys like normal and started my workout. First the tread-mill to warm up my muscles, and then the weights. I may be small for my size, but I can lift and hold my own. Captain stayed with me throughout my work-out like he has the last few times I've been here, so having him by my side shouldn't have been different. It should have been exactly the same as before, only this time my body was all too aware of him.

I'd waited—hoped, actually—for him to mention the breakfast he left for me. But when he didn't, I let it go, not wanting to make it seem like it was a big deal. Instead of bringing it up, I decided to play it cool and pretend that my body wasn't screaming for his touch as we worked out. All day he's kept his dis-tance, and it's eating me alive. Normally he'll find ways to touch me and I'll pull away, but now that I welcome it, it's not coming. Maybe now that he's had a taste he doesn't want any more. He went back home and thought everything out and has changed his mind. I'm more work than I'm worth. I've heard that more times than I want to remember over the years.

I was anxious to get in the ring because I knew this way I could put my hands on him. But it's not the same as when he's the one doing the touching. Instead of making a grab for me or getting us tan-gled up in one another, he deflects all my moves and

blocks me when possible. Going down and taking the
loss without really fighting back. It doesn't feel like
he's letting me win; it feels like he's trying not to
touch me. And that thought makes me a little angry.

"You gonna let me win all day?"

Captain stands and moves to the other side of the
ring, watching me. Just as he's about to say something, a buzzer goes off and the guys all push away
from the ropes.

"Time's up, Turner," McCoy yells, and I let out
a breath.

Our session is finished for the day, and I'm over-
loaded with emotions. I want to get out of here as
soon as I can, yet I want to stay and yell at Captain.
What is wrong with me?

I duck under the ropes, grab my water bottle and
take a drink. I pack up my stuff and say my goodbyes
to the guys as they head out before me. As I throw
my stuff in my gym bag, I feel him behind me, and
I know if I turn around I won't be able to take the
look on his face. It will only remind me that I'm an
idiot for wanting someone so perfect. I'll hate myself, because I can't have him. I'm not good enough
for a man like him, and my past is nothing but trash
that follows me around.

"What?" I say, not turning to face him. He reads
me so easily I don't want him to see I'm upset.

"You owe me another round."

I flip around at his words, angry that he wants to
get back in the ring. What the hell? I just took him
down without him so much as touching me, and now

he wants another chance. No, thanks. I don't want his pity. I know I'm being a brat because I'm always running hot and cold, and it's completely hypocritical, but it still pisses me off. He's the one who started all this. With his touches and sweet words. Maybe a little crush I had on him blossomed and now it feels like he's the one running. He's taken away the little touches I'd grown accustomed to. He made me crave them and now I'm pissed I'm not getting my fix.

"You didn't get enough nap time in on the mat? I thought that's what you wanted."

Reaching behind his head, he grabs the neck of his sweat-dampened shirt and pulls it off. Up and over it goes, revealing his smooth chest and tight abs. His wide rib cage does nothing to hide his muscles. The dark tattoos that wind up his arms flex, and I swear to God if I had panties on they'd disintegrate. Jesus, this guy looks like the *after* picture on one of those workout videos.

I swallow audibly.

"Just one more round. I think I needed to find my rhythm." His words are punctuated by the sound of the gym door closing. The guys all left in a hurry to enjoy the rest of their Sunday.

Squaring my shoulders, I reach up and tighten my high ponytail and bounce on the balls of my feet a little. "Let's do it."

The old Italian ladies in the restaurant had a name for me. They called me Difficile. I found out it meant tough, and I kind of liked it. They didn't say much to me, or about me, but knowing that they thought I was tough meant something. I wasn't one to back down from a challenge, and I sure as hell wasn't going to stop now. Captain throwing down the gauntlet was the one sure way to get me into the ring.

I watch as he goes in first, bending between the ropes. I watch his ass, and I give him a smirk when he straightens and catches me checking him out. I duck in and stand up, bouncing all the time. My body is still loose from the workout, and we don't have on gloves. When we spar, we don't throw punches. We disarm, restrain and contain. So as we both put our hands up and start circling around the ring, we wait and see who's going to make the first move.

For once, I chase all my feelings out of my head and focus on what's in front of me. Other than the small distraction of the perfection that is his body, my mind is sharp. I mimic his speed around the mat, waiting for an opening. He's at least twice my size, so I'm at a disadvantage when it comes to strength. But with the right moves, any man can be brought to his knees.

This isn't like earlier today. The ring is charged now, and I feel it coming from him. He's going to come at me, and when he does, I need to be ready. I can tell that when he gets ahold of me, this won't be so easily won.

Just as the thought enters my mind, he strikes.

His hand comes out, and I try to block him, but he takes me off guard and goes for my upper thigh. I spin and kick, barely getting free of his large hand as he takes a step back and out of my reach.

"My mother always told me not to play with my food," he says, getting low and moving around the ring again.

"You plan on having a meal up here after I send you crying back to your mama?"

He laughs big and loud, and I can't help my matching smile.

"Oh no, kitten. I plan on eating something up here, and the only tears being shed will be tears of joy."

I could try to read into what he's saying, but his hand comes out lightning fast, and I have half a second to react. His fingers graze my waist as I slip to the side and come up behind him, knocking him off balance and skirting away.

"What's wrong? Got tired of losing in front of the boys?" I pout as we start to dance around the ring again, and once more he laughs. God, I hate how much I love the sound of it.

He looks at me with intense eyes and his smile turns wicked. "I don't care about getting my ass kicked by you in front of my guys. What I do care about is them seeing me on top of you and what might happen when I get you on your back."

I push away his words and try to not let them affect me. "Don't you mean *if* you get me on my back?"

He licks his lips and we dance around again. "No, kitten. I mean *when*."

The slow throb between my legs has nothing to do with what he's saying. Nothing at all. At least that's what I keep telling myself. God, why did I let myself be alone with him? He's all sweaty and meaty, and Jesus, I want to climb him like a tree. I'd be his little monkey mate and do tricks on his shoulders for money. What is wrong with me?

The distraction is enough for him to exploit an opening. This time he grabs my thighs with both hands and flips me to my back. The mat is a trampoline that's been strung tight, so although it sounds loud and painful, falling on it doesn't actually hurt.

What hurts is the ache in my lady business as he moves between my legs and cages me in. How does he keep doing this, and why does it keep turning me on?

"So, as I was saying." He leans down, his lips a breath from mine, and I'm coiled with anticipation.

I open my mouth and my eyelids grow heavy as I think about all the things I want to do to him right on this dirty mat. But as the fantasy starts to come to life, our cell phones ring.

Captain pops up and I do the same, both of us grabbing our phones, which are off to the side.

"Paige, oh my God, I'm engaged!" Mallory screams over the phone, and for a second, a tiny beat of my heart, I'm beyond jealous.

I look over at Captain and he looks at me, and in that moment something passes between us.

"Mal, if you ask me to wear pink, I'm going to murder you," I say into the phone, my eyes still on Captain.

He blinks and then looks away, getting off the mat and walking in the opposite direction. Mallory is going on about her engagement, and then, finally, the part of me that loves her, the part of me that is beyond excited for my best friend, kicks in, and I smile while I listen.

SEVEN

Paige

"Fucking hell." I roll over and look at the clock. When I got back from working out with Captain, I cruised the internet for way too long, digging for information and finding nothing. I was going to need help and there was only one person I could think of who could do it. I'm not sure if he will or if he'll tell Captain about me asking. I'll have to come up with a plan. I rub my eyes, still feeling drained even though I slept. That hour nap is not going to cut it. It doesn't help that I'm feeling sexually frustrated and my emotions are being pulled in every direction. I want to tug the covers back over my head and sleep until tomorrow. Preferably with Captain wrapped around me so I wouldn't be restless.

A loud bang comes from the living room, making me spring from my bed. No one can break into this building, so whoever's banging on my door is someone who was allowed up. The security in the building is the best, and no way did someone who isn't supposed to be here get in. I secretly hope it's Captain, but I push that thought away. I don't see him doing this. Though after the last forty-eight hours, I'm starting to rethink what he's capable of. He's getting me off balance and I can't read him. One second I think he's running hot, then the next he's cold as ice.

Maybe Mallory is moving some of her stuff. I head for the door, ready to give the movers a mouthful. I fling it open, to find Mallory standing there with a Red Bull. She holds it out to me, and I know it's some kind of peace offering for something she's about to do. I didn't think we were meeting today; I was sure Miles wasn't going to let Mal out of his home for as long as he could keep her there. But maybe he wanted to ensure all her stuff was in his place as soon as possible, hoping that would make sure she couldn't change her mind.

"Don't stab me," she says with a bright smile. She looks like she's glowing. She's in yoga pants and a shirt that's too big for her, so I assume it's Miles's. Her hair looks like she just got out of bed, and her face is clean of any makeup. I've never seen her this happy before. And no matter how much it hurts that it's not just me and her anymore, I can't help but be happy for her. I grab the Red Bull and pull her in for a hug. I don't want her to worry about me, though I know she will. This is her moment and I won't get her down by throwing my shit on her shoulders.

Her body relaxes and she hugs me back. "I know we were going to go out and talk about wedding stuff, but…" She trails off, making me pull back and look at her. "Miles didn't want me going far, so he kinda…" She looks toward the living room.

Oh God. When Miles does something, it's never

half-assed, especially when it comes to Mal. No one knows that better than me. I've been on the front lines for him, pretty much stalking her, for over four years. I shake my head, wondering what he's up to, this time. I laugh as I pop the tab and take a drink. I walk into the living room and come up short.

"Jesus."

"Yeah, I probably shouldn't have told him pink was my favorite color."

Mallory didn't have to tell him anything. Miles knows all when it comes to her.

I can't help but laugh harder at the sight in front of me. The room is crowded with a variety of wedding-related paraphernalia, all in pink. I walk over to a rack by the sofa and pull off a wedding gown. "This is terrible. I didn't even know they made pink wedding dresses!" It's so ridiculous it's funny, and I can't stop laughing.

Mallory scrunches her nose. "It's not terrible," she counters, making me laugh even harder, and her smile widens.

"You got engaged hours ago." I put the dress back on the rack and look around the rest of the room. There are samples of everything needed for a wedding, and a stack of books to go with them. My apartment looks like a wedding planner's office. "Did he have this shit in storage, ready to go, for when you said yes?" I think the chances are high, but then again you can get anything at any time when you have money like Miles does.

"You know Miles," she says.

Yeah, kind of. I know how he is when it comes it her. I came into Mallory's life because of Miles. He'd hired me years ago to be her secret bodyguard. I fed his stalker habit when he hired me to be her roommate in college and watch over her while she went to school. That quickly changed from her being a job to her being the most important person in my life. The only friend I had, and it had all been a lie. One that blew up in my face when Mallory found out, and I thought I'd lost her.

Though she started out as a job, it wasn't that way anymore, and she knew it. Even as mad as she was at me, the job brought us together. We never would've crossed paths without Miles, and I'm thankful. Two people who didn't have anyone else at the time bonded quickly, and we've been glued to each other since day one. But now she has Miles, my half brother, and that's the most important thing in her life.

Miles and I were brought together for one common reason: revenge against our father. But I don't think he's after that anymore. Now all Miles wants is to let it go and be with Mal, but I can't. Our relationship revolved around this plan, and it's all Miles and I have as far as our relationship goes. He was good to me. He pulled me off the streets and gave me a job. He sent me to school and made sure I had what I needed, but our relationship is based on the bond we formed over hating our father. Now we don't have that anymore, so I'm not sure what will happen in the future.

Miles isn't the brother who invites you over to hang out. We don't really talk unless it's about Mal, and he's cold to most people. I've never gotten that chill to melt, and I've given up. I'd tried at first when he came into my life. I had a spark of hope that maybe I could have some normal type of family. But he never let me close, and it probably didn't help that I'd had some resentment toward him when he found me. He was the other family. His mom was the woman my mother used to cry over, wanting to be her, thinking the grass was greener on the other side. No part of my father was green and happy. I'm sure Miles's mom, Vivien, didn't make out much better when she was with him.

Miles and I don't really do anything together. In fact, now that I think about it, he doesn't really even have a use for me, and I wonder what that will mean. I don't think he'll fire me from his company, but that would only be because of Mal. He wouldn't do anything that might upset her.

The thought cuts deep, and all of a sudden I feel a little bit lonelier. I put a smile on my face, not wanting to make this moment sad. This is important to Mal. Having grown up in foster care, she has always wanted a family of her own, and this is the first step toward it.

"So he wants to get married tonight?" I tease. She lets out a little huff and I'm guessing I'm right.

"I told him I wanted to hang out with you and talk about the wedding and other stuff. So he had everything brought here for us to hang out and go through."

"Do you even want all this shit?" I pick up some fancy-looking plate that was part of a dining set.

"No. I mean, who am I going to invite to a wedding? I think he thinks I want to do some big deal. I don't. I just kinda want to be married."

I put the plate down. "Did you tell him that?"

"We haven't done a lot of talking since I said yes." Her face blushes a cherry red at her own reference to sex.

I shake my head and drop down on the sofa. "Miles doesn't even like people. I'm sure he'll be happy with something super-small."

She walks over to the stand with all the dresses and pulls off the pink wedding gown.

"Put it down, Mal. I love you. I can't let you wear that."

She puts it back on the rack and comes over, plopping down next to me.

"You moving out?" I ask the question I already know the answer to.

She ignores my question and asks her own. "You okay?"

"I will be."

She grabs my hand. "Don't do anything crazy, Paige. I know you want your piece."

I glance over at her. She's the only one I've told about watching my father kill my mother. I didn't tell her about all the other things I've heard about him over the years. Things I heard him say he did, too. I didn't want to taint sweet Mal with all that. I gave her the basics. My main reason. That I stood there and did nothing before I ran. I never told a soul what I'd seen. Partly out of fear, and partly from shame. The guilt eats at me, and sometimes I feel like it's alive inside, slowly taking over, piece by piece. Sometimes I welcome it and other times, like when I look at Captain, I wish I didn't have it.

"Maybe you should tell Miles."

"No." I cut her off. Not going to happen. This is mine, and not only that, I don't want to pull him back into this. I don't want Mal in it, because if Miles is, she is. Miles is done with our father and I want to keep it that way. I don't want Alexander's sights anywhere on Mal, because that's where it will end up if he and Miles go toe to toe again.

"I know you can't let it go. I get that, I really do. If someone hurt you or Miles, I'd want to make that person pay, too. I'm just—"

"Let's not think about this today," I push. We should be fighting over what ridiculous dress she's going to try to make me wear. I should be trying to persuade her to choose a huge and ostentatious menu, while she tries to do everything on a small, simple budget.

"I've never seen your face like that, Paige. You looked so lost last night."

She keeps trying to push me back there. Back to somewhere I don't want to go, because I still feel shame about that, too. I'm pissed at how easily I froze in front of my father last night. How many years have I been so good at hiding things? How come it's all starting to show? Maybe I'm cracking. Maybe I'm not as strong as I thought I was. How many nights had I lain in bed thinking of all the things I'd say to him whenever I came face-to-face with him again? Throw my own threats in his face and show him he didn't scare me. That I was going to haunt his dreams now. He'd lie awake at night, scared to close his eyes in case the nightmares would come. But I didn't give him that. Instead, I gave him the fear he loves to see in people.

"I was fine. Captain brought me home." She raises her eyebrows in surprise as I try to change the subject. Yeah, that's how I can get her off this. She's always eager for Captain information and wants to talk about this thing I have for him. Now that she's happily in love, she seems to want the same for me. I bet she's already planning double dates. I almost snort at the idea. I give her more details, knowing it will keep her off topic. "He stayed the night."

"Oh my God!" She claps excitedly and I shake my head.

"Calm down. We just slept." I can practically see little hearts floating over her head. "I don't know what's up with him. One minute he's kissing me and the next he's on the other side of the room."

"He's hard to read. His face is always the same. Like a stone that sees all, but I know he's into you. I mean, the only time he ever cracks a smile at work is when you're poking at him."

I want to ask if she thinks something between him and me could really work. She's the one who dubbed him Captain America. We'd joke about how perfect and all-American he always looked. That kind of perfection wouldn't want me once he started to peel back my layers. At one time I thought I could fake it until I made it, but if I've learned anything over the past few days, it's that Ryan is able to see through me too easily for my liking.

I shrug like it's no big deal. I get up from the sofa and walk to the rack of dresses, pulling off one that's actually white.

"This will rock on your body," I tell her. It would fit her like a second skin, and Mal has all the right curves for something like it.

"I'd have to get married tomorrow or it'll never fit." She stands, putting her hand on her belly. "We read the test wrong Friday. We didn't wait long enough. I'm pregnant. You're going to be an aunt." Her face lights up, and now I know where that glow is coming from.

I rush over to her, embracing her in a hug, knowing how disappointed she was, even if she tried to hide it, when the test was negative. Mal shows everything on her face.

"I still can't believe it," she murmurs next to my ear. I can hear tears in her voice as I pull back and look at her. She's so freaking happy it makes me smile even wider.

"I know what this needs," I tell her. She sniffs and gives me a watery smile. I know she's happy, but it's not the time for tears. It's time for fun. "I'm going to try on that pink wedding dress."

Mal bursts into laughter.

EIGHT

Paige

WHEN THE ELEVATOR DINGS, I look up from my phone and see Miles and Mallory step out. It's Monday morning and things are back to normal. Well, as normal as they can be now that everything's changed. Mallory is getting married and having a baby, and I'm too happy to worry about how this is going to affect me.

Standing up, I feel Captain move in beside me. I try to ignore the way my body heats at his proximity and focus on my job.

I woke up bright and early this morning to get ready for the day. I dressed in my usual attire for work: a white button-up collared shirt and black slacks. I change it up a bit with my shoes, unable to stop wearing ridiculous heels. Thank God Miles has always provided me with a hefty salary, so I can afford the things I like. I should probably wear something more sensible, but shoes are my weakness. Well, shoes and food. For a second I think about the kiss I shared with Ryan and realize I could easily be addicted to that, too. Probably already am.

Shaking off the thoughts of him and his gloriously

naked chest, I straighten my shoulders and tuck my phone into my red leather messenger bag that matches my shoes. Today I'm wearing my favorite pair of Miu Miu Mary Janes, with heels that look like big screws. They give me the height I need and make me feel industrially sexy. Is that a word? It is now.

I've been waiting down here for about fifteen minutes, during which time Captain was watching me from across the street. I wondered when he'd come inside, but I guess he was waiting until the happy couple needed their security detail.

"Good morning, kitten."

His low voice sends a shiver of pleasure right between my legs, and I have to blink a couple times before I can respond. No one could have heard him say the words, and I'm sure if he repeated it to a stranger they'd seem normal. Possibly playful. But to me, the memory of the last time he called me that has a whole mountain of meaning attached to it. I remember his deep voice whispered in the dark, and all those desires come flooding back.

Thankfully, I've taken my mind out of the gutter by the time Mallory and Miles approach us. It's then I realize I never responded to Captain, and it's too late. I smile at everyone but him in greeting. Those green eyes will make my knees weak right this second and I need to compose myself first.

"We're going to drive in this morning," Miles says, pulling Mallory close to him as they exit the building. Mallory flushes a deep shade of red, and I try not to think about how messy the back of that limo is going to be when they get to our building.

I step outside and make sure Miles and Mallory are safely tucked inside the car before it pulls away from the curb. I watch them leave and then decide to walk to work. The morning is cool and I don't mind the few blocks it takes to get there. There's another security detail in place at Osbourne Corp that will greet them when they finally peel themselves off one another and get to work. But before I can take two steps, Captain's warm palm wraps around my hand and his body moves beside mine.

I'm obsessed enough to know that he was standing beside me the whole time I watched their limo leave, but I thought I could walk away without incident. Why is this man my undoing?

"I'm going to walk to work today, if that's all right." I don't make a move to take my hand from his or to look into his eyes. I'm powerless at his touch, and if I see anything on his face that's close to desire, I swear to God, I'll climb his body like a stripper pole.

"I saw that. Thought I might walk with you, kitten."

"You can't call me that." My eyes are on his shiny shoes, and for some reason my heart feels like it's longing. Hearing him call me that sweet name makes me wish for something I can't have. Something special and sweet that I'm incapable of being. But I can't stop the want from stirring inside me.

"Why not?"

When he cups my chin with his other hand, I take a breath and look up at him. His dark greens are bright and soft. He's looking at me like I've made his day by merely being alive, and it's a shot to the heart. I take an involuntary step into his space, and his warmth welcomes me.

I've lost my voice trying to find an answer to a question I didn't want him to ask. He puts me in this fog where I don't remember why he can't call me that, or why I can't belong to him. I get too close and I forget everything but my need to be with him, and my desire to let him protect me.

A passing bus blows its horn next to us and I blink a few times, breaking the spell. I step away from his touch, dropping his hand and feeling his fingers on my chin slip away. The distraction is exactly what I needed, and I hate that I got it. I wasn't strong enough to do it myself, so maybe I should send that bus driver a thank-you note. I'm cold without Captain's touch, but I'm doing this to protect myself and it's the right decision.

I walk in the direction of Osbourne Corp and feel him at my side. This time I tuck my hands in the pockets of my dress slacks, grateful that I've got them. Pockets are usually in short supply in women's clothing.

We walk in silence for two blocks, our steps in sync, and the rhythm is soothing. His silence and the click of my heels in time with the weight of his boots go a long way to calm my nerves. When we get to the coffee shop nearby, I look over and nod. He smiles at me, and my ovaries melt. Jesus, that man has a face Adonis would be jealous of.

"Red Bull, vanilla latte, blueberry muffin and a

chocolate scone?" He asks the question, but he knows he's right.

"Remembering my breakfast order is creepy, but I'll give you points for being efficient," I lie. It isn't creepy at all. It's sweet and makes me want to pull him to me for another one of those kisses. *Stop it, Paige*, I inwardly yell at myself. I have got to let this kiss stuff go. It's taking up too much of my thought processes. It can't be normal to think about a kiss this much.

I watch as he walks inside the shop and orders all that food. He's going to get a large coffee and a bagel and cream cheese for himself. He never eats the bagel, always offers it to me. It's annoying how much I like that.

I watch from outside as he gets his coffee and waits for the food. My eyes are trained on his full lips as he brings the cup up to his mouth, forms a little O and blows on the hot brew. Then he licks his lips, and I swear everything below my waist throbs as he puts his mouth on the lip of the cup and drinks. Watching him should not be turning me on, but I have to cross my arms because my nipples are now on high beams. I'm picturing all the things that man can do to me with his mouth when I hear someone say my name from behind me.

"Paige? Is that you?"

Turning around, I'm shocked when I see Patrick. He was one of the kids who lived near the restaurant I grew up in. We would play together in the back alleys when we were eight and talk about running away.

He came from a shitty home like I did, and when he disappeared when I was ten, I had assumed the worst.

"Patrick?"

Recognition dawns between us, and we both smile as we step forward for a hug. I wrap my arms around his neck and his wind around my waist. I could cry with relief. Patrick was the closest thing I'd ever had to a friend, but we were small kids. I have an overwhelming feeling of nostalgia seeing him, and a longing for a childhood I never had.

"What happened to you?"

"Where have you been?"

"This is crazy!"

We talk over each other, both asking the same questions at the same time. I stare at him. His big blue eyes and shaggy black hair give him that little-boy look still. He's just a little taller than me, and just as skinny. He's dressed in a Red Hot Chili Peppers T-shirt and jeans, and I want to laugh.

"I think you were wearing this exact same thing last time I saw you," I say, and playfully slap his arm.

His smile is soft, and he nods at me. "Yeah, could be. I'm down this way to meet a friend for breakfast." He smiles and shakes his head. "God, it's so crazy running into you. Not a day goes by I don't think about you. Let's have dinner, maybe—"

"No."

We both turn to see Captain standing there, holding my bag of breakfast and scowling at Patrick. I want to laugh at his absurd expression, but I also feel the need to step in front of Patrick to protect him from Ryan's wrath. So I do a little of both.

Laughing, I shift so I'm standing in front of Patrick and take out my phone. He gives me his number and I text him mine. "I've got to get to work, so text me later and let's set something up. I'd like to talk. It's really good to see you."

"Yeah, I'm running late, too. Great to see you again, Paige. Really great."

He leans in for a hug, and I give him one back. I can practically feel the glacial stare Captain bores into my back, but I ignore it. I release Patrick, and he walks into the coffee shop, waving to someone inside.

"Who was that?" The question feels accusatory, like I'm in trouble. I can see the jealousy on Captain's face. His jaw is locked as he waits for my answer.

"Just an old friend I haven't seen since I was a kid." I take a sip of my latte and walk the rest of the way to work thinking about Patrick. Captain must sense where my mind has gone because he doesn't ask me any more questions. I'm sure he'll do his own digging once we get to our office, but until then he stays silent.

Patrick knew about my situation with my mom and dad, so I'm sure he'll have questions. I don't know that I'm ready to go down that path again, but it might be good to talk to someone who already knows about my past. Telling Captain everything isn't going to be easy, and maybe I don't have to. This could be a way for me to work through what I want without the pity I know Captain will give me. Patrick and I grew up the same, so I'm not worried about him feeling sorry for me. We both had it bad back then, and something about sharing that darkness seems familiar.

We walk into the building and scan our badges, and I make my way to my desk and set down my things.

I feel Captain's eyes on me, watching my every move. He's got questions of his own, but I'm not ready for them. The one thought that keeps running through my mind is that I felt more when Ryan looked at me than when Patrick had me in his arms.

NINE

Paige

___

JORDAN RAISES A dark eyebrow at me from over the top of his many monitors. I look away and scan the room to see if anyone else noticed. Captain is staring intently at his computer, which he's been doing since we got to the office. I'd bet you anything he's running a search on Patrick. I would roll my eyes, but it's something I'd do, too, if I was him. His job is to keep Miles safe, and part of that is knowing everything about everyone around Miles. But a deeper part of me hopes that it's jealousy making him do it. At work, Captain always does everything by the rules, and to think he's breaking protocol and looking something up to check on me makes something warm inside me. I love the idea that I can make him do things he shouldn't be doing. That he'd break the rules just for me.

Clearly Jordan has noticed me staring and is wondering what the hell I want. Jordan doesn't like to be stared at, but he's the only person I know who can get me what I want. Well, at least get it to me the fastest, and I'm not sure he'll help me. If I know anything about men, it's that they love a good damsel in distress, especially men in this line of work. It's what they do for a living. Protect people.

I'm supposed to be reading about a new company Miles wants to take over. I'm in charge of learning all the ins and outs about it and who it might piss off if the buy goes through, but all I'm doing is waiting for the right time to get Jordan alone. I tried to gather information on my father on my own, but there wasn't much. I need to be able to track him, find out more about what he's doing and where he's living. What I will do with this information, I don't know, but I need something, anything. I need to be more prepared for him.

I cast my eyes toward the door, and Jordan's forehead crinkles. The scar that runs from his temple down his cheek pulls tight. I've always wondered how he got it. He isn't like the rest of the men here in Security. Sure, he holds his own, but he's normally behind a computer screen, so that scar and how he got it have always piqued my interest. I'd get it if it was McCoy, Grant or Sheppard. They all spent years in the services, and I know Sheppard even used to run a SWAT team. Scars on them add up, but not on Jordan. In fact, I don't know much about Jordan at all. The others like to talk. Him, not so much.

Not waiting to see if he'll follow, I stand up. Captain looks up at me, and I answer before he can even ask.

"Ladies' room."

"Maybe if you laid off all the Red Bull…" Grant

says, and I ignore him. They're always giving me shit about it, but they drink my weight in coffee.

"I could use a drink," Jordan mutters, standing up.

"Grant, you don't want to see me without my Red Bull," I tease in return as I leave the room, Jordan not far behind. I don't worry when I grab ahold of him and pull him into the ladies' room. I'm the only woman on the security team, and Security takes up the whole floor. We don't need the space, but only we are allowed on this floor, so I know Jordan and I won't be interrupted. He comes easily and sports a bored look on his face. Almost like he wants to get this over with. Probably wants me to stop staring at him, thinking I'm looking at the scar he tries to hide behind his hair. He sometimes lets it hang over that side of his face on purpose.

"Jesus, Turner," he mutters, shaking his head at me.

"I know, right? I bet this bathroom is way cleaner than yours." I crack a smile, but he gives me nothing. God, this guy is a stone. Not even a smirk.

"I need your help," I tell him, finally getting his attention. The bored look fades away and curiosity takes hold. I don't often ask for help, even though I'm new. It's hard for me. Even harder when I have to ask a man. He stands a little taller, like he's gearing up to protect me. "I think this guy is stalking me and, well…" I trail off, like I'm so frazzled I can't finish the rest of my sentence. I wring my hands to play up the effect.

"Okay, I'm sure the team can find out—"

"No." I cut him off. "This is really embarrassing." I shift from foot to foot. "You see, we kind of had this one-night stand and I think maybe he recorded us." Jordan's eyes go a little wide at that. "He's threatening to send the video out if I don't go out with him again."

"Are you fucking shitting me?" Jordan squares his shoulders like he's ready to fight.

"Thing is, I think he's bluffing. I got really drunk and I'm pretty sure we didn't, you know…" I let the words hang once again. "But I'm not totally sure."

Jordan runs his hands through his shaggy hair. "Give me his name and some information. I'll check him out and let you know."

That's not going to work. I have to watch him do it. "There's a time crunch, and he could send this video at any time." I let my eyes go wide, playing it up. These guys never see me as anything but tough, so I know this has to be freaking him out. Maybe even making him uncomfortable. But I'm banking on him helping me. I don't believe that anyone who can hack a computer like Jordan can doesn't have some experience in illegal activity.

"All right, all right. I'll check now."

I rattle off the information about a guy I'd met at a bar a week ago with Mal. I give Jordan all the details I think he'll need to track him down easily enough.

"All right, follow my lead, and if I find anything, I'll destroy it." He pulls open the bathroom door and we both walk back to the main office.

"I'll show you a few shortcuts I use for the recognition software. It can cut down some time when you're short some info," Jordan says to me as we enter the office. Everyone looks up as we walk in and then goes back to what they were doing. Everyone but Captain. His eyes stay on me as I follow Jordan to his desk.

He has more computer screens than any of us. Most of us have dual screens, but he has five. I stand back as he sits down, and I pretend to fidget with one of my nails, not looking at his screens, but at his hand on his keyboard. I surreptitiously watch as he types in his passwords. Everyone has three sets of passwords to gain access to their own computer. Each password is five characters long. It's set up that way so no one can ever keep up if you type it in front of them. But I can without a problem. My brain takes in each hit of the keys and locks the memory away.

"See, if you go in here…" Jordan says, as he does nothing of the sort. He says one thing, while he hacks away, pulling up this guy's driver's license and any information he can find on him. Next I watch him pull up the guy's emails. Most are related to his job at an architecture firm; a few emails are from some date sites. When Jordan doesn't find anything there, he goes for they guy's phone. God, I hope he's never done this to me. What does Miles use him for? I push that thought away and focus on what's happening now.

I watch as he pulls up all available information on this guy. You really forget how much of yourself you keep on your phone. He comes up blank, like I knew he would. But that wasn't the point. The point was to learn. To remember how to do what Jordan did. And I learned a lot.

"That should do it. You know the codes and how to use them. It will cut a lot of time for you." I look down at him and he gives me a half smile, like he's happy he couldn't find anything, and guilt slices through me. But I block it out. I have enough guilt to worry about, and this small thing is one I can live with. The guilt I carried for my mother, I wasn't so sure of, because I'm not really living at all.

The thought makes me look up at Captain, who's once again got those eyes on me. Maybe he's never taken them off me.

Sitting back in my own chair, I debate when I can get the office to myself. That's going to be the tricky part, but I shouldn't be watched so carefully anymore, like when I first came back to New York. I was always with Mal, whose main guard most of the time was Captain. He's going to be the hardest to slip past. I'll have to do it in the middle of the night, but I don't know how closely things are monitored here.

Maybe it will be something I can delete once I have access to Jordan's computer. But what will it matter if I get the information I need? Do I want to get fired? No. But it's a price worth paying for what I'll be getting.

It's what this is all about. Miles might have fallen off his path, but I haven't. We teamed up to take down my father, and Miles believes he's done that, stripping him of his businesses and leaving him with nothing. But I know most of those were fronts. They were what made him look like he had legit dealings, that he rolled with the elite of New York. Sure, it would hurt, because Alexander was always about his ego, asserting his power over people to make himself feel like more of a man. He wouldn't be happy looking like he'd failed, but he could still move on with his life. My fear is that he could keep doing the other things he'd had his hands in. Most of his illegal activities had slowed with his attempt to go legit, but I know Alexander, and he would never leave it completely. The drugs, the whores, the money, they were all too enticing. There's no way he gave it all up. He's rotten to the core, and he wouldn't ever walk away from that.

I don't know how much Miles knows, but he didn't experience it firsthand growing up, like I did. Father Dearest hid that from Miles, treating him like his golden boy, until Miles found out how he'd really treated his mother. The only reason I even know that is because Vivien told me. God knows Miles wouldn't have had that little heart-to-heart with me.

I'm not even sure why Vivien told me. She always tries to get close to me, which is unsettling. For some reason it always feels like a betrayal when I'm with her. Even though I know Vivien wasn't wrong, I'd already failed my mother so much, so liking Vivien was like adding one more sin to the pile—a pile that was starting to crash down on me, the weight becoming unbearable at times.

"Kitten." I look up from my computer to see Captain. He startles me from my thoughts, and I glance around the room. Everyone is gone, making me wonder how long I zoned out.

"How many times do I have to tell you to stop calling me that?" I snap, taking my anger out on him, before I grab my bag and leave the office.

TEN

Paige

MY PHONE BUZZES in my hand, and I scowl when I read the text. Glancing around, I don't see Captain, but it's clear he must see me.

Captain: You should stop in that diner for dinner. I hear they have good meatball subs.

Me: Stalker

Captain: You like it. Make sure you tell them no sesame seeds on the roll.

I want to stomp my foot because he knows me too damn well. Better than I know myself sometimes. How he knows all this is beyond me, but I guess we spend so much time together it was bound to happen.

Me: Why don't you order it for me, since you know everything?

Captain: Already did, kitten. See you at your place in ten.

I growl at the cat emoji he sends next and I curse
again. I shoot a look into the diner to my right and
can't see if he's really in there because of the glare
on the glass. At first I think he's joking, but what if
he isn't? I stuff my phone in my bag and quicken my
steps to my place.

By the time I get home, I'm a little sweaty. I go into
my apartment and clean up a bit. I try to tell myself
it's not because he's coming over, because clearly I'm
not letting him inside. I'm just straightening up at a
very fast pace for no reason at all.

Looking around the living room, I see all the wedding shit is still in its place. I give up on that immediately and go to my room, putting away my clothes
and making my bed because I forgot this morning.
Not because Captain is going to see it. Or push me
down on top of it.

The thought of him over me has me squeezing my
thighs together in excitement. The image of him in
my room again and doing so much more than sleeping takes hold, and I feel the pool of desire between
my legs. Just as I debate if I have time to masturbate,
there's a knock on my door.

"Shit." I pull off my heels and throw them toward
the closet and walk barefoot to answer the door.

"Go away," I say through the closed door, and the
fucker laughs.

"Open up, kitten."

"No." I cross my arms and stand there like a brat.
I don't know why I'm pretending I don't want him in

here, because I do. I just don't like that he assumes he can come and go so easily.

"You going to make me eat this whole thing myself?"

My treacherous stomach rumbles, and I remember that I haven't been to the store. There's a piece of moldy cheese and a can of Red Bull in my fridge, and my stomach knows it. I let out a huff and open the door a crack.

I look down Captain's big muscled frame to the huge bags of food he has in his paws. The smell of Italian spices and marinara hits my nose, and my mouth waters. I clear my throat and try to act cool.

"Leave it." I prop my hand on my hip and wait expectantly.

"That's cute. Move your sweet little ass out of the way." I stand back in surprise as he kicks the door open and walks right in. "Could have used my key, but my hands were full. Lock it, will you, kitten?"

"Why do you keep calling me that?" I do as he says, half annoyed, half turned on. Did he kick in my door to bring me food? Talk about a wet dream.

He places the bags of food on the table and I walk over, reaching out to open them up. But before I can, Captain is in front of me, pushing me back against the wall and placing his hands on either side of my head.

"What the—"

My words are cut off as he leans down and places a soft kiss on my neck. The warm sensation sends a shiver all over my body, and without thinking I tilt my head to give him more of my skin. The slick heat of his tongue trails down to my collarbone, and a pulse thrums between my legs. My hands move to his chest, feeling the ridges of his pecs, and I run my palm across his dress shirt. His nipples harden at my touch, and I wonder if he's getting hard anywhere else. He presses his lower body against me, and I know exactly where he's affected the most. I push my hips forward, trying to mold our bottom halves together, forgetting every reason I've ever had for not wanting to be with him.

"I keep calling you kitten," he says, pulling one of my legs up his hip so my pussy is rubbing against his thigh, "because it gets you wet."

The shudder of my breath does nothing to disprove his theory as he starts to move me up and down his leg. Captain has never talked dirty like that to me before. He's made it known he wants me, but he's normally a gentleman about it. This is different. It's dirty. And a small part of me likes the idea that maybe he just does dirty with me. That something about me makes him talk to me that way. That he can't control himself and I bring out his barbaric side.

He grasps my hips and guides me over the hard ridges of his upper thigh. The width of it opens me up, and even though we're both wearing pants, it's the perfect pressure in the perfect place. He's controlling my movements, but it's exactly what I want, so I don't stop him. His mouth is at my neck, and I move my fingers from his chest to his hair so I can hold his mouth in place.

His grip on my hips is nearly painful, and I know

he's going to leave marks on me. I should care, but instead all it does is ratchet up my desire, and I give in to what he wants. His back and arms flex and strain with his effort, and I feel like he's a caged beast waiting to be unleashed. Somewhere in the back of my mind I know this is crazy, but it feels too goddamn good to stop him.

"Ryan," I whisper, and I let my head fall back against the wall.

The delicious pressure building between my legs as Captain makes me hump his leg is too much, and I explode. The orgasm rips through me, and I scream with pleasure. I come as I cling to him, and let him use my body the way he sees fit. This wasn't planned or thought out; he came in and took from me what he wanted. Something about the loss of control is so freeing, and I ride the wave of pleasure and try not to analyze it.

He licks a place on my neck and it feels tender, like maybe he bit me, but I was too busy climaxing to notice. I don't really care, now that I'm in blissful paradise. He places soft kisses all the way up to my ear, and I hum in contentment.

He pulls back a little to look down at me, and those forest green eyes see straight through to my soul. Leaning down, he presses his lips to mine in a kiss that's more gentle than I would have imagined. I thought he'd be starved to receive his own pleasure, but instead he gives me that one soft kiss and steps away from me.

I miss his warmth the second it's removed, but he

reaches out, takes my hand and leads me over to the table. I walk on shaky legs as he sits down and then pulls me onto his lap. The bags of food are in front of us, and he reaches out and opens one, like nothing happened over there against the wall.

Looking to where we were and then back to him, I open my mouth and then close it again, unable to articulate my thoughts. After a few tries, I finally manage a sentence.

"You can't come in here with food and give me an orgasm."

He looks into my eyes and gives me his big, straight-teethed, all-American smile, and I want to slap him. Or maybe kiss him. Just for letting me know he can come here and do just that.

"I got you a foot-long meatball sub, some fries and cheesecake. Next time, I'll feed you first. You're hangry."

My lower half grumbles from being hungry and then clenches at the thought of more pleasure. I slip forward, plop down on the seat beside him and put my feet in his lap. I don't know why I do it, but he smiles at me and rubs them while I eat.

"You going to tell me who that guy was this morning?" Captain asks, after we've sat in comfortable silence for a few minutes. He hands me a beer from one of the bags he brought and goes back to rubbing my foot with one hand while he eats with the other.

"No," I say around a mouthful of meatballs. He waits, and after I chew it up and swallow, I take a drink of the beer he handed me and sigh. "I assumed you already looked him up."

"Obviously," he says, without a hint of apology in his voice.

"Then what's there to tell?"

"I'm curious about what he was to you. What he might want to be to you now."

I roll my eyes but try to imagine seeing Captain with another woman. I don't get to the point where he touches her before I've clawed her eyes out. Maybe he's pretty spot-on with the kitten name.

"He's an old friend from an old life. One I have no intention of going back to. He went missing from my neighborhood as a kid, and I worried about him for a long time. Seeing him today was good. It answered a question I didn't know I was still asking."

He looks at me and nods as if he understands. "Promise me, Paige. If you see him again, you'll take me with you." I start to take my foot from his lap, but he holds it tighter, not letting me go. "I mean it. I'm not going to stop you. I just need to be there."

He gives me a long, hard stare, and I can see the need there, but also fear. So I nod and go back to eating my food. I don't understand all these emotions passing between us. Or what the hell has happened tonight. But I'm pushing it aside and enjoying his company while it's here. God knows it's going to be lonely enough when he leaves. With Mallory moving in with Miles, it will be so empty. I need to have a meeting with Miles about the place here, to see if I can stay. He pays me a salary through his company, but I want to make sure that plans haven't changed, with Mallory getting married and them having a baby on the way.

"Hey. None of that," Captain says, tucking a piece of hair behind my ear.

I look up, and he touches my chin before sitting back and rubbing my feet again. I don't know how he knew where my thoughts had gone, but he could sense it wasn't a good place.

"You got a TV in your room?" Captain takes a sip of his beer, and I'm confused.

"Why?"

"Because I want to watch the fight, and you've got pink shit all over your living room."

I laugh and nod. "Yeah, there's a little one in my room. But I didn't ask you to stay."

"It's like getting cheesecake. You don't have to ask for it to want it." He winks at me, and my cheeks heat. How does he always keep me off balance? "I'll let you have some of my cheesecake if you let me watch TV in your room."

I think about it for a second and then pull my feet from his lap, standing up so I'm able to look down at him. He's sitting and I'm still only a few inches taller than him.

"Fine. But you keep your pants on."

His smile is so deliciously wicked, I want to straddle his lap right this second. But instead I pretend I'm unfazed, snatch the box of cheesecake off the table and stomp down the hallway.

ELEVEN

Paige

"WHAT HAPPENED TO the pants rule?" Captain asks when I come out of my closet dressed in a long T-shirt. It's an old-school one that I've had so long it's got a few small holes in it, but I can't seem to part with it. Mal has a matching one. We would wear them on veg-out nights when we would stay home and try not to move from the sofa. We had those nights quite often.

I'd thought about trying to find something sexy to put on, but I really don't have much. Besides my shoes, dressing up isn't really my thing. Until recently, when I needed to look professional for work, I had nothing but workout clothes and club clothes. I've tried to pretend that I haven't been trying to get Captain's attention, but he seems to like the way I dress. I've bought a lot of things with him in mind, but I haven't ventured into sexy underthings. Yet. I also debated putting on the shirt he'd left here. I wonder if it would turn him on to know I've been sleeping in it.

"I could have on shorts under here." I reach up, pulling my hair out of my ponytail and letting it fall loosely before shaking it out a little. God, he looks good in my bed. I'd never thought about a bed's size before, but now I'm happy I only have a queen-size. His big frame takes up most of it, and we'll have to be pressed together so that I can fit. He didn't even try to take up only one side. He's stretched out in the middle, his shoes long gone, the sleeves of his shirt rolled up like always and the buttons around the neck undone, showing off part of his chest. Maybe I should have made a fully dressed rule, because I want to pounce on him. Seeing the little patch of exposed skin turns me on. What would I do if he was naked? Jesus, his nickname for me is starting to go to my head. I want to roll on top of him and rub my body over every inch of his. Just like a kitten.

"But I don't," I finish as I crawl onto the bed. I go for the cheesecake, but he grabs it first, smiling at me. "Ask Mal about the freshman year food incident and you'll never snatch food from me again."

I narrow my eyes at him, making him smile more. Normally that look sends most men running, but never once has it worked on Captain. In fact, I think he likes it, because he always smiles when I do it. That only makes me more irritated. Or makes me swoon a little. I don't know which, and I'm not digging to find out. Never has a man been so easy with me. Nothing I do is ever off-putting to him. I wonder how long that will last when more of me starts to come out. There are parts of me he keeps finding, no matter how hard I try to keep them hidden. If only I could manage it for a little longer so I can have a few more of these days to tuck away in my memory.

Mal is the only person who's ever stuck around.

The only person who's ever stayed, even when some of my truths came to light, though I did have to fight to keep her. But Captain is different. He's fighting *for me*. No matter how hard I push, he stands there, unmovable. I could say that's even more irritating, but it's not. Instead, it's giving me a funny feeling I've never felt before. It's settling. A feeling I've never had. To think I could have someone who would always be there, no matter what I did.

"Give me your best shot, kitten."

His playful smile warms something inside me, and without thinking, I lunge for him. I catch him off guard, making him drop the cheesecake. But before I can dodge his grasp, he has me on my back with his big body over mine. He's above me, caging me under him, with my hands pinned above my head, his fingers locked into mine.

"Maybe if you're good and give me a piece of you to eat, then I'll give you a piece of cheesecake," he teases, before moving his mouth to my neck and taking a small bite. It causes me to wiggle under him as desire spreads through me.

"I thought if I let you watch the fight in my room, you'd share." I make no move to try to get out from beneath him. In fact, I try to wrap my legs around him, but he's so big it's almost impossible.

"Fuck the fight."

He takes his lips away from my neck, and I see a flash of his deep green eyes filled with desire before he claims my mouth with his. His tongue pushes past my lips in a searing kiss. His normally controlled body shakes slightly and I can feel him fighting to control himself, wanting to pull back from me. Wanting to pull back from where we are going.

"Don't fight it," I whisper against his lips as he starts to do so. "I like it when you let go. Let the perfect gentleman you always try to be slip away for me. I like this dirty, deeper part of you that comes out to play with me. I like that I make it come out."

"I promise he only comes out for you, kitten."

"Show me. I need this," I plead, looking up at him. I want him to snap, make the world melt away for me.

He captures my wrists in one strong hand. His mouth comes back down on mine, and I moan into his mouth, letting him take me and push me farther into the soft bed. Something about him makes me want to let go, to not think about anything but getting lost in him. So I do. I drop my legs from around him and let them fall open farther, giving him the invitation to do whatever he wants with me.

His hand moves under my T-shirt and up my thigh. It trails up slower than I'd like, the torture bittersweet as I rock against him, wanting more. Wanting his hand between my legs. He growls into my mouth, deepening the kiss as his tongue makes love to mine. There's still a restrained need in his body, and I want him to unleash all of it on me.

He pulls away abruptly, and I try to sit up, needing his mouth. I have to have it back on mine. I don't care if I need oxygen. I want to keep kissing him forever. I want to stay in this moment forever.

"I want to feel all of you." I yank at my hands, and

he reluctantly frees me. I wrap them around his neck, pulling him back to me and taking another kiss. He claims my mouth, and I've never been so taken. After we're both breathless, he breaks the kiss and rests his forehead against mine.

"Kitten." He says my name like a prayer, with so many emotions in his voice. I can see him fighting himself, and I want to make him snap. Why do I love pushing him so much?

I drop my hands from around his neck and go to the buckle of his pants. I fumble with his belt, pulling it free. I go to fling it across the room, but he snatches it from me.

"Hands on the headboard," he growls, his tone catching me off guard. "I'll give you what you want, but you'll do as I tell you."

His words send a thrill through me, all the way down to my toes, and I swear I can feel them tingle. My dirty Captain is coming back out to play. I slowly raise my hands to the headboard. I wrap my fingers around the metal bar and do as he says.

He flashes a predatory smile as he wraps the belt around my wrists and through the bars. My heart pounds in my chest and my body clenches with want. I have to bite back a moan as I watch him do it. Don't get me wrong, I always thought sex with Captain would be good, but I didn't think it would go like this. He didn't strike me as kinky, but maybe I'm so vanilla myself that I think this is a kink.

I lick my lips, wondering what he'll do next. I can't find any words as I stare at him in anticipation. All too slowly he sits up and looks down at me. He locks his jaw, and I can see all that control he's trying to hold in as he pushes my shirt up my body, exposing me inch by inch, and I wonder if he is torturing himself, too.

When I'm fully bared to him, he cups my breasts with his rough hands, and they fill them perfectly. I arch my back for him, loving the roughness of his hands on my smooth skin.

"Captain," I moan, begging for more. "Please."

"You call me Ryan when I have my hands on you, or I'll stop." His thumbs brush over my nipples, then halt as he waits for me to do as he tells me.

"Ryan. Please. I need more."

"Good girl," he says, his voice thick with need. "I know what you need, kitten." He slides his hands down my body, making my sensitive skin tingle with every touch. "I wanted to taste all of you tonight, but I can't. I don't think I can stop myself if I have a taste. I'd want to cover every inch of you with my mouth and make sure you were covered in my smell. But right now, instead of that, let me give you what I can."

"Oh God," I breathe shakily.

A whimper escapes as he reaches into his pants. I suck in a breath in an attempt to ground myself. He pulls out his cock, wrapping his hand around it and stroking the long, thick shaft. It's insanely erotic, watching him touch himself. I grip the bar on the headboard tighter, wishing I could touch him. I have the urge to do that for him.

My inner walls clench with a need to be filled as

he stares down at me, stroking himself. I can feel my panties dampen at the sight, but I can't look away.

Suddenly he grips my hips, pulling my ass onto his thighs, opening me up even more to him. He pulls my simple white panties to the side as he glides the head of his cock against my clit, barely grazing it. My whole body jerks at the sensation. He slides his fingers to the lips of my sex, opening it and baring all of me to him. A string of words I can't understand come out of Ryan's mouth as I throw my head back, thrusting my chest into the air as he moves back and forth.

"God, you're beautiful," I hear him say, making me look back at his face. His eyes are trained on me as he continues to rub the head of his cock against my clit. Back and forth, driving me crazy, pushing me closer to my climax. I start to move my hips with him, thrusting and grinding, miming sex.

"Ryan." His nostrils flare at the sound of his name. His dark green eyes seem darker than normal, and he looks primal. His thighs spread even more, and my legs go with them, opening me impossibly wider as his hand moves to my hip, his fingers digging into me. It's a possessive hold, so tight I swear I can feel it all the way to the bone, the perfect bite of pain.

And just like that, the climax slams into me, making me cry out his name. Ryan jerks against me, and the warmth of his release coats me as we both reach our peak together. The heat of his seed on me and his possessive grip stretch the orgasm rolling through my body, reaching heights I'd never thought possible.

I explode from every inch of my body, and when it finally ends, I'm exhausted.

My whole body goes lax and my eyes fall closed. I don't know how long we stay like this, but I can feel Ryan's eyes on me the whole time. He's staring down at me, but I can't summon the power to open my eyes or ask for my hands to be unbuckled. I'm not sure I want to be let go.

His fingers brush against me as he moves my panties back into place, and then he cups me. I feel like I've been marked on some unspoken, primal level. His release makes the panties stick to me, and I can't say that I hate the sensation. I hear him shuffle around for a minute, then my wrists are free. He runs his finger along where my hands were bound, massaging them. Then his mouth is there, kissing them, and it makes me smile.

When he's finished, he places his lips on mine in a kiss so soft I melt a little more into the bed, and sleep starts to take me. I would protest when he pulls away, but he takes me into his arms, wrapping his big body around me. His legs tangle with mine, and it's better than the kiss. Having him wrapped so tightly around me is comforting and safe.

"Want your cheesecake, kitten?"

"No," I slur, because in this moment, there isn't anything in the world I want more than to fall asleep in Ryan's arms.

TWELVE

Paige

WHEN I WAKE in the morning, I know instantly Captain's not in the room. I've gotten to the point where I can feel him, no matter where he is. Rolling over, I see a note and a little butterfly flaps its wings in my belly.

> Kitten,
> I'm taking Mallory to meet with a wedding planner. Miles asked to walk to work with you this morning, so get your pretty ass up and get to it.
> Missing you,
> R
> PS your snore is adorable

I want to crumple up the note, but at the same time I want to hug it to my chest. How can he be so annoying and sweet at the same time?

Just like last night. He was sweet in the dirtiest way, showing me a side of him I didn't even know was there. I like that I get that from him. Everyone else sees him as calm and cool, but I get to see something else. Like I have my own part of Captain no one else gets. Only I can draw it out of him, and he does it to me, too. It reminds me of the night he brought me home and told me he wanted the Paige I hide from the world, and I found myself wanting to give it to him.

I jump in the shower and make quick work of getting ready. When I'm out, I blow-dry my hair a little and then pull it back into a low ponytail. I knot the length around the band, making it look like I have some kind of hairstyle, when really this is the easiest thing.

I pull out a long-sleeved blue dress shirt that makes my eyes pop, and a pair of long black slacks. It's my basic uniform of a button-up and slacks, but the fun is always in the shoes. Today I grab my royal blue pair of Manolo Blahnik's and slip them on. They match my shirt and my eyes, and I wonder if Captain will like it. I shake the thought from my mind.

When I walk to the front door, I see a bag on the counter. I wonder how he left to get me breakfast and then came back and set it on the counter without my waking up. I must have been more tired than I realized last night.

I open the bag and smile at the baked goods inside. He even brought me a Red Bull. I walk out the door, going to the lobby to wait for Miles to come down so I can escort him to work. When I get downstairs, he's already waiting on me and talking to the front desk manager, and I check my watch to be sure I'm not late. I'm actually fifteen minutes early, so I wonder what's going on.

"Morning," I mumble around a mouthful of muffin.

"Hi," he says, smiling and then eyeing the bag.

I hold it out to him politely in offering, but thankfully he shakes his head. I don't know that I could have parted with any of the food Captain got for me. Something about him getting it makes it feel extra special.

"I thought I'd come down early and we could walk to work together. Mallory wanted to meet the wedding planner first and seems to think that it would be for the best. Something about me scaring her off if I went with her."

"You don't say." I raise an eyebrow. Miles laughs, and I realize he's never done that with me before. The strange sound is nice, and for a second I forget our history and laugh with him.

"I also thought this might be a good chance to talk."

My smile drops along with my stomach. It's the fear that's been sitting in the back of my mind. Now that he has Mallory, he doesn't need me anymore. His little spy is no longer useful. Hell, I think I actually made things worse for him since we've gotten to New York, even plotting to sneak out with Mal one night. I'm surprised he didn't fire me on the spot that time.

"Let's walk. It's nice out this morning."

I nod and slip my bag of breakfast into my shoulder bag. I'm not so hungry anymore, and I feel like I'm going to be sick. But better to get this over with as soon as possible and while it's only the two of us. Mal would probably make him keep me on, and I don't want to be here just because I'm his soon-to-be-wife's best friend. I want to be here because I'm wanted. Not because I'm pitied.

"Paige, I've always known what you mean to Mallory and how important you are to her. I knew that even before she found out the truth about how I'd influenced her life. I saw the relationship you two had forged over time, and I don't want to interfere with that. Even if at times I'm a little jealous of it."

We walk at a slow pace, but I look ahead, staying quiet and listening to what he has to say. This must be his way of letting me down gently.

"And before Mallory, I had a hard time expressing my feelings to people, including you." I can feel Miles look over to me, but I don't acknowledge it. "I know that we're in a strange situation with our relationship to each other and our history. But I wanted to clear that up now that Mallory has agreed to marry me and we're going to have a baby. I'm on a new path."

I know he is. He isn't after our father anymore, but I'm sure he knows I still am, and I'm guessing he doesn't want that around him or Mal. I can't take the anticipation anymore and I stop in my tracks, turning to him. "It's fine. I'll have my stuff out by the end of the week. Do I still have a job or not?" Miles looks at me with wide eyes, and I cross my arms, waiting for him to speak up. "Rip the Band-Aid off already. I'm a big girl and I can deal with it."

"Paige." He pauses, and his mouth opens and closes a little, like a fish. He lets out a disgruntled breath and then tries again. "Paige, that's not what this is. I know I'm bad at this, but I'm trying, so be patient with me, okay?"

I shift my weight to my other foot, not understanding what he means. He pinches the bridge of his nose and curses, then looks at me again with eyes so like my own.

"I'm trying to say that I care about you as a sister and as a friend. That I know I've been cold and distant for a long time, but it was my own ass getting in the way. You're not only important to my Mallory, but you're important to me. To the family we're building. One that you are part of." He reaches inside his jacket and hands me an envelope. "This is the deed to your apartment. I'm giving it to you. You're still employed through Osbourne Corp, but if you choose to seek employment elsewhere, I won't stop you. But know that I would be truly sad to see you go. You're an asset to the company and to your team. To everything Mallory and I are trying to build together."

I take the envelope and hold it in my hands, feeling tears sting my eyes. What is happening?

"You and I have a common enemy, and I know our original plans changed for me. But if you need help with anything…" He gives me a hard look and something like understanding passes between us. "Anything at all, you tell me, and I'm there for you. I can never repay you for what you did to get my Mallory to me, so I hope this is a start. I'm grateful that I have you, and I hope now that things are settled between us, we can start to mend our broken past."

I hug the envelope to my chest and look down at

my shoes, nodding. I don't want to cry, and I'm afraid if I look at him I will. "Thank you," I whisper, and as if in understanding, Miles starts to walk again.

The rest of our journey to work is silent, and by the time we've arrived at Osbourne Corp, I've got my emotions under control. When we pause outside the glass entrance, I turn to him.

"Mallory was right about you."

Miles nods, a smile pulling at his lips. "She usually is."

"I'm not done with him," I say, and Miles nods again. "I'll do what I can on my own, because I want to keep your hands clean. But he's got things he needs to atone for."

"I'm here if you need me" is all he says.

We walk inside and part ways, and I slip into the ladies' room before going to my desk. When I walk inside, I go into the first stall, lock the door behind me and lean back against the wall. I put my hand over my mouth and let out the sob that I was holding in the whole way to work. All the worries that I didn't know were hiding so close to the surface finally release, and I let them go. It's like a weight has been lifted from my heart and I feel lighter. I allow myself a few moments to get it all out of my system, and then I take a shaky breath.

A giggle escapes my lips, and I realize I'm happy. The worry of being pushed away from Mallory and from my home is gone. In its place is a dream of the future. One where I'm part of a family and have people who care about me. There were times in my life when I thought this was never possible, and to have it at my fingertips is something I didn't dare allow myself to hope for.

I walk out to the sink and wash my face, thinking about the path that's stretching in front of me. If this is possible, then what else could be? I finish drying my hands and suddenly an image of Captain and me together forms in my mind. Would this be possible, too? Could I have a life with him despite my past?

Walking out to my desk, I see McCoy, Grant and Sheppard are already in their seats, and I hear Jordan making coffee in the break room off to the side.

Captain's chair is empty, and I'm reminded that he's with Mallory this morning. I wonder how it's going and think about texting Mallory but realize she probably needs to pay attention. Dropping my bag and sitting down in my chair, I decide to text Captain instead.

Me: I do not snore.

Immediately the chat bubble pops up, like he's been waiting all morning for me to text. Something about that makes me smile, and I feel that little butterfly again.

Captain: I've got video evidence.

I cover my mouth with my hand, and I think he's got to be lying.

Me: Bullshit.

Captain: Does this look like the face of a guy who lies?

He sends a pic of himself, and I can't help the goofy grin that spreads across my face. God, what this man does to me. Then I see the attached video and my mouth pops open. That fucker recorded me sleeping, and he's right, I do snore.

Me: Oh, you're dead meat. You wait and see. Payback is a bitch with red hair.

Captain: I look forward to it. How about tonight? I got passes to the new brewery that opened up in Chelsea.

Me: If you're trying to bribe me with beer, it won't work.

Captain: They have hot dogs, too.

Damn it.

Me: Fine. You win.

Captain: Always do. See you after lunch. X

The kiss on the end of the text feels silly. But at the same time I reach out and touch it, like he actually sent a kiss. I put the phone down and then drop my face in my hands. This isn't supposed to be happening. I'm not supposed to be falling for him like this. None of this is part of the plan.

I wish someone would tell that to my heart.

THIRTEEN

Paige

"You going to get this shit out of here?" I ask Mal as I prop my ass up against the counter in the kitchen, looking over at the bridal explosion that is my living room.

"Are you going to tell me what's up with this little number?" Mal drops one of the bridal books she's holding and runs her eyes over my outfit as she joins me in the kitchen.

I have on a pair of white shorts, ankle boots and a dark purple crop top, which if I move just right will show a little bit of my stomach. It's not something I'd normally wear, but I find I'm doing a lot of things lately I don't normally do. Besides, my new favorite thing is to get Captain worked up. I like seeing how far I can push him before he snaps. Get him to use that dirty mouth of his on me. When he doesn't hold back his emotions, I don't have to decide if I should give in and enjoy our time, or if I should stay as far away as possible. When I'm not the one holding the power, it leaves the decision up to him. It's a useless game, because I know what choice I'm going to make. But apparently I still like playing the game.

I shrug, trying to downplay it. "Going for a few beers."

"I miss beer." She puts on this fake little frown, making me roll my eyes. She's been pregnant five minutes. How can she miss anything?

"Yeah, you look real broken up about it." She places her hand on her stomach, and her face lights up. It's been like that for the past few days. She only pretends to pout, so I bet it works on Miles. Speaking of which… "Where is your shadow? I find it hard to believe he's let you out twice in one day."

She waves her hand as if Miles is nothing to worry about. "Back to beers." She wiggles her eyebrows. "Captain?"

"Yeah, he suckered me in with beers and hot dogs. How can a girl say no to that?" I do a fake swoon, but Mal smiles bigger, knowing it's probably the perfect date to ask me on.

"Maybe you should have a snack or something. I mean, this is a date, and sometimes when you eat, you get a little…" She chomps her teeth together like she's trying to make an animal face.

"What are you doing?"

"You know, like a crazy tiger." She brings her hands up, doing some swiping motions, the worst tiger impression I've ever seen.

"Does your tiger have rabies or something?"

"Sometimes I wonder if you do." She pushes away from the counter. "Come on, let me do your makeup." I groan at the idea. This is a game we've played for years, but she has nothing to barter with. "I'll get all this stuff out of here if you let me. All the pink will be removed from this apartment before you come back home tonight."

I weigh her offer. I could simply throw all the shit in the hallway.

As if reading my thoughts, she trims her deal. "Just mascara and this lipstick I got that will match your top." Without waiting for a response, she heads for her old room.

When I enter, she's digging through one of her makeup bags. I glance around her room and think about how fast things have changed. We haven't really been in New York long, but for some reason it feels longer. Most of Mal's stuff is still here. From what I can tell of the clothes she's been wearing, Miles must have filled her closet with new ones at their place.

Mal stops rifling through her bag and places her head on my shoulder, her fingers locking with mine. "It's going to be weird not living with you," she finally says. I lean my head against hers, thinking the same thing.

"You're just a few floors up," I remind her, and myself.

"I know. I know. Still." She pulls me over to the bed, and I sit down as she starts putting mascara on me. "What will you do with the room?"

"Nothing." The word is simple, but it holds so much weight. I can't think of a single thing to do with the room. Nothing. What does that say about me? What am I going to do? Make up some secret room where I plot my father's death? Coat the walls with pictures and maps like you see on all the spy movies, because that's literally the only thing going on in my life right now? It's my one driving goal. I haven't ever thought past the point of getting my revenge. What would I want after that? If there even is an after. The reality is I could be in a room like this, only smaller, with bars on one side. But now it seems like there are a lot of possibilities if I want them. The risk count is higher now. There's more to lose.

"Pout your lips," Mal demands, and I do it. "God, Captain is going to lose it. Maybe he'll even let you hold his shield." The lame joke makes me laugh. "Take it. It looks great with your eyes." Mal hands me the lipstick, and I look in the mirror.

The dark plum lipstick does look good. Hell, it looks freaking sexy against my pale skin. I look like a woman. A lot of the time I feel like a girl, given how small I am. Maybe I should cover up the freckles on my nose.

A knock sounds from the other room, and I glance over at the clock. Captain isn't supposed to be here yet.

"It's Oz. I'm surprised he lasted this long."

I follow Mal out of the room and open the front door. Miles immediately pulls her into his arms, his mouth connecting with hers. I watch as Mal blushes, still shy about a public make-out session, but she doesn't push him away. She lets him kiss her, and even though it's a little gross, I'm happy for her. Weeks ago I would have told someone who was making out like that to get a room, but now envy lights inside me. There's a new want that's taken hold, and I know who put it there.

Finally, he gives her one last kiss and they separate.

"Hi, Paige." He smiles and hugs Mal close.

"Hey." I give a half wave, not sure what else to do. I still feel a little off after this morning's conversation. Mal looks from me to Miles, and he wraps an arm around her waist, pulling her even closer.

"I have movers coming," he says, and beams at Mallory.

"You've said that ten times today, Oz. I know and everyone in the whole building knows you have movers coming today. You're moving me upstairs and never letting me escape."

Miles doesn't seem bothered by Mal making fun of him. He merely pulls her to the side to let the movers in and starts giving orders.

"How'd the wedding planner go this morning?" I ask Mal, ignoring everything else going on.

"You don't think they're packing my panties, do you?" Mal says offhandedly, not answering my question. Miles lets out a weird sound, and after Mal's tiger move in the kitchen, I wonder what animal sounds these two are going to teach their kid. Miles releases Mallory and goes to her room, I assume to collect her underwear.

"Don't bring up the wedding in front of Oz. He's already trying to get information, but it's a surprise. He's always surprising me, and I want to be the one doing it this time…" She trails off as Miles returns with a box in hand.

"I'll toss these," he tells her.

"You will not!"

I can tell Miles wants to say more when he flicks a glance my way, but he stops himself. Thank God, because I don't want to hear about whatever my brother wants to do to my best friend.

A knock on the open door makes us all turn to see Captain standing in the frame. He's changed from his work clothes. His suit is gone and he's dressed in a pair of jeans and a gray polo that fits tight across his chest.

"Paige." He walks over to me, and before I have a chance to wonder what he's doing, he leans down and kisses me. It doesn't last long, but the message is obvious. We're together. He just made that clear in front of Miles and Mallory.

"Osbourne." Captain nods to Miles, who studies us for a second. Mal has those stupid dancing hearts over her head again, and I want to pop them.

"Ryan," Miles says, and an awkwardness fills the room.

Everyone but Mal seems to notice. Suddenly she's in planning mode. "We should go on a double date. To dinner or maybe a ball game. Oz gets the best seats. Or—"

"Baby, let them be," Miles says. Mal fake pouts and Miles changes his mind. "I can get good seats."

He's easily swayed by her, and Mallory smiles. God, they're so freaking cute I want to punch them. I think it's more the effect Mal has had on Miles that's so intoxicating to see. To want something like that.

That a woman has the ability to light up a man's whole world is fascinating to me and awakens a strange yearning inside me.

"Mal, I'll text you later. Big guy might not even make it through the night," I say, tossing my thumb in Captain's direction.

"Don't take food off her plate and you'll be okay," she informs him.

"I know how to handle my kitten," he says, lazily wrapping his arms around me. Butterflies take flight in my stomach at the "my" and I blush. I don't know whether I want to slam my boot onto his foot or climb him like a tree. Mal's mouth drops open and she stares in shock.

"Let's go, baby. I have dinner ready," Miles says.

"You're staying here, sir?" Captain asks.

"We won't be leaving the building."

Captain pulls out his phone and sends a text. Being my nosy self, I look and see Grant was the recipient.

"I'll have Grant make sure Paige's place is locked up and all the movers exit the building."

"Sounds good. We'll be taking the car in the morning," Miles says as he pulls Mal from my apartment. She's looking over her shoulder, her mouth open. Maybe Miles can distract her enough so she doesn't blow my phone up all night.

"Let me grab my bag." I step away from Captain and scurry down the hall to my bedroom.

I barely make it through the door before Captain is on me, kicking the door shut behind him. He grabs me in his arms and presses me against the closed door.

lame kiss, and I'm sure he was just being nice last night. He says this is the beginning of us, but it's not. I'm going to make that clear and then move on.

"Lame kiss, my ass," I growl as I grab my bag and leave my apartment.

SIX

Paige

"You look nice under me, Captain."

I reach out a hand, helping him off the ground. Captain's cheeks are red, and the guys around us are giving him shit, but I feel like I could conquer the world.

We're in Midtown Manhattan off Forty-first Street and Bryant Park. There's a small warehouse here we use for group training sessions on weekends. Along with me and Captain, there's McCoy, Grant, Sheppard and Jordan. The four guys are all part of Miles's security for Osbourne Corporation and are his personal detail when Captain and I can't be there.

Today we're sparring, and Captain teamed me up with him. I don't know if it's the sugar rush or the caffeine I had this morning, but I've been on point. I would have thought after last night he would go easy on me, but he doesn't hold back. In the back of my mind, I wonder if he knows I'm trying to prove something, and is just letting me get it out of my system. Either way, this is the third time I've taken him down and I could still use another round.

The warehouse is bare, with a ring in the middle

I love how easily he can move me around. It makes me feel desired and feminine, something I've never thought of myself as.

"I'm starting to think this wall-pinning situation is our thing," I mutter.

"Anything that involves you is my thing," he says, before his mouth falls onto mine. He kisses me like he hasn't seen me in days. Like we didn't spend the afternoon at the office flirting before I gave him the slip to come home and change before our date.

When he pulls his mouth from mine, he releases me, and my legs drop to the ground.

"Put some pants on," he says, looking down at me.

"Okay." I push past him, grabbing my purse, then I make a lunge for the door, flinging it open and racing down the hallway. He catches me before I get to the front door and throws me over his shoulder. I think he's going to take me back to my room, but he doesn't.

"Guess we'll just have to walk around like this so I don't have to worry about anyone thinking you don't have a man."

Captain opens the front door, and I try to wiggle free.

"Sir."

I hear Grant's voice, and it makes me freeze. "Shit," I mumble. Now everyone is going to know.

"Don't let anyone in Paige's room. It's the first door on your right down the hall. Text me when everything is clear."

"Of course, sir," Grant answers as Captain carries me in a fireman's hold toward the elevator.

"Turner," Grant says as we pass him. I give a small huff as a response.

When the elevator doors open, Captain walks in and then puts me on my feet, hitting the button for the lobby. The doors close, and I cross my arms.

"Everyone is going to know now," I murmur.

Captain wraps his arm around me, pulling me into him. I go easily, like I do every time he touches me. My body does whatever he wants.

"It's cute you think those men don't know you're already mine," he says, and then he kisses me.

FOURTEEN

Ryan

I TAKE HER hand in mine and we walk the couple blocks to Upright Brew House. When we get to the entrance, she looks at me and looks back at the building.

"This isn't a brewery. It's a restaurant."

"I know," I say, tugging on her hand and walking inside. "Reservation for Justice."

I look down at Paige, and I can almost see steam coming out her ears. She's so adorable when she gets angry. I like working her up, as she seems to like doing to me. It's all the sweeter when I get my hands on her and she melts for me. Only for me. The hardness she tries to give the world slips away, and I get the Paige she tries to hide. So full of passion and a sweetness of her own kind.

"You tricked me. This is a date!" she gasps. She looks around. "Do they even serve hot dogs?"

I have to bite back a smile. She can fight it, but I know she wants this date. She wants to be loved. I'm willing to do that for her. Break down those walls she puts up to protect herself. She'll soon learn she doesn't need them. I'll always protect her. Been doing it for so long I don't think I could ever stop. It's part of who I am now.

I pull her to my side as the hostess shows us to our table. When we sit down, Paige looks around, and I can't take my eyes off her. She's so beautiful with her dark blue eyes and auburn hair.

"That hostess needs to keep her eyes to herself," Paige says, loudly enough for everyone around us to hear. My eyes snap back to the woman, whose face flushes before she rushes back to the hostess desk. I hadn't even noticed her, but clearly Paige noticed her noticing me.

"Kitten, I'm all yours. No need to get jealous."

"I'm not jealous," she lies, and fuck, does that turn me on. Her getting worked up over me even if she doesn't have anything to worry about. I know I get worked up over her. Have been doing it for years. It's been hard being away from her all this time, having limited contact with her. Praying no fucker was trying to take her from me. Thinking about it gave me fucking nightmares. Even though I knew I needed her out of New York and away from her father, the shit still hurt, but I'd always put her before me, and at the time it was best she was away.

She stares at me for a second, a half smile pulling at her lips. She looks down at the menu, trying to hide it. It's clear she likes hearing that, so I make a note to keep reminding her that I'm not going anywhere. That I am hers. "Okay, they've got a cheeseburger. You're forgiven," she says, looking over at a nearby table.

Her gaze trails up to the ceiling, where the wood

is stained like hexagonal puzzle pieces. I'm sure it's nice; it looked that way in the pictures. But why would I look at it when I have the most beautiful thing in the world in front of me, someone I've been trying to make mine for what seems like forever?

The waitress comes over, and Paige glances down at the menu, then at me. "What are you drinking?"

"We'll both have the seasonal white, please," I say, without taking my eyes off Paige. She lets out another breath, like she's annoyed, but nods, and the waitress walks away.

"Why didn't you just ask me out on a date?"

I smile at her and take her hands across the table, pulling them to me so I can hold them. "Because you like to fight me instead of doing what you want." I raise an eyebrow in question, but she doesn't deny it. She likes when I take charge. Too many years spent doing everything on her own. "Plus, every time we're alone, you maul me."

She tries to take her hands away from mine, but I hold her fast. I'm not letting her go. Because we both know she doesn't want me to, and I don't want to let her go, either. Never do.

"I do not! That is totally the other way around." She denies the charge, but her cheeks flush. The little freckles on her nose stand out even more, and she looks younger than she is. She looks innocent.

"When I know you don't just want me for my body, then I'll let you have your way," I tell her.

She smiles at that and then shrugs. "You're no fun." She gives me a wink that goes straight to my cock. She got me to break last night. I just wanted to lie in bed with her. Get her used to me being around and not going anywhere. But then having her little body under me, begging for me to do things I've been dreaming about for years… A man can have only so much control, and I snapped. And she was right. It's been a long time since I've been with a woman—long before she even came into my life. Sex was never something I'd craved before her. But with her I do. I can't stop myself.

The waitress comes back with our beers and asks if we've had a chance to look at the menu.

"We'll have two of the Angus burgers with bacon and cheese. She'll have mayo and ketchup, but no onions or pickles, and I'll take it how it comes. We want a dozen wings, half mild, half hot, an order of truffle butter popcorn, and cut fries. That should be it."

Paige starts to say something, but I do it for her. "And then we'd like to see the dessert menu when we're finished."

She sighs loudly enough that it makes the waitress laugh, but she jots it all down and walks away.

"You're the worst," Paige says, and I let go of one of her hands so she can take a drink of her beer.

"I'm the worst because I know everything about you."

For a second her eyes grow wide, and then she looks away. "You don't know everything."

I know everything. But I don't need to tell her that. "I know what's important. Like the way you take your burgers and what kind of beer you like. I know when you lean back in your chair at work you twirl your hair with your left hand. I know that you like to take the stairs two steps at a time, even though your legs are half the length of most people's. I know you like the smell of lemons and prefer food over flowers. I know your eyelashes flutter when you're having a bad dream, and I know that a kiss below your ear will stop them from coming." Her deep blue eyes are locked on mine, and I run my thumb across her wrist.

"I know that you feel something for me that scares the hell out of you, and I know I won't take you until you recognize what that feeling is. I know that in the end, you're going to be mine, but you're terrified of seeing that far ahead. That it's going to take you some time to get used to me being around. That I'm not going anywhere. That I'd never hurt you. I know all of that, Paige, and so much more." I lean forward a little so that my words are only for her. "I know I've loved you since the first time I saw you, and one day, you'll say it back. That soon you'll see that I really do love you. That they aren't just words. I'm going to prove it to you. Make you fall in love with me."

Small tears form in the corners of her eyes, but she doesn't let them fall. She's a fighter, that's for damn sure. And it's my most favorite thing about her. I want her to let me fight beside her. With her. Show her she's not alone.

After a moment of holding my hand, she takes a breath and smiles at me. "You don't know what color underwear I'm wearing." She raises her chin a little in a smug challenge. She's teasing, because she doesn't know what else to say. She needs time to let all I said settle in, and I'll give it to her. I'll give her anything she wants as long as in the end she's mine.

I bring her hand to my mouth and kiss the knuckles. "You're not wearing any, kitten."

She tries to fight the smile, but she can't. Instead, she looks at my mouth, which is running back and forth across her hand as I feel her skin against my lips.

"How is it you know everything about me and I don't know anything about you?"

I pause my movements and smile at her. "Too busy being dazzled by my incredible personality?"

"That can't possibly be it."

The waitress comes over with our food and to offer us another beer. Reluctantly, I let go of Paige's hand so she can eat, but I don't have much of a choice, as she really doesn't play nice when it comes to her mealtime.

"So tell me, then." She glances at her burger and then back to me quickly, like she's shy about asking.

"I was born in Ukraine and placed in an orphanage as a baby. My mother was a prostitute, from what I could find out, and she couldn't keep me. I was adopted by my parents, who couldn't have children and had already adopted two other kids from that area. I was three months old when they brought me to America, and I grew up in Chicago, Illinois."

Something passes between us, and I see understanding in her eyes. "So you have siblings?"

"Yes. I'm the baby of the family."

She laughs as she looks over my big body. "Some baby."

"I have an older brother and sister, but we're not very close. We love each other, and I go back home when I can, but my work keeps me busy." I pause to take a bite while Paige thinks about which questions to ask next. She probably has a dozen to choose from.

"What's with the tattoos?"

I smile and wipe my mouth, thankful for an easy question. "You don't like them?"

"No, I do. You just don't seem like the type."

I shrug and look down at my arms. "I got most of them after I came to New York. You're right when you say I look all-American, because that's what most people say. I think I did it to rebel against that." It also helped to blend in when I worked with thugs. I was a little too pretty, as many had said before. I needed something with an edge. I hold out my arm for her to see. "Did it work?"

She rolls her eyes, but she still smiles, and that's all I ever want.

"I love cold weather, the Packers and chocolate chip cookies. I can't stand champagne, I don't trust cats and I'm skeptical of people who don't walk barefoot in their own home. I have a birthmark on my left foot, I've never met a piece of bacon I didn't like and I have a very strong attraction to your ass."

Paige howls with laughter, and I sit there watching. The way her head tilts back and exposes her throat. The way her hair falls to the side. The way she places her hand on her chest. She's laughing with her whole heart, and it's the most beautiful thing I've ever seen.

I wish I could tell her more. I wish with everything in me that I could lay it all out on the line. But I need her to fall in love with me first. I need her to see what's standing between us and give in to it. Because when I finally come clean, I need to know the bond holding us together is strong enough that it won't break. All the other shit doesn't matter. How I grew up or where I came from. Small details of my life. Now is what matters. The choices I make today. At least, I pray that's all that matters to her.

We talk about work, and she asks me simple things that don't require me to lie or hold back the truth. She finishes her food and some of mine before the waitress brings out the dessert menu.

"What are we having?" I ask as she looks it over.

"You're not going to order for me?"

"No." I shake my head, and she smiles excitedly. "Dessert is the most important meal of the day. I would hate to deny you the pleasure of choosing."

She hands the menu back to the waitress, ordering one of everything. "Life is short."

She leans back in her chair, and I want to kiss her so badly. I need to pull her into my lap and hold her soft body against mine. But this isn't the place for that, and I meant what I said to her earlier. Until she tells me she loves me, I won't take her. We've been getting too close to that happening, and it needs to stop. I want more from her than a quick fuck, and I want her to respect that.

By the time the desserts arrive, I've finished telling her a story about my first time taking the subway and getting lost.

"So you paid a homeless guy twenty bucks to take you to the drugstore?" She laughs, scooping up some ice cream and taking a bite.

"It may have been profiling, but I assumed he'd know where to find one. I had a head cold. What else was I supposed to do?" I love seeing her smile, and I would tell her stories like this all night if it kept that look on her face. "Besides, he ended up being a she, and she offered more than the directions. If you know what I mean."

We laugh some more, and then Paige tells me about her first time on the train with Mallory and how they sat in seats that faced away from the direction the train was heading, and she got scared they were going the wrong way.

"I was yelling at the ticket guy that we needed to get off the train, but he was really nice and explained that it happens all the time." She takes a deep breath and rubs her belly. "This has been the best surprise date I've ever had."

"I would have to agree. You ready to go?"

"I don't want it to end." I can see the truth in her eyes, and I reach out, take her hand and lead her out of the restaurant.

"Let's go for a walk. The night's not over yet."

We take the path to the park. The sun has set, but the lamps light the way along fountains and trees. It's a beautiful night, and holding her hand isn't enough, so I wrap my arms around her and pull her to my side.

"What's happening?" Paige whispers, more to herself than to me.

"Whatever you want to happen, kitten. I'm not going anywhere."

FIFTEEN
Paige

"Fuck." I HEAR the muttered word as I slowly open my eyes, the morning light peeking through the curtains of my bedroom. I smile against Captain, his chest hair tickling the side of my face. I give a little wiggle of my hips, feeling his morning wood press into me as I breathe him in.

This is how I've woken up the last few days, with my body on top of his. I can't ever get close enough to him. It seems I'm a cuddler. Who would have thought? Maybe years without much physical contact has my body soaking up every bit it can get while it lasts. He grips my hips to stop me from grinding against him. Instead, I sink my teeth into his chest, giving him a playful bite. He murmurs another *"fuck,"* but this time his voice is so deep I can feel the vibration.

I sit up on his lap, looking down at him laid out on my bed. I still can't get used to it. He looks like a Greek god with all his thick muscles. Too bad he won't let me do what I want to him. He looks like he's been awake for a while. Probably has. Captain is a morning person, and it's the only fault I've found with him over the past few days. That and the fact that he's hardly touched me since the night with the belt. I'm getting frustrated. This is totally ass backward. Isn't the man supposed to be pushing for sex and not the woman?

I stretch my arms over my head, doing my best to tease him, and the hands on my hips tighten. His face turns hard as his eyes narrow on me. He jerks his hips, making his cock dig into me, and a soft moan leaves my lips.

"Kitten," he warns.

"What?" I bat my eyelashes, like I have no idea what I'm doing.

"You're pushing it."

"Really?" I rock my hips slightly. "'Cause it feels like I'm rubbing it." I lean down, a breath away from taking his lips. And right before I almost kiss him, I spring off the bed. Two can play this game.

Well, I *think* I can play this game. Or at least I'm trying to. Captain is the only man I've ever tried to seduce before.

If I've learned anything over the past few days, it's that Captain likes to kiss me. It's like he can't go more than twenty minutes without touching his lips to mine. He even steals kisses when we're at work. It's cute and silly and maybe a little juvenile to sneak off for a make-out session. But I can't get enough of it, even when I pretend like it's annoying me. He smiles every time I tell him "no, we can't do this at work," then he kisses me again. I think what I love most about it is that he's normally all business on the job. But with me, I come first. His need to kiss me overrides everything else. It's adorable, and I don't care that it's immature.

He makes a grab for me, but I dodge him, slipping into the bathroom and locking the door.

"Think I can't get in there?" He uses his firm, no-nonsense tone, and I roll my eyes.

"I'm naked," I tell him, pulling off my T-shirt and panties and turning on the shower. I know he won't come in now. I hear him growl before saying something about breakfast. I giggle.

I jump in the shower and make quick work of my morning routine, throwing on some navy slacks, a white button-up silk top and lilac Prada wedges. I gather my hair into a ponytail and then join Captain in the kitchen. The man knows that the way to my heart is through my stomach, and he's not pulling any punches. We work around my kitchen like he lives here and knows it even better than I do. I guess he probably does. He's cooked here more than I have.

"I don't even know where you live," I say, taking a bite of the eggs with extra cheese. The flavors hit my tongue. God, this man can cook. How does he do everything so perfectly? He has to have another fault besides being a morning person.

He smiles. "A floor down."

"What?" I say, louder than I intend. "Does *every-one* live in this building?" What the hell? I really shouldn't be shocked by this. No wonder he can pop out of nowhere sometimes.

"I've worked with Miles for years. It's easier this

way." That makes sense. It's easier to be close. He's been guarding Miles since before I came into the picture. Captain has always been around. I wonder how close they are. Probably not super-close. Miles doesn't really let people in. Not until recently, anyway, and that's a major work in progress as it is.

"God, I used to dislike you so much." I shake my head, thinking back to the times I saw him before Mal and I came to live in New York permanently. I hadn't seen him that often, but it was enough. He was with Miles so much that when I checked in, he'd be there. Sometimes he was worse than Miles with the questions. Sometimes, after I'd report to Miles, Captain would call and grill me again. He'd even shown up at our school a few times, wanting a detailed rundown of things. He'd demand I show him around the campus so he could see where all our classes were. He even inspected our dorm room. Sometimes I wasn't sure who was more obsessed with operation Keep Mal Safe—Captain or Miles.

"You wanted me." It finally hits me. That's why he was such a pain in the ass! "That's what all the questions were about! I thought you thought I was incompetent!" I throw my hands up in the air, shocked I hadn't seen it sooner. How did I miss it?

"I told you, Paige. I've loved you since the moment I laid eyes on you." He makes no apology for his words or actions. He's not even a little embarrassed at being caught half stalking me.

My stomach flutters again. That's the second time he's said the *L* word to me. Mal is the only other person who's done so. I think I felt it, but I wasn't sure how to communicate it to her.

"She's starting to get it," he says, standing up from the breakfast bar and placing a kiss on top of my head. I sit there, running through all the conversations we've had over the years. They always focused on what I'd been up to. Where I'd been going. How my classes were panning out and if I needed anything. Anything at all.

"You're like Miles. Two peas in a stalking pod." I debate if I should be irritated, but I bet those little hearts Mal gets dancing over her head are dancing on mine right now. I was always jealous of how much Miles obsessed over Mal, worrying about every tiny thing. I don't think Captain is that bad, but I like his way better. It's subtle and less controlling, but still possessive.

He comes over, moving in on me, and I lean back. "You're going to kiss me."

It's not a question, but I answer it, anyway. "Nope."

I jump off the chair and go in search of my bag to take to work. I can feel his eyes on me as I check to make sure I have everything I need. I have to bite the inside of my cheek to keep from smiling. It's been five minutes and he's already losing it with the not-kissing thing. Why didn't I think of this sooner?

By the time we make it to our office building, I remember why I haven't gone on a kissing strike sooner. Because I like it as much as he does. Making out on the couch like teenagers, it's like making up for lost time. It's a simple thing girls do, and I'd missed out on it. Now I wonder who's going to break first. God knows if Captain really wants a kiss, I'm going to be pinned to a wall. So my best chance is to beat him to it.

When the elevator door closes, I throw myself at him. He catches me easily, pulling me to him. He grabs my ass, his fingers digging into me. I go straight for his mouth, kissing him like I haven't seen him in years. I pour everything I have into it, giving him all the emotions he's made me feel over the past week. I tell him without words that I think I'm falling in love with him, too. I want him to finally give in and give us both what we want. I want to share something with him I've never shared with another person in my life.

I rub against him, needing to get closer. I run one hand through his short hair, and I pull a little, gripping him as possessively as he holds me. I feel aggressive and passionate, and I want to leave a mark on him.

When I hear the elevator ding, I push back and put some distance between us. Taking a breath, I adopt a straight face, but I glance over and see that Captain looks shocked. Probably because I've never attacked him like that at work before. He's the one always grabbing me here.

I give him a smirk, proud of myself. "Better make sure that one holds you over," I tease, before walking out of the elevator, leaving him standing there, surprised by my actions.

Well, that was the plan, anyway. I don't make it half

a step before I'm being grabbed back into the elevator and pinned against the wall. Captain reaches over, slams his fist against the button to close the doors, and the elevator does what he demands. Then he slams the emergency stop, and a shiver of desire snakes down my spine.

"Kitten, I promise you that you don't want to tease me." He makes it so there isn't space between us, pressing me farther into the mirrored wall. "You don't know how many times I've jerked off in the shower this week, thinking about taking you, having you, making you mine. I've been doing it for years, but it's worse now because every morning I wake up with you in bed next to me, your sweet smell all around me. Knowing what your body feels like. What you sound like when you moan my name." My breath catches at his words. "You breathe and I'm fucking turned on. So when you pull a stunt like this where you tease me, I have to think real hard about why I'm not ripping your panties off and fucking you right here, right now."

"Holy shit," I whisper.

"Now give me your mouth."

I do as he commands, kissing him once again. This time it's as hard and raw as before. Only, I'm not in control. He kisses me like nothing else in the world matters and we have all the time he wants. I'm a puddle of molten need, gasping for breath, when he finally breaks our connection.

"Don't ever deny me when I want your mouth," he growls, then finally pulls away, leaving me dazed. I didn't know a kiss could make the earth spin in the opposite direction.

After a second I get my footing back and straighten my shoulders. "There isn't a time when you don't want my mouth."

"Then you better buy stock in ChapStick."

I laugh at that, and he lets me go. He hits the button to our floor. The elevator opens and we step out, and both of us walk into the office like nothing happened. We take our seats. Only McCoy is here. Everyone else is out on duty. He glances up at us and raises his eyebrows. I wonder if my lipstick is all over my face now.

"I deleted the feed," he finally says, and I groan. He totally saw what Captain and I just did in the elevator.

"Watch yourself, McCoy," Captain growls, standing from his chair, suddenly angry.

McCoy puts his hands up in a gesture of surrender. "Told you I deleted it, man. Not like I fucking watched it."

"Cool it," I snap to Captain. He takes a breath and then slowly sits down, his eyes still on McCoy, clearly pissed that someone saw our make-out session.

"Sorry, I'm a little on edge," he tells McCoy. I have to fight a smile, because I know why he's so on edge. Me. I know what he wants from me. A clear commitment that I'm in this for real. Not playing a push-and-pull game anymore. And I want to give him that so bad. The past few days have been some of the best of my life. The tension drains from the room, and we all go back to our computers.

I respond to a few emails, then check in on Mal's schedule. I'm normally on her detail when she leaves the building, but she's just been going from work to home. She doesn't need me when her driver is our security, so I haven't had much to do.

When I pull up my calendar, the floor drops out from below me. How could I have forgotten? The date stares back at me, and a cloud forms in front of my eyes. It's the anniversary of the day I lost my mom.

"Fuck," I whisper to myself, dropping my head and taking a few breaths. I get myself under control, because I'm not going to lose it here at my desk.

I told myself I was going to enjoy Captain while I could have him. That when he finds out what I want to do to my father, he'll leave me. Hell, I don't even know if I'll get to stay around after. If I make it through, I might have to run. It's why I kept him at arm's length from the beginning, because we are two different people who come from two different worlds.

But somehow when I decided I would take what I could from Captain, he'd taken me. I've been living on this little fluffy cloud, forgetting all about my mother and how I have a duty to repay what was done to her. How could I do that to her? I owe her justice. It's like I'm back in that room watching her die, standing there helpless all over again. Then the night flashes through my mind, playing scene by scene.

I close my eyes tightly. I don't know how long I sit there making myself watch it over and over again in my head. Reminding myself of what I did.

Nothing.

I'd done nothing to save her. And what am I doing now to avenge her death?

I pull out my cell phone and text Mal.

I need a favor.

SIXTEEN

Ryan

SOMETHING IS WRONG with Paige. I've been watching her all day, and she's not herself. I've gotten her alone twice to ask her, but she brushes it off, saying she has a headache. I'm not sure I believe her. A mask has dropped over her face, making her harder to read than normal. By the end of the day, she isn't any better, and I'm starting to worry and feel completely on edge. Every muscle in my body is strung tight as I wonder what's going on in that head of hers. She's been playful these past few days as I pulled the real Paige out piece by piece, but that playfulness has all but disappeared now.

"Kitten, maybe I should take you to the doctor," I say, putting the back of my hand on her forehead to see if she has a fever. She doesn't feel warm, but this isn't like her. I don't like this shit, and something about it is eating me. It feels off, and I always trust my gut.

She glances around and then back at me, knocking my hand away more forcefully than I expect. The motion burns deep in my gut. The playfulness slips away even more. She's slipping away. I can feel it.

Usually when she bats me away, it's a halfhearted attempt. Almost an invitation to keep touching her. But that felt different. "To put it bluntly, I started my period today. I get really bad headaches and cramps, so if you don't mind, I'd like to be alone tonight."

Her statement surprises me. I didn't expect her to say it, but it's not like she's got the plague. I don't know what most guys' reactions would be, but I don't care. It's just a period. Every other person on the planet has one. It's not like she's going to give it to me, and if I'm with her, I can take care of her. Get her anything she might need.

"Look, let's go home and I can rub your feet and you can rest. I'll make us dinner." I'm already thinking about what I can do to make her better. Maybe she's irritable and needs to eat. That happens more than not. I can Google what helps with that time-of-the-month shit. I'm sure there is something I can do for her.

She looks annoyed and shakes her head as if shaking away the idea. "No, I'd rather be alone. I'll see you in the morning." Her words are final, and I'm shocked, pissed even, as I watch her stack those blocks back up around her. She thinks they're going to stay, but I won't let them.

"Hey." I grab her arm, but she jerks it out of my grip. What's happening? Why is she being so aggressive? She's pissed, that much is clear. I can see it in the tight lines of her body. She's rigid, almost breakable.

"Seriously, Ryan. I'm fine. Give me some space tonight. Is that so much to ask?"

The fact that she used my real name makes me take a step back. I don't appreciate her tone, or her insinuation that my being with her is somehow an inconvenience. "I wanted to make sure you were all right. I can see you have that under control." It takes everything in me to force those words past my lips.

This is about her father. She has that same look on her face she had that night at the party. I take a deep breath to calm myself. I need to give her a little space. A little time to breathe, but not much. She isn't walking this road alone, as much as she wants to, or at least thinks she wants to.

She grabs her messenger bag and avoids eye contact. "I'm fine. I'm not feeling great today, and I'd appreciate a night off."

"Absolutely." The word comes out cold, but she doesn't react. I clench my fists at my sides so I don't reach out and grab her and pull her to me.

I try to give her what she's asking for, even though I think the reason is bullshit. There's something else there, but with Paige, I can't push her. Not yet, anyway. I need to figure out what's happened. What's changed in the last few hours. My mind runs through everything that's gone throughout the day and nothing comes to mind.

We walk out of the building together, and I make sure she gets home safe. When she says goodbye to me at her door, I throw my hands out and let it go. Obviously, she isn't ready to talk about what's really going on.

I take the stairs down one floor to my apartment

right below hers. I let myself in, dropping my keys by the door, and walk to the living room. It's sparse and cold in my place, and suddenly I hate every inch of it. Mostly because it doesn't have Paige in it.

I flip on the TV that shows the feed from all the cameras in the building. I pull up the one that's on her door. I sit on my couch, wondering if she's okay and trying to think of what the hell happened after we got to work. I lie back and look up at the ceiling. We're separated by only a few feet, but for some reason it feels like we're miles apart.

That's okay, kitten. I'll let you push for a minute, but I'm coming for you.

SEVENTEEN

Paige

"HEY, I'M HERE. What's going on?"

I grab Mallory and pull her into the apartment, closing the door behind her. She gives me a wary look but doesn't push. I've gone over this a hundred times in my head, so hopefully she'll be okay and won't ask a lot of questions. I don't want to have to lie to her. I swore I would never do that again, and I won't.

"I told Captain I needed to be alone tonight. I said I got my period and I wasn't feeling good."

She looks at me in puzzlement and tilts her head to the side. "You hardly ever get your period. You've been irregular since I've known you."

"I know. That's not the point," I say, hating that she knows me so well. How does she know exactly when I get my period and when I don't? That's some creepy friendship shit right there.

"Paige, what are you up to? Is this another secret mission?" For a second she looks excited, and I think back to the night we sneaked out on Miles and Captain. She gets way too excited about pushing Miles's buttons, but after doing the same to Captain, I can't say I blame her. It is fun seeing them squirm. And

I'd be lying if I didn't say it was nice to watch them chase after us. I wonder if Captain will chase after me when he finds out what I've done.

I shake off that thought, because it derails me. I need to stay focused, something I haven't been doing, and I don't have much time.

"No, tonight is a solo operation. Next time, I swear," I add when I see her face drop into a pout. "I need you to stay here, and if Captain comes knocking, tell him I called you to come down and stay with me. Tell him I'm asleep in the bedroom and I can't come to the door."

"What if he wants to talk to you?" she asks, already accepting without question what I'm doing. God, I love this woman.

"Make up an excuse. Say I'm taking a shit in the bathroom, I don't care. Just convince him that I'm fine, but that he doesn't need to check on me." I grab my backpack next to the door and shoulder it on. "I don't think he'll come up, but in case, I need you."

She puts her hand on my arm and gives it a squeeze. "Yeah, absolutely, Paige. I got your back."

It feels good knowing that she'll always be there for me, even if we aren't together like we used to be. I want to tell her all of this, but I don't know if I can. Something about this feels like it's only mine, and getting her involved beyond this will just complicate things more. I don't want to drag her into this. It would only drag Miles in, too. This is my mess, something I had to make amends for, not them.

"Thanks, Mal." I lean in and give her a hug, holding

her tight before turning to leave. When I put my hand on the doorknob, she stops me.

"Will you tell me what this all about someday?"

I look over my shoulder and smile at her. I don't answer, I only shrug and walk out the door. I wait a beat, making sure I hear her lock the door behind me. When I know she's good to go, I'm on the move. I love Mallory, but there are some things I don't know how to share.

I USE THE service elevator in our building, in case Captain happens to be watching the cameras. I'm not sure where all of them are in this building, but I have a good idea. I dressed in all black and boots, trying to blend in. I avoid the cameras as much as possible, sidestepping down the hall where I know the blind spots are. I know this building is a fortress, but every palace has its weaknesses. I slip out through the basement garage and then haul ass up to Osbourne Corp.

I don't know how much time I have, and I'm basing it on the assumption Captain will show up on my doorstep around bedtime to check on me. If I know him like I think I do, I need to be back home and in my bed before that happens, because he won't take no for an answer. Mallory is merely being used to slow him down. I've probably got an hour before he's kicking in the door. Tops. The thought makes my stomach flutter. He's probably so concerned and worried about me, and I'm here doing this behind his back. Worse, I'm using him.

Mallory had told me Miles had a late meeting,

so she would be good until midnight. I was hoping Captain would be on his detail and I wouldn't have to lie, but he wasn't. McCoy was. But I have a feeling Miles will somehow get out of his meeting earlier, to get home to Mal as soon as possible. Either way, the pressure is on to do this fast. Our guys are crazy, so I'm not leaving anything to chance.

When I get to the building, I use the side entrance by the garden that Miles made for Mallory. There's an emergency exit there, and it's an access point. Only three people have clearance to use this door as a way to enter the building: Miles, Mallory and Ryan. I take the badge from my back pocket and scan it, watching as the light turns green.

I didn't want to steal Captain's badge, but it seemed the only way. I don't want to be caught on camera getting into the building, and if the scans are done on all the entrances, it will show that Captain's badge was used. It may ruffle some feathers, but no harm, no foul, right? As the head of Security here, he comes and goes at all hours. I don't think anyone will even notice or question that he'd come late in the evening.

When he grabbed my arm earlier today, I broke free and made a show of being irritated that he was trying to grab me. It was the only way I could think of to distract him so he wouldn't see I lifted the pass from him. I'll leave it in his desk tonight, so he'll think he left it at work. He's going to be pissed, but as long as he doesn't find out it was me, I'm covered. Maybe he won't hate me then. I don't like lying to him, but it's better for both of us. It doesn't put him in the middle of anything if he doesn't know any better. Everything can fall on me.

Making my way up the stairs to our floor, I avoid the cameras in the stairwell. I know there's no way to do so in the elevator, so this is my best bet. When I get to our floor, I secure the entrance behind me and go over to Jordan's desk. I sit down and click a few keys, bringing his computer to life. I unzip my backpack and take out my laptop and some cords, linking the two computers together. I enter all three of Jordan's passwords, remembering exactly what they were from the day he showed me. Once I'm in, I open up the software to copy everything I'm seeing to my laptop. If someone digs, the searches will come up on Jordan's computer and it won't lead back to me. I'll wipe all the information after I'm done and I get what I want, but it will show that his was the one accessed tonight and not mine. *Sorry, buddy, but a girl's gotta do what a girl's gotta do.*

Once I'm all set up, I pull everything I can find about my father. Miles has a folder of information about him. I mainly need locations, phone numbers, emails and things that will lead me to him. Or lead me to a weakness he might have. He's gone off the grid since Miles took a lot of his companies out of commission. Those companies that were fronts for a lot of his dirty dealing, and he's hiding, letting the dust settle. There are files here that can be accessed only by encryption software, and I use that to go in and pull up Miles's files, as well. They could be love notes to Mallory for all I know, but I've seen Captain looking at them, and I want to have them copied onto my personal drive, too. I can look through them thoroughly when I get back home, but tonight is about gathering as much information as I can. I have a feeling that after my little break-in, I won't get this opportunity again. Captain will watch his badge more closely, and Jordan may suspect someone was on his machine. Worse, I may get caught and never be allowed in the building again, and I need as much as I can get on my laptop.

It takes me only a few minutes to scan through and add the files I want. It takes another few seconds to mirror all the data from Jordan's computer onto mine and close down the programs. Once I've got what I need, I wipe Jordan's computer of everything I've done and load my laptop back into my bag. I put it on my shoulder as my pulse races, but I've got what I need. I'll finally be able to end this. Put it behind me. Maybe have a future with Captain if he'll still have me. God. Captain. Just thinking about losing him makes my whole body ache.

I push Jordan's chair back exactly how I found it and check his desk one last time to be sure there's nothing out of place. I smile, thinking that it's all going to plan, and turn to leave.

And as I do, I run into a brick wall. My Captain.

"Hey, kitten," he says, looking down at me. "Have something of mine?"

EIGHTEEN

Paige

CAPTAIN STARES DOWN at me, his face nothing but hard
lines. An unreadable mask. There's no emotion to it,
and he's giving nothing away. He's still in the same
suit he wore to work today. His green eyes look darker
than ever. I grab the strap of my backpack tighter and
stare back, unsure what to say to him. I don't want
to try to explain this. I knew we weren't forever and
that's why I was savoring all the moments I could
with him, collecting each of them to replay over and
over again in my head when he was long gone from
my life. For when he wanted nothing to do with me.
He'll regret ever telling me he loved me, because the
person he thought he loved isn't really me.

It's tearing at my heart, because I never thought
about the fact that I'd have to relive the breakup along
with all the good moments. This is when he finds out
who I really am deep down inside, and he walks away
from me. Seeing him staring down at me, I feel the
weight of it hit me in my chest. The reality of losing
another person I love.

Love.

The word bounces around in my head. Holy fuck. I love him and I lost him.

"I—" The single word leaves my lips before he cuts me off.

"Not a word," he says, his tone completely flat. He's unreadable, and I don't know how to react. His big hand engulfs my wrist, and he pulls me along behind him as he turns to leave. I don't fight, though maybe I should. The urge to flee is strong, because facing the reality of what I've done is closing in on me. I'm good at running when I get scared. When I can't handle what's happening. The silence in the elevator is deafening. I don't know if I hate it or welcome it.

He hasn't told me it's over. Yet. So in this moment of limbo, he's still mine, but I know what's coming. I want to lean into him. Take his mouth in one last kiss. I remember this morning with the two of us in this very elevator, and it was completely different than it is now. My eyes fall closed as I replay it in my mind, feeling the tears start to build up behind my eyelids. I fight with myself to not let one slip free.

When the ding sounds, I open my eyes and Captain is pulling me from the elevator and out of the building. He holds my arm as we walk down the street to our building, and I wonder where he's taking me. To my apartment, to his, or maybe even to Miles's, to tell him what I'd done? He's probably going to tell him to fire me, shattering yet another relationship that was starting to build.

Maybe I should run. I could take the backpack and go. It has the information I need, and it's what started me on this path almost five years ago. I let myself become distracted and forgot about the one person I owed. I let Captain and the thought of us sidetrack me and help me forget the horrible things I witnessed. He filled my mind with so much sweetness, it took up all the space. The memories of every touch we shared pushed forward and eclipsed the dark.

"Don't even think about it. You won't make it two feet," Captain growls, cutting through my thoughts.

Somehow he knows exactly what I was thinking. His anger shows in his words, and it's the first spark of any emotion I've gotten from him since he caught me. When we finally make it to our building, relief hits me when I see him push the button to my floor. The elevator ride is far quicker than I'd like it to be, and he soon pushes me into my apartment.

I look around but don't see Mal. I wonder what happened. He came faster than I thought he would. Part of me had hoped I wouldn't get caught at all and that I'd still have a few more days with him. That maybe I could get my revenge and be able to keep him from finding out what I'd done. The thought of keeping him and having something of my own makes my chest ache.

He finally lets go of me when the door shuts behind us. I hear the lock click into place, the sound echoing in the silent room.

"Don't ask me for it." I tighten my hand on the strap of my backpack, unsure of what I'll do if he demands I give it to him. I'm weak. I don't know how I'll react if he asks me to let this go. If he finds out what I was doing and he makes me choose… Because deep down I think I'll choose him, and what does that say about me? That I wouldn't do right by my mother? That I could move on with my life while she's dead and gone?

I don't want to have to choose. It's easier to beg forgiveness than ask permission. He reaches out, and I think he's going to make a grab for it, but he cups my face, and I lean into his palm, closing my eyes, letting his warmth seep into me. Every time he touches me I melt so easily. How he does it, I have no idea, but he does. With one touch I want to curl into him and soak up a lifetime's worth of affection.

"I don't want the backpack, kitten."

A sob threatens to break free at the nickname. If he's still calling me that, it has to mean something. A flare of hope takes hold in my stomach, making me open my eyes to look up at him.

"You don't run from me." He leans down, getting more into my space. "You don't even fucking think about running from me."

Gone is the patience he'd been giving me. White-hot anger burns through him now, but it's not about what I'd assumed.

"I stole your badge," I blurt out, not understanding what's happening here. We seem to be focusing on two different things.

"Did you hear me, Paige?" He ignores me, the fierce heat still in his eyes.

"Did you hear *me*?" I snap, not sure if I'm mad

that he didn't respond or mad that he called me Paige and not kitten, the nickname I'm supposed to hate.

"I don't care about the badge." His eyes flick to my shoulder. "Or the backpack." He moves farther into my space, and I take a step back, uncertain of what's going on. I can feel the anger pulsing off him like a living thing, filling up all the space around us.

His whole body goes solid at my retreat, and he takes a few calming breaths. I've never seen him like this. Like he's about to lose it. It's probably because the woman he thinks he loves deceived him.

Taking me by surprise, he picks me up in his arms and pulls me close to him. He buries his face in my neck and I feel his warm lips on my skin. This big beautiful man is engulfing me in his strength and need, and it's almost more than I can bear.

"I didn't mean to scare you, kitten. I'm sorry." His words are muffled against me, but I hear them. Unable to help myself, I wrap my arms around his neck and run my fingers through his short hair. I feel some of the tension leave his body, and the quaking intensity of him lessens.

"I saw it in your eyes. You thought about running, just taking off, didn't you?" He leans back and looks at me, and I nod. His hands are at my back and his fingers dig into me like I might disappear right in front of him. "I told you I love you."

I have to bite my lip to keep it from trembling. Every time he says that, it's like a balm on my soul, making me feel not so dirty.

"You think I don't know you want to hurt your

father? Kitten, I don't miss one fucking thing about you. I know every breath you take."

I shake my head. "It's not like Miles. I don't want to ruin him," I tell Captain, trying to make him understand. It's worse. I'm worse. I want something darker. It's the only thing that will stop the guilt, stop the nightmares. But part of that's wrong. Captain stops my nightmares now.

I have to make him see, to get this over with. I can't take the torture of him walking out. I want it done already. "I watched my mother die right in front of me. I stood there and did nothing. Then I ran." Like I wanted to do again tonight. To run as far away from all of my self-hate. I'm always trying to run from the memories, knowing that it's impossible.

"Oh, kitten."

I try to push back from him, but he won't let go of me. His grip on me is unbreakable, and it makes me hope he'll never let me go, no matter how hard I pull. That he'll keep holding me.

"Nothing. I've done absolutely nothing to make him pay for what he did to her. I didn't do anything to help her then, and I need to make that right. I watched it all happen while I remained frozen. Then when I could move, I ran."

"And my girl remembers everything. Bet you even make yourself relive it over and over, don't you?"

"Don't say that," I snap. "I'm not your girl. Don't you see it? That's what I'm trying to tell you. I'm not good for you. I'm not who you think I am. Part of me is spoiled, and it won't ever be made right. I won't stop until I make him pay." Even as I throw the words at Captain, I dig my fingers into his shirt, not wanting to let go. I'm telling him he should be leaving, but I'm clinging to him. My body and heart are at war.

"Kitten, you can keep trying to push me away, but you're going to learn real quick I'm not going anywhere. I don't want to lose you, so I'm going to give you the revenge you want."

"You don't mean that. I don't think you understand that I want to—"

He cuts me off before I can finish. I'm about to finally give voice to what I've been dancing around. "I'll kill anyone who gets in the way of you and me. The way I'm seeing it right now is he's standing in my fucking way. He's making you push away from me. That makes him as good as dead."

Tears start falling, breaking free of the dam I'd built when he found me in the office.

"Don't cry, kitten." I wrap my arms and legs around him, burying my face in his neck as I let all the tears flow free. "It's you and me. No matter what. I love you, Paige, and if this is the path you need to take, then I'm going to plow it clear for you."

I hold on to him tighter, letting free all the welled-up emotions inside me. I never want to let go, and I never want him to release me. He carries me into the bedroom, where my back hits my bed, and he comes down over me.

He's not leaving.

"I'll never leave you," he says, and I realize I said the words out loud. "Is this why you keep me at arm's length? You think once I got to the core of you, I'd leave?"

I nod into his neck.

"Look at me, kitten."

I reluctantly pull back, sure my face is a red, blotchy mess. His hand cups my cheek as his thumb wipes at my tears.

"I've been taking things slow with you. I was worried I might spook you with how strongly I feel for you. That shit is done. You're mine, Paige, and you're not going anywhere without me. I'll fight for you, and soon you'll see how true that is."

I don't get it. Why is he so willing to do this for me? Why does he want to work so hard to be with someone like me? I'm sure he could walk into any bar and find a girl with not even a tenth of the baggage and shit I carry around. Someone who doesn't have a chip on her shoulder. Maybe I should question him and his motives, but I don't. I should probably tell him I won't let him help me, but instead I take all his promises to heart. I should scream at him to pull himself from my mess, but I can't let him go. When the reality of losing him hit me, the pain was far worse than I'd thought it would be. It's numbing, and I hate it. I want to believe him and put my trust in his hands. I want him to be my safety net and my shield. The thought of a life without him is impossible to bear, and I won't waste another second on denying him. Denying myself.

"I love you," I whisper.

I want him to know, because I've never loved

anyone like I love him. Never wanted to get lost in someone's soul and tell him all my secrets. I don't care anymore. I have nothing to lose. I'm taking him and never letting go.

NINETEEN

Ryan

HER DEEP BLUE eyes are filled with so many emotions as I stare down at her. The thing I see most in them is hope. Hope that I'm true to my word, hope that I don't let her get away, hope that I won't break her heart as she gently places it in my hands. My thumb continues to brush away tears, but inside, the adrenaline is pumping through my veins.

She loves me.

I'm unable to move as I hover over her, listening to her breathe. It's a moment I want burned into my memory so that I can recall every single detail for the rest of my life. I take in her scent of lavender, imprinting her into my soul. There's a part of my mind that worries she's giving in only because she thought I'd cast her aside, but that doubt is quickly dashed. It's only my insecurities that are trying to push through, and I ignore them. I knew that if I could get her to fall in love with me, then nothing else would matter. And so it shall be. I will make this the way it's supposed to be and forget about the part of me that has doubt. The bigger part knows that she's finally being honest with herself. I've known for a long time she felt the same way I did. She's just been slower at getting to the point than I have.

"I love you, Paige." Leaning down, I rub my nose against hers and close my eyes. It scared the shit out of me when I thought she might run tonight, slip away from me and out of my grasp. The thought was unbearable. I know I haven't been with her for years, but I always had eyes on her. Knew where she was and what she was doing. If I lost that, I think I might go insane.

She moves her hands to my neck, and then our lips connect. It's soft and tentative at first, as if she's exploring me for the first time, making sure I'm really here, still a little unsure that I want her. But there's a passion under the surface that's beginning to create waves. A heat churning between us that I can feel building.

Her lips are full against mine, and when I open my mouth, I feel her tongue sweep inside. She's trying to take charge, but neither of us really wants that. She likes when I'm in control, even if she doesn't admit it. But I feel the need in her kiss, and I know what she's after. She's trying to force me into what she wants, but she should know by now that it doesn't work that way. I know what she needs. I set the pace for us because I want this to be perfect for her. I want everything to always be perfect for her.

I reach behind my neck and take her wrists, gently pulling them away. I press her hands above her head, softly but firmly.

"Not tonight, kitten," I whisper, staring into her

gorgeous blue eyes. Fighting myself. I've wanted her for so long, and even with all the tempting things she's done to turn me on and try to get me to take her, her *"I love you"* was the fucking sexiest thing she's ever done for me.

I sense an intensity inside her that matches my own, but I don't want her like this. I don't want our first time to happen after I caught her sneaking around and made her spill her darkest secrets. I want it to be special and perfect, like she deserves.

"Don't make me wait any longer. Please, Ryan, haven't we danced around this long enough? I've given you what you wanted. Make love to me."

I close my eyes, hating to deny her anything. "I want it to be special. You deserve candles and rose petals. Our first time will be with us the rest of our lives. It will be the memory that sticks with us when we're old and gray and sharing Jell-O." She smiles at me, and there couldn't possibly be a more beautiful woman on this earth. "We're going to tell our grand-children one day about how we fell in love, and I want our whole story to be exactly what you deserve."

She wiggles one wrist free and brings her hand up to my cheek. "Everything about us is messy. The way we met, the way we fell in love." She smiles like she surprised herself in saying that so easily. "The way I try to push you away when we both know all I want is to be in your arms. I've never had anything in my life as perfect as you, as perfect as this. Make love to me."

I drop my head to her chest, resting my forehead

there. Breathing in her smell, I feel her other hand come free of my grip and dance across my back. She tugs at my dress shirt, pulling it from my pants and up my spine. She tugs it up to my shoulders, and I reluctantly let her take it off me. She discards it, and then I look down as she grips the hem of her own shirt. She pulls it off her body in one fluid motion and wiggles beneath me to unclasp her bra. She takes it off and throws it to the side with our shirts, and I let out a breath. She's naked from the waist up, and it takes everything in me not to look down at her breasts. I want to so badly, but if I do, I might lose control.

"I love you, Ryan." She says the words, and they're like warm honey spread over my skin. She thinks I'm the perfect one, when it's really her. She thinks she's the one who's been hiding things. I've known all the secrets she thinks she held from me. In reality, I'm the only person in the room with secrets. I'm not as perfect as she thinks I am. I should be the one baring myself to her right now, but she's the one stripping herself bare.

I close my eyes tightly, the tenderness of her words making my heart jump. She moves her hands between us, and I feel her fingers undoing my belt and then my pants. She pushes them down my waist and over my ass, exposing my cock. I keep my eyes closed, because I don't know if I can control myself.

"I can't stand it anymore. I want to be connected to you in every way possible." She places a soft kiss on my chest as I feel her move, taking off her own pants.

"Show me you'll never let me go. That I'll always have you, no matter what."

Unable to stop myself, I glance between us, seeing her push down her panties and kick them off. She's naked under me, and I can't stop staring at her perfect body. She's so small compared to my size, but her curves are mouthwatering. Her full breasts with hard pink nipples look like they were made perfectly to fit in my hands. My cock bobs between us, and a pearl of come beads at the tip. My need for her has surpassed any feeling I've ever had in my life. I want her more than I want my next breath, and I can't hold back much longer. I've been holding back so long. The walls are cracking.

She takes my shaft in her hand and strokes me from root to tip, then back down, and grips me firmly at the base.

"Fuck." I hiss through gritted teeth. Then she tells me what she wants through squeezes of her hand.

"Make." Pulse. "Love." Pulse. "To." Pulse. "Me." Her words are breathy as she spreads her legs wide.

"Goddamn it, Paige." I grasp the headboard and thrust into her grip. The little vixen is getting the best of me. She's the only person in the whole fucking world who can do that. "If you let me in your pussy, I won't stop. I'll be like a predator that's marked its prey. You won't ever be free of me."

She nods, a wild look in her eyes that does nothing to slow my desire for her. I tighten my grip on the bed and look down at her exposed pussy. She's glistening with need, and I can see that she's ready for me. Ready for this. She's right in saying we've been building up to this moment. There's no need for foreplay when we both know what we truly want.

"Move your hand," I say, tightening my jaw. She does what I demand, taking her hand off my cock. "Legs around my waist, and arms on my shoulders." I want her wrapped around me completely, every inch of her body touching mine as we join together. Again, she does as instructed. "I love you with everything in my soul, and nothing will ever change that. Nothing."

She nods, her eyes looking to mine, full of anticipation. "I love you, too." The words come easily from her now.

"I'm clean, kitten, and I know you are, too. I want you skin on skin, with no protection."

She hesitates for a fraction of a second, and I want to ease her fears. I take a hand off the headboard and grip her chin so she doesn't miss a word of what I'm about to say.

"You're the only one I've ever wanted this with. And the only one I want for the rest of my life. That means everything, kitten. Love, sex, marriage, kids. All of it. You'll give it to me because you want the same damn thing, too."

Her big blue eyes look deep into mine, and a knowing passes between us. I know that's what she wants. I see it in the way she looks at Miles and Mallory. She wants that, and I can give it to her. I even saw it when she was messing with me and told me she was knocked up, and I told her that baby was mine. Her eyes had lit up for a moment before she masked the want, but I'd caught it.

"I do," she whispers, and I can't help but think that with just those two words, she's agreed to so much more.

"I do," I repeat, and connect us in the most intimate way possible, thrusting inside her fully in one long stroke.

"Shhh," I say against her lips when she cries out. She's a virgin, so I thought this might hurt. I try to hold still and let her adjust. I take her lips in a soft kiss, trying to do all I can to ease the pain. Whispering to her over and over that I love her, wanting her to get used to the words. Her body squeezes around me, and I fight back my release. I want to make this good for both of us, so I move my mouth to her neck.

I lick under her ear and then nibble my way down to her collarbone. I keep myself fully seated inside her, letting her fit to my size. When I get to her breasts, her breathing has evened out, and she relaxes a little under me. My mouth latches on to one of her nipples, taking the hardened peak softly between my teeth. I suckle her, then bite down a tiny bit, and I'm rewarded with a moan. She starts to wiggle her hips a little, opening her legs wider as I move my mouth to her other breast.

I have to possess her in every way. Something inside me is screaming for me to own her. I know that it sounds crazy, but I can't help myself.

"You're mine now, Paige. There's no turning back."

I'm a selfish beast, because I know exactly what

I'm doing. I will dominate every inch of her if it means she can't ever walk away from me.

With my mouth on her, she becomes as soft as warm butter under my touch. Her body relaxes, and I begin to move, letting her feel every ridge. Her tight walls surround my cock, and I've never felt a more perfect grip. The warm, wet heat of her channel welcomes every thrust. Her nails dig into my shoulders, and I beg her to mark me. I want the world to see that I belong to her, to my Paige.

She pulls me away from her breasts, and I take her mouth in a kiss that's almost as feral as my need for her. Thick, hammering passion beats down on my back, and I take her like a savage. I know I should be tender and I should slow down, but I can't hold back anymore.

"Harder," she moans in my ear, and sweet fucking Christ, it's like she's been made for me.

I thrust harder, letting our bodies meet their primal needs. To love, to fuck, to breed. I want to get inside her so deep that I never leave, and I want her skin to absorb my scent. I want the two of us to share one set of lungs and never take a breath without the other. The need is beating between us like a living thing, and she clings to me, begging me for more. Begging for what only I can give her.

She's saying my name and telling me she's close. Her orgasm is like a wildfire and she can't control it. I'm afraid if I go over with her, I'll be split in two, but I can't keep it together any longer. Her thighs grip my waist, and her nails drag down my back as she shouts her passion into the room. Her climax grips my cock, and I roar into the pillow as I release deep inside her.

It's the single greatest moment of my life, and I've never felt more connected to another person. It's as if our hearts combine in that moment and fuse into a bond that can never be broken.

We lock eyes as we both gasp for air, the two of us recognizing that this is bigger than we could have ever imagined. That what we had thought of as making love turned out to be the joining of souls. It's more powerful than anything I've ever felt, and there is no going back.

Our eye contact doesn't break as I slowly move inside her again. Tonight is the beginning of the rest of our lives, and I want to spend it making sweet passionate love to the woman under me.

I only pray that when she finds out my secrets, this will be enough to bind her to me.

TWENTY

Paige

"OH GOD." MY BACK arches off the bed. I want to be closer to Captain. Need my body as near to him as possible. I don't think, I react.

"Ryan," Captain corrects, growling against my pussy. His broad shoulders have my legs spread wide to give his massive size all the room he needs as he eats me. He devours my pleasure as if it was his own. The vibration of his voice rolls over my clit, making my orgasm push forward, wanting to break free. Captain knows this, but he pulls back. "Say it."

He likes to tease me. Maybe not *tease* exactly, but he likes to get what he wants. Long gone is the polite man who'd been holding back on me. When he took my virginity hours ago, something within him broke open. It's animalistic, and I find every part of it intoxicating. I love when he takes control over my body and does whatever he wants with it.

I release my grip on the bar of the headboard, my fingers going to his hair. I try to thrust my hips upward, wanting his mouth back on me. His hand grasps my hip, locking me into place. Why does that shit, his controlling nature, turn me on?

"I love you." I give him the words I know he wants. I've said them to him so many times throughout the night, he should be sick of it by now. But if he likes hearing me tell him that as much as I like when he says it, then I'm dead wrong. I could listen to him tell me he loves me over and over again and probably orgasm from only those words.

"All of it, kitten."

I grip his hair tighter. "I love you, Ryan."

"That's my girl," he says, before his mouth lands on my clit again. He sucks me in possessively, the pleasure exploding into an orgasm that I've been teetering on. It finally breaks free as I chant his name into the room, my whole body going lax.

He slowly crawls up, leaving a trail of kisses along the way. His morning stubble abrades my skin, and I'm sure I have his mark on every inch of me. When he reaches my mouth, he kisses me deeply, and I taste myself on him. The kiss turns soft and lazy as he moves his mouth against mine, then his body shifts over and settles against me. He pulls me tightly into his arms, and I close my eyes, smiling.

"Morning," he says in my ear.

"Hmm" is all I can muster in response. The man has worn me out more than any workout I've ever done in my life. And for the most part since last night, I've been on my back. He moves his hand from my hip, up my stomach, and then cups one breast. He can't stop touching me, but I can't keep my hands off him, either. I always want some part of me wrapped around him.

"My kitten is docile after a night of good lovin'."

His words only make me smile more. I am. I want to lie here all day. I'm relaxed and sore all over. But a good sore. Every time I move today, it will remind me of him and all the things we did last night. The passion that exploded between us that had been building up for years has finally detonated. No more walls or secrets. Everything came tumbling down last night. I bared myself to him, and it felt good. It was freeing to finally let someone really see me.

"I fed you. Are you going to feed me now?" I tease, turning in his arms to cuddle against him. I bury my face in his neck, and something about it is comforting. Safe. Nothing can touch me when he's wrapped around me. I wish I could stay here forever.

"Have I ever let you go hungry?" he asks, rubbing my back rhythmically.

I don't think I want to get up for food right now. It's the weekend, and we don't have anywhere we have to be. I throw my leg over his body, crawling on top of his big frame so I'm straddling him. My face is still in his neck. He wraps both his arms around me, holding me close. God, he feels so good against me. I was stupid for ever fighting this, for missing out on even one moment of what we've shared.

"You're not going anywhere. I changed my mind," I tell him, burrowing farther into him. I want to soak all of him up. His smell, his warmth, anything I can get.

"Do you know how long I've wanted this?" he says lazily, making my heart do a little flutter.

I sit up, wanting to look down at him. The morning light spreads across the bed, and he looks me over. I'm not shy about my nudity and let him look his fill. I rest my hands on his chest, running my fingers through his short chest hair.

"You've really wanted me all this time?" We talked about it the other day. I'd even made a joke about him being a bit of a stalker, like Miles was with Mallory. That all these years when we both worked for Miles, he'd wanted me, too. I loved the thought of it.

"From the very start," he confirms.

I bite my lip, wanting to ask more. I suddenly feel extra territorial.

"What is it, kitten?" he pushes, knowing I have something I want to say. It's crazy how well he reads me. Maybe even a little scary. No, not anymore. I'm not hiding from him. I'll give him all my secrets. I know they are safe with him. I can feel it.

"Last night was my…" I try to say it, but my cheeks warm.

A grin spreads on his lips. "I know. Why do you think I haven't taken you again? I know you're sore." He runs his hand up my thigh. We haven't had sex again since last night, but we've done other things. Well, he did things to me. Explored every inch of my body with his mouth and hands, over and over again. Like he thought he might have missed a spot. It felt like he was marking me. "Even if you try to tempt me by sitting naked on top of me." He rubs small circles on my thighs with his thumb, making goose bumps break out on my skin.

"I guess what I'm asking is…" I look around the room, feeling a little unsure of myself. I'm insecure because this man looks like a Greek god below me, and he's between my thighs. He's the definition of perfection. I don't know where to begin with a man like him in my bed. I let him take the lead, and I gave up all control.

"Eyes on me."

I snap my eyes back to him. "Have you been with anyone recently?" I finally spit the words out. I hate the idea that he wanted me, but might have still been with someone else while he waited. The thought of him with someone else makes me sick, but even more so as I think about how he felt about me. The idea of him harboring those feelings, but still being with someone else, nauseates me.

The moment the words are out of my mouth, I want to snatch them back. I realize that I don't want to know the answer. I start to dig my fingers into his chest, but Captain moves. He sits up, coming face-to-face with me.

"It was me who came up with the idea that you wouldn't be allowed to date when you were watching over Mallory in college. I told Miles it might distract you, but really, I knew it was the only thing that would keep me from coming for you."

My mouth falls open at his confession. I never really wanted to date. I'd always had a little crush on Captain. He'd been the only man to spark my interest, after watching how my father treated my mother for years. I wanted nothing to do with men before Captain came along. Going to a college full of privileged males didn't help, either. Rich men thought they could do anything and get away with anything. I think that's part of why I'd always had a crush on Captain—because he seemed so good. Like a man who would cut off his own arm before he'd ever hurt a woman. He's a protector, and I crave that, deep down.

I didn't want to date anyone, but it didn't mean he had any right to stop me. Especially if he was dating. The thought makes my blood boil. I dig my fingers into his chest more, wanting him to feel the bite of my nails.

"Retract the claws, kitten." I feel his hard cock jerk under me, and I narrow my eyes at him.

"It's been a long time." Still, I keep glaring at him, giving him the look that normally sends people running. But not him.

He smiles the stupid, perfect smile that melts me, the one he gives me when he thinks I'm being cute. "For years, there's only been one woman in my bed, shower, at my desk, maybe a few times in my kitchen."

"Ryan." I growl this time.

"You. If you only knew of all the things I dreamed about doing to you, you might run." He rests his forehead on mine. The teasing smile drops away. "Paige, you're the only woman I've touched since I laid eyes on you. There was no way in hell I'd give someone else even a small piece of me, knowing what I felt for you. You've owned me for years. All of me."

I tilt my head up a little, giving him a soft kiss.

Then I bite his lip, making him jerk. Before I know what's happening, I'm on my back with him looming over me. His big body hovers over mine.

"Just giving you a taste of what would happen if I get jealous. You know, so you make sure it doesn't happen," I say, raising my chin in challenge.

"Hmm. You might want to rethink that, kitten. I like your teeth on me, if you haven't noticed." He grinds his erection against me, and the friction is delicious. I wrap my arms around his neck, wanting to stay connected.

"I'm sorry. I'm finding myself very territorial with you all of a sudden. Maybe because I've never really thought of anything as mine but you. I think you're mine," I tell him, wanting to put it all out there. "I don't think I could bear to lose you. When I thought I did last night, for a moment—"

"You'll never lose me." His words cut me off. They hold so much confidence.

"It's wrong for me to let you get mixed into my mess with me."

"It's wrong for you to not let me," he throws back. "You think I'm going to let you kill him?" His words are low and challenging.

I thought about it for so many years. I've implied what I want to do, but the words have never come out of my mouth. They're always right there but never slip free. It's like if I voice it, then I'm bringing them to life and becoming like him. The day my mother died, I just stood there. Then when I saw my father again, for the first time in ages, I stood there once more. Paralyzed. Maybe I don't have what it takes.

"You don't think I can do it." It's not a question.

"Paige, you can do anything you put your mind to. Your strength was one of the first things I noticed about you."

"Then why?" I ask, looking up at him. He looks like a warrior ready to go to battle for me. My warrior.

"You've had enough darkness touch you. I know you want your piece of payback, and I'm going to help you get it. But I'm going to shield you as much as possible while we do it. When it's over, it's over. And I'll spend the rest of my life filling that beautiful brain of yours with memories you'll want. There'll be so many, and they'll be so beautiful that they'll block out the ones you can't let go of. I'll give you so many you'll have no choice but to replay those in your mind."

"You're already doing that," I admit.

"You're going to let me shield you? Help you get where you're going? Be a team?" he presses, always wanting my words. He needs to hear me say what he wants. "Let me take care of you, kitten. Let me make everything right. I can give you everything you could ever want."

God, that sounds good. Not even my mother took care of me like Captain wants to. I was always the one taking care of her and picking up her broken pieces. The thought of a life where I have a partner, someone to stand beside me through the storm, is a welcome relief I didn't expect.

"If I let you do this, then you have to do something for me."

"Anything," Captain agrees, without a second of hesitation.

"I want you to make love to me while wearing the Captain America costume. Complete with shield."

The intense moment is broken as he smiles and puts his weight down on my chest. I can feel his body shaking with laughter, and I wrap myself around him and close my eyes. If this is what love feels like, then I never want it to end.

TWENTY-ONE

Ryan

A KNOCK ON the door startles me awake, and I realize that I've somehow fallen asleep with Paige on top of me. I squeeze her lush ass with both hands and grind my erection into her stomach before I roll us over. I kiss her cheek and pull the covers over her, then grab my pants and tug them on.

I make my way to the front door, look through the peephole and smile. Mallory is standing there with a basket in her hands, so I unlock the door and swing it open.

"Morning," she says over her shoulder as she comes in. Miles is out in the hallway, talking on his cell, and he waves to me. I give him a chin lift in hello and leave the door slightly ajar. "I brought you guys brunch. Miles and I went out early and thought we would drop this off on our way back up."

"Do I smell food?" Paige walks out of her room with a blanket wrapped around her and her hair all on one side. She would look comical if I didn't want her so badly.

"You've got the nose of a bloodhound," Mallory says. "Looks like everything worked out last night."

She looks at me in my shirtless state, and I bring my hands up to cover my naked chest. Mallory glances over at Paige, who laughs and rolls her eyes.

"We'll leave you two alone," Miles says from the doorway, dragging Mallory behind him.

"Wait, I want girl talk!" Mallory pouts as she exits. She yells for Paige to text her as I close the door behind them and lock it for good measure.

"What happened last night?" Paige asks as she digs into the basket of food.

"Do you need a reminder?" I walk up beside her and kiss her bare shoulder.

"Yes." The word is breathy, then she clears her throat. "Maybe in a second. Tell me what happened. Before you found me."

"I knew something was off with you last night. I went home and I debated about what to do, and then I decided to come check on you. I had this feeling that you were going somewhere, and when I got to your door and Mallory answered, I knew. She didn't even open her mouth. I took one look at her and guilt was written all over her face. I told her if she went straight home, I wouldn't tell Miles."

"Bet she hated that," Paige says, pulling the containers out of the basket.

"He found out, anyway. He was walking in just as I was leaving. He always knows where she is. But I didn't stay to listen to what happened. I knew my badge was missing, and I knew you had plans to sneak back in. You're the only person who gets close enough to me to be able to take it from me."

"How did you know?" she asks, pulling down plates and serving us food.

"Kitten, I keep telling you that I know you better than you know yourself. You gave me the slip, but not for long."

"I'm surprised Miles isn't pissed," she says, looking down at her plate.

"Nah. He knew where she was the whole time. There's enough security in this building to guard the president. It's not like you asked her to go to a bar so you could hit on men." I give her a smirk, and she throws a grape at me.

"I only did that once. And it wasn't to hit on men." No, maybe it wasn't, but half the bar was eye-fucking her by the time I showed up.

"Get over here and make it up to me." I grab her by the waist and put her up on the counter of the kitchen. Pushing her blanket off her, I let it pool around her hips. I spread her legs, exposing her fully, and look at her sitting naked in front of me. "Delicious." I still can't get over that she's here naked in front of me for my taking. For so many years I've wanted this. Worked toward it. I thought it would never come.

"What do I have to do to make it up to you?" Paige looks at me with hooded eyes, her dark auburn hair flowing down one shoulder. She smells like lavender, sex and me. My mouth waters to taste her again. She might have been a virgin last night, but Paige isn't shy. Even better, she likes it dirty, something I didn't know I liked until her. She brings out a barbaric side of me.

"I think you're probably ready to take me again, aren't you?"

She bites her lip but spreads her legs wider, scooting to the edge of the counter.

"That's what I thought, kitten. Always ready for me." I unbutton my pants and kick them off. As I stand naked in front of her, my hard thick cock points angrily at her pussy. It's the place he wants in most, and he's dripping for her.

I grab one of her ankles and prop it up on my shoulder as I press my aching head to her opening. I thrust in firmly, letting her take all of me in one long slide, then give her a second to adjust.

"Relax, kitten. I'm going to take you deep like this. I want your eyes on my cock as it goes in and out of you. I want you watching me take you, and I want you to see it pulse when I come inside your pussy. Sucking every drop of me into you, where it belongs."

I feel her clench around me at my words and watch as her eyes drop to our connection. I slowly drag out of her and then thrust back in quickly. We both moan at the sensation of me taking her. As I pump in and out in even motions, she pants with need. I keep rocking at the same tempo while I bring my thumb up to her exposed clit. At the first touch she cries out my name but doesn't orgasm. She's overly sensitive from my mouth, but she doesn't tell me to stop.

My cock is slick with her passion, and my entry is so easy. She's unbelievably tight, even after taking her cherry, and I don't know how much longer I can last. I grab her other foot and put it on my shoulder so both her legs are up in the air. Her ass is on the edge of the kitchen counter, and she's got her palms braced behind her for support. But she's not going anywhere. I've got a grip on her hips, and we watch as our bodies become one over and over.

Turning my face to the side, I lick her ankle and bite down on the inside of her foot. She cries out my name, and it turns me on even more. I do the same to the other foot, and I feel her clench around my cock.

"I love you, kitten. I love you so much."

Her back arches, and she screams as she comes on me. It's the green light I've been waiting for, and I thrust into her hard one last time, filling her up with every drop I have. Marking her deep inside her body.

I take her legs off my shoulders and wind them around my hips. I pull her upper body to mine and hold her as we both try to catch our breath. It's fast and intense, and it's the best fucking thing I've ever felt.

"Every time I touch you, it's better than the last," I say, kissing the top of her head.

She looks up at me with eyes glazed with a lust-filled fog, and she smiles. "You're not so bad yourself."

I kiss her lips and take my time tasting her sweetness. When I've decided I need to feed her before I fuck her again, I pull out of her and take a step back.

"Why is that so hot?" she asks, looking down at my cock and seeing our mixed pleasure coating me.

"I love hearing you say I'm hot, but to which part are you referring?"

My cock bobs between us, and she licks her lips

"Seeing my come on you, mixed with yours. Your cock covered in us. I don't know why, but seeing it makes me want you all over again."

"Because you like seeing that you marked me, too," I tell her.

She slips off the counter and slowly drops to her knees in front of me.

"Paige," I say through gritted teeth. I hold out my hands to keep her from getting closer, but I'm backed into the counter. "What are you doing? Get up off the floor."

"I think you know what I'm doing." She runs her hands up my thighs, and they tremble under her touch.

"Get up, Paige. You don't need to do this." I don't know why, but her on her knees in front of me isn't something I want. She should kneel for no one. "I mean it."

"Just a taste," she says, looking up at me. The sight of her below me has my cock flexing with need, but my heart aches to pull her off the floor. "One little lick."

I clench my jaw and fist my hands, not wanting her to think she has to do this. My woman should be worshipped. And I don't know if I can control myself like this.

The heat of her tongue on my cock has me closing my eyes. It's like fire running along my shaft, and then I hear her moan. The sound goes straight to my balls. Her mouth opens around the head of my cock, and I have to look. I glance down at her and see her mouth stretched wide around my girth. I unclench my fists and reach out, grabbing her hair with both of my hands. I hold her head still while she sucks on my cock, and fuck me, it's the most erotic thing I've ever seen.

"You want to suck my dick?" I ask her, and she nods. Her mouth is still full of cock, and I feel her tongue graze the tip. "Take it all the way to the back of your throat, then, kitten. Clean it off." She takes as much of my length as she can, breathing through her nose when it goes as far as she can reach. "Fuck."

She hums in delight, as she nearly has me coming undone.

"You get this one pass, so you better enjoy it. I don't like seeing my woman on her knees. Not even for me." She rubs up my thighs, to my balls, rubbing them and cupping me. "Suck me off, and then I want to come on you."

I see her slip her hand between her legs at my words, and I hear how wet she is. The thought of me marking her has her turned on, which only makes me want to do it faster.

"Deep breath," I say as I grip her hair tighter and pull her down on my dick. I move in and out of her mouth, and it takes only a few pumps before I'm ready. "Sit back on your feet."

She does as I ask, her hand still between her legs, as I pull out of her mouth and jerk my cock off. Thick spurts of come shoot out and land on her chin and neck. I see a drop land on her breast, and I reach down, rubbing it in. I fall to my knees in front of her, rubbing the come all over her with one hand while the other goes to her pussy to help her get off.

"You're mine now. Come on my hand, kitten. I want to smell your pussy on me all day."

Her wetness clenches around me, and I lean forward, kissing her. My tongue sweeps into her mouth, and I can taste my own pleasure. She's coated in me, and it's the biggest turn-on of my life. She whines into my mouth as she comes for me, the sticky sweetness covering our entwined fingers. When the last tremor is released, I bring my finger up to her mouth and wipe the wetness on her bottom lip. I taste the two of us together, and it's fucking perfect. Just like my Paige.

"Good girl. Now let's eat."

She blushes but melts into me, and I have to bundle her up in the blanket and carry her to the couch.

We lie there all day, eating, kissing and petting each other. I take her off and on, unable to get my fill. There are conversations that we need to have and plans we need to make. But today is for loving my kitten. And if there's one thing I do well, it's love her.

TWENTY-TWO

Paige

My phone buzzes in my bag, and I lean down to grab it. It's Monday, and Captain and I are back at work. He's been giving me glances all day that have me squirming in my seat, so I wonder if he's decided to send me a dirty text.

I'm surprised when I see Patrick's name on the screen. With everything that's happened lately, I'd completely forgotten about him. I feel like an asshole for not getting in touch when I said I would. I slide my thumb on the screen and read his text.

Patrick: Hey, Paige. It's a long shot, but I wanted to see if you were free for lunch today. We can meet at the same coffee shop as last time, if that will work. Maybe around noon?

Normally Captain and I have lunch with our team or alone. But I always eat with Captain. Now that things between Captain and me are serious, I don't see a way around not inviting him along. I walk over to his desk and lean my hip against it. His eyes travel down my tight black top to my black-and-gold palazzo pants. I've got on my gold Dior stilettos that Captain fucked me in before we left my apartment this morning. When his eyes land on them, I see an eyebrow rise, and I know he's thinking about it, too. I feel a pool of warm liquid swirl around the lower half of my body, and I have to clear my throat to concentrate on what I'm saying.

"Eyes up here, sailor."

Captain leans back in his seat and puts his hands behind his head. This makes his dress shirt stretch across his muscles and chest, and fuck, I want to straddle his lap.

"I wasn't in the navy, but if you want to pretend, I'd gladly welcome you aboard." He spreads his thighs a little, and I roll my eyes at his lame joke.

"Later. Right now I need to ask you a favor, and before you say yes, I need you to agree to all the terms." I narrow my eyes at him, and he crosses his arms. "I want to have lunch with my friend Patrick. Simmer down," I say, when I see him open his mouth. "I want you to come with me, but I need you to play nice."

"Oh, I'm going," Captain says.

"I literally just asked you to go. What I need you to do is be nice. Patrick was an old friend of mine, and I want to catch up. I'm not saying I want you two to be besties, but I would appreciate the support. Think you can handle that?"

"Yes."

He agrees too fast, and it makes me skeptical. "You promise? No alpha bullshit chest-beating?"

He uncrosses his arms and stands up, looking

down at me. Even with my skyscraper heels, he's still a head taller, and I have to admit it's intimidating.

"You like it when I do my alpha bullshit."

I audibly swallow and feel my pulse move to the juncture between my legs. No matter how much I try to deny it, he's right. The shit turns me on like crazy. But that doesn't mean I have to tell him so.

"I like it when you give me what I want. And I want to go to lunch at noon with Patrick." He huffs, and I place my hands on his chest. "And I want you by my side. Okay?"

"Okay."

I reach up and playfully smack the side of his cheek and turn to walk away. I can feel his eyes on my ass, and I walk with a little more bounce in my step than normal to tease him. I don't know why I love pushing his buttons, but it's truly the greatest pastime of all.

When I get to my desk, I text Patrick back.

Me: Sounds great. Hope you don't mind, but I'm bringing my boyfriend.

I feel silly typing "boyfriend," but I guess that's what Captain is. Patrick texts back a thumbs-up emoji almost instantly. I look over at Captain, and of course he has his eyes on me, so I open my desk drawer and take out a lollipop.

When I pop it in my mouth and suck on the end, he looks like he could spit nails. His grip tightens on his desk, and I wink at him, turning back to my computer screen. I love making that big man suffer.

By the time lunch rolls around, I've eaten no less than five lollipops to torture Captain. When it's time to leave, he comes over to my desk and jerks the candy out of my hand and throws it in the trash.

"Let's go before I take you in the bathroom and spank your little ass."

"Promises, promises," I say, grabbing my bag and brushing past him. I make sure he feels the curve of my ass against his crotch, and I swear I hear him curse under his breath.

We get in the elevator, and I feel the need between us charging. I plan to maul him when the elevator doors close, but just as they are about to, a hand comes through and Jordan stops them from shutting all the way. He hops in and looks at us, smiling. He has no clue that the sexual tension between us is so tight it's about to snap this elevator in half.

"Get out," Captain says, and I put my fingers in front of my mouth to stifle a laugh.

Jordan looks between us and then slowly steps off the elevator. The doors shut, and Captain pushes a code, locking them closed and stopping us from moving.

He turns to me and slowly walks over, pressing me up against the wall. "You want me to take you right here? Because I'll fuck you anywhere I want. And with the way you've been teasing me today, it looks like you're begging for it."

My breathing is shaky as his hardness rubs against me.

"If you behave through lunch, I'll bring you back

here and give you what you want. I'll bend you over and take you hard, just how you like it. I'll make you come on my dick and tell you all the dirty shit you love to hear. But don't bait me, kitten. Because you and I both know that's a dangerous game."

He steps back and hits the button for the main floor, and the elevator moves again. By the time the doors open again, I'm still flustered, but Captain doesn't have a hair out of place. He takes my hand and pulls me from the elevator as people step around us, trying to get on. Once we get outside and the fresh air hits me, I'm able to take a breath and get my head clear. Jesus, that man makes me dizzy.

When we get to the coffee shop, we walk inside and see Patrick at one of the tables off to the side. He's wearing dark-rimmed glasses, and his hair is messy, but he still has the same smile from when we were kids. He's still as skinny, but only now he has some facial hair. I walk over and start to give him a hug, but Captain steps in front of me.

"Hi, I'm Ryan, Paige's fiancé. It's nice to meet you."

I'm shocked on so many levels. For one, because he cut me off like we were in traffic. Second, because when did I agree to marry him? And third, because I'm kind of melting that he did all of the above. God, what is wrong with me?

"I'm Patrick. Nice to meet you." He gives Captain a genuine smile and meets his eyes. It's friendly and nonthreatening.

I lean around Captain and wave to Patrick, and he waves back.

"I already ordered at the counter if you guys want to. Or you can sit and order later," Patrick says.

"You sit, Paige. I'll order."

Captain watches me as I take my seat, and I swear he's doing this so I don't make a move to touch Patrick. I indulge his alpha tendencies and sit down across from Patrick. From where my seat is, I can watch him go get in line and wait to order our food. He keeps glancing over at me, and it's kind of adorable.

"I'm really glad you came today. It's been hectic with work, but I wanted to try to reach out," Patrick says, taking my eyes away from Captain.

"Me, too. I've had a lot going on, and I completely forgot. So I was really happy you sent a text." I glance back over to where Captain is and see that there's a woman beside him in line. She's checking him out, but he doesn't look her way. The line is long and it's moving slowly, so he hasn't taken a step forward.

"So what have you been up to since the last time I saw you?" Patrick's question pulls me back to the conversation.

"Wow, a lot actually." I tell him about college, trying to keep it somewhat light and upbeat, but I want to know what happened to him. It's been sitting on my mind all these years. "What happened to you when we were kids? You disappeared." I want to know more about him. He was the one who up and vanished.

Patrick smiles at me. "I got picked up for shoplifting and then got put into foster care. But I got lucky.

I was adopted by a really great family that helped me work through some shit and got me involved with the Big Brother program. That's what I do now. I give back and pay it forward."

"That's a relief. I always thought something bad happened to you," I tell him, glad to hear everything was fine.

"Yeah, we had it rough growing up, for sure," he says, taking a drink of his tea.

Looking back over to Captain, I see the woman edging closer to him. This time I see her not-so-accidentally brush against him, and he turns around to look at her. I'm too far away to see what she says, but she leans in and touches his arm. I feel myself growl low in my chest as a territorial wave hits me. Who does this bitch think she is? Captain says something and turns back around, ignoring her, and it eases some of my anger.

I open my mouth to say something else to Patrick, but I see the woman take her phone out and point it at Captain's ass. Fiery anger rises up my neck as I see her snap a picture of his butt.

"Oh, hell no." I stand up out of my chair so fast, it hits the wall. Captain turns to look at me when he hears the noise, and concern is etched all over his face.

The woman isn't paying attention, and I stomp over to where she's standing. Before she can look up, I snatch the phone out of her hand. She turns to me, a mix of anger and embarrassment on her pinched face.

"What do you think you—"

"You shut the fuck up," I say, cutting her off. The room goes silent, and I can feel eyes on us. "I saw you snap a picture of my man's ass. Number one, nobody messes with what's mine. Number two, how dare you? If you were a man and this was a woman, imagine how this would play out. You'd be called a pervert and I'd get the cops involved. Just because you're a woman doesn't give you the right to objectify someone or take their picture without their consent. Have some respect, and don't be an asshole. Especially when their fiancée is standing ten feet away." I smash the phone down on the tile floor and watch it shatter into a thousand pieces.

"You owe me a phone!" the woman screams, but nobody backs her up. She's alone in this, and she knows it.

"I don't owe you shit. You took a picture of my man, I took your phone. We're even. But I suggest you get your ass out of here before I want to get more than even."

I put my hands on my hips, waiting for her to make a move. She looks around for half a second, then decides to leave. I stand there making sure she stays gone, and I feel Captain's big hands come around my waist.

"Fiancée?" he asks, and I wave my hand like I'm batting the word away. "And here I thought you liked objectifying me," he says, so low only I can hear him.

Seeing the show is over, the coffee shop's patrons

go back to what they were doing. I turn in Captain's arms and smile up at him.

"Only I get to treat you like a piece of meat. Now get me a sandwich. I'm starving."

He squeezes my ass and laughs before he lets me go, and I walk back over to where Patrick is sitting.

"Sorry. Didn't mean to cause a scene," I say, shrugging.

He laughs a little and shakes his head. "You haven't changed at all."

"What do you mean?"

"When we were kids, you used to get so pissed off when people would touch your things. I understood it, though, because neither of us had much. So what we did have was precious. I guess it's that way with you still."

I give him a half smile, thinking he's right. "Yeah, I guess so. And I do love that man." I glance over and see Captain wink at me, and I feel the love in my chest.

By the time our food is ready and the three of us start eating, we're through the small talk of introductions and what we're doing now.

"So what happened with your mom and dad?" Patrick asks, looking over at Captain and then back at me. He's is trying to gauge what Captain knows, and I appreciate him protecting that.

"She passed away. He split," I answer, trying to sum it up as quickly and painlessly as possible. I don't want to go into any more detail than necessary.

Patrick was a part of that life, but it was a long time ago, and I don't really want to dig it up.

"Sorry to hear about that."

We tiptoe around the bad times in our lives, trying to focus on the good. We tell Captain stories about growing up, and talking about it brings some of the better memories back to the front of my mind. The more we talk, the happier I am that Captain came and that we did this. It lets him see another part of me, and it reminds me that I'm not all doom and gloom. There are pieces of me that are still good and bright. Just like the pieces he's given me.

A dark-skinned guy with long dreadlocks walks into the coffee shop and smiles over at our table. I don't recognize him, but he comes straight to Patrick and gives him a kiss on the cheek.

"Hey, baby. Sorry I'm late." He looks over at us and offers his hand to me. "I'm Amos, Patrick's husband."

We shake hands and Amos joins us for the rest of lunch. It warms my heart to see Patrick so happy and in love. It's clear that the two men are head over heels, even after Amos tells us they've been together since they were twelve.

Captain takes my hand under the table and squeezes, and I know it's time to go. When we say our goodbyes, it's with promises to do this again, and I mean it. It's nice having a part of my past that isn't dark and dirty. It's a relief to be able to hold on to something from that time, to have a memory that doesn't remind me of what I did or didn't do.

On our walk back to work, Captain brings our

joined hands up to his mouth and kisses mine. My steps are light, and I feel like a weight is being lifted.

Neither of us mentions the *F* word the whole way back.

TWENTY-THREE

Paige

WHEN WE GET back to the office, I take a step toward my desk, but Captain tugs on my arm. I follow him down the hall, thinking he must want to talk to me. He was quiet on our walk and didn't say anything in the elevator on the way up.

We go around the corner, and he pulls me quickly into the women's restroom, slamming the door and locking it. He grabs my hips and turns me to face the sinks. I feel his hand push on my shoulders, and I lean forward, gripping the counter. I look up to the mirror in front of me and see his angry reflection behind me. He grabs the waistband of my pants and pushes them down my hips, taking my panties with them. My lower half is exposed to him, but it's not enough. He kicks my feet apart, and he stares down at my ass as he undoes his belt. The sound of the zipper is loud in the room.

"Holy shit," I breathe, feeling adrenaline and excitement spike through me.

His motions are jerky, and when he's free of his pants, he grabs his hard cock and strokes it.

"You think I forgot about how you teased me

today?" I feel his wet tip rub on my ass cheek. "You're lucky I don't fuck that mouth of yours to teach you a lesson, but you'd like that too much."

My mouth waters at the thought of sucking him off while he's mad. He'd be aggressive and probably lose control.

"Look at you, kitten. Bent over and getting wetter by the second. All I have to do is remind you that you're mine and you're soaked for it." He touches me between my legs with his free hand, and his fingers coat themselves in my desire. Suddenly his fingers are gone, and I feel a stinging slap on my ass. "You ever pull a stunt like sucking on lollipops at your desk again and I'll make my dick your candy for a week."

"That's like threatening me with food. You're doing punishment wrong, Captain."

There's another smack, and damn if it doesn't make me hotter.

"You call me Ryan when your pussy is out. And just because I get off doesn't mean you get to. I'll make sure you go a week without a single orgasm to ease that ache between your legs."

Fuck. He's got me there.

As we look into the mirror, our eyes lock, and I nod. He seems to take that as an agreement and lets go of his cock, using both hands to grab my hips.

"Now, if you keep quiet and give me what I want, I'll let you come. You going to be good for me, kitten?"

"Yes, Ryan." I don't tease him anymore because I can see how close to the edge he is. I'm dripping with anticipation of the hard fuck he's about to give me, and I don't want to do anything to derail it.

His powerful thrust fills me almost to the point of pain. His big cock is longer and thicker than my body is made to take, but somehow I adjust. As if he knows I need a second, he pauses long enough for me to catch my breath before he pulls out and hammers back in. His strokes seem to go on forever as the length of his shaft pulls out and then possessively pushes back in. He owns every inch of my body, and the thrill of being taken is like a drug. I'm dizzy with lust as I watch him take me. His face is savage, and the feel of his grip balances between pleasure and pain. My tall heels give me some height as I'm bent over, but my feet lift off the floor slightly as he fucks into me. A sheen of sweat covers my body as I try to muffle my pants and cries of pleasure. Normally I can be as loud as I want, when he makes love to me at home, but this isn't the place for that. We're right beyond our offices, and something about that makes this even hotter. He wants me so badly he can't wait to get somewhere private. He has to get inside me without a moment of hesitation.

He releases my hip and brings his hand up to cover my mouth. It's what I need as my orgasm rips through my body and I scream my pleasure into his palm. He knew I was close before I did, and he knew I wouldn't be able to stop myself from shouting.

"You can't keep that sassy mouth shut, can you?" he says, giving me an evil grin in the mirror. He looks wild as he thrusts into me one last time and grunts out his release. The sight of him climaxing so hard sends more tremors through me. He's like an animal that's come to rut, and the primal part of my body is loving his rough treatment.

I'm like a goddamn cat in heat getting mated by her king. And I can't say that doesn't turn me on.

My legs are shaky as he pulls out slowly and then bends down to pull up my panties and palazzo pants. I brace all my weight on the counter as he rights my clothes and then his. Afterward, he turns me around and I fall to his chest, completely spent. I want to lie down and take a nap, but instead he makes me stand here.

"God, I love you," he says, taking my lips in a tender, sweet kiss that is the complete opposite of what we just did.

I love that we can have both. The tender, sweet lovemaking where I'm on the verge of tears, and the hard, fast fucking where we are desperate for one another.

Once he's kissed me so thoroughly that I want him again, he holds my waist and helps me back to my desk. He sits me down in my chair and pushes it in, then walks over to his desk and sits down. He acts like nothing happened in the bathroom, despite the fact that he had to carry me out here like I'd lost the ability to use my legs.

I look over at him and see he's got his elbows on his desk and he's looking at me with hooded eyes. It's then I realize he's got two fingers held up to his nose and he's smelling me. Without thinking, I lean back in my chair and pull out a lollipop. I've always liked a challenge.

"I WANT TO plan this out," I say, taking a bite of my sesame chicken and pointing a fork at Captain.

"What is there to plan? I told you I'd take care of it."

He rubs my feet, and I want to moan with how good it feels, but I don't want to give him the satisfaction. We've been going back and forth about this since we got home, and neither of us is giving up much ground. We've skated around the subject of my dad for long enough. He knows that I want him to pay for what he did, and I want to be as much a part of that as possible. Captain thinks that I shouldn't be involved.

"I've got information about where he is. I found everything you need the night you caught me in the office. I've waited long enough, and I don't want to wait anymore." I point to the laptop on the table beside me, as if he can't see it's right there.

He looks at me intensely, but understanding passes through his beautiful green eyes. "I will do this for you, because I don't want any of his darkness to touch you. If you step down this path, there's no going back, Paige. I'm going to protect you from what this will do to you. When it happens, you won't know about it. And I'm not going to sit here and plan out every detail of something that could take away the light in your eyes."

He leans forward and puts his hands on my knees,

getting so close that he's almost in my lap. I want to hold him to me and tell him that he's right, but a part of me wants to fight for what I think I should be doing.

"You remember every detail of everything that's ever happened to you, kitten. Don't let this be something else that you won't forget. I will give you the revenge you want and the closure you need, but I refuse to let you get your hands dirty. I love you too much to let you do that to yourself."

He sits up and kisses me on my forehead, then takes our empty plates to the kitchen. I sit there, listening to the water running as he washes dishes and cleans up. I think about what he said and how I know he's right. But I also think that if I don't do this, then it will feel like I'm standing idly by all over again. If I don't make some kind of effort to plan this out, then what have I truly done to avenge my mother besides find a man to do it for me? Does that mean I'm like her?

Captain's phone rings. "Justice," he says, and I hear him rumble a few words before ending the call. He walks out to where I'm sitting and slips on his shoes. "I've got to run upstairs for a second. Miles wants me to look at the baby monitor. He said he's having problems getting it hooked up. I swear that man is crazy. He wants his baby's crib camera circuited to the building's security feed."

I smile at him as he leans down and gives me a quick kiss before he goes. I see the laptop beside me and decide that if I give him the information, then I'm doing some kind of good. This way he won't have to take time digging on his own. I reach over and pull up the encrypted files. There could be a few things that Miles already dug up when he was closing his business deal, so it could save me some time starting here. No sense in looking up information Miles already found.

It takes me a few minutes to decode some of the folders, and after a few failed attempts I finally find one that's marked AO. I take a guess that the initials stand for Alexander Owens and click on it. When it opens, I have to run another encryption. This must have something I need, otherwise why would it be so difficult to get to?

Once it's unlocked, I see pages of documents on Alexander, and a lot of it is business related. This isn't necessarily a bad thing, because it could narrow down where he's working and possibly staying. I make my way through a few of them and then see that Miles has pages of notes to go with each document. Miles has always been thorough. I read through a few and then organize them by date. I search through everything until I find a phone number.

I do the search like Jordan showed me, locating his phone, then hacking into it. I start with his text messages. I stop cold when I see Ryan's name. I start to read them.

My heartbeat quickens and my palms sweat. What the fuck am I reading? There's another entry a few days later.

Ryan reporting in on what's happening at Osbourne

Corp. Months and months of texts that stopped a little over a month ago when Captain stopped responding to my father.

"Hey, kitten. You miss me?" My whole world drops out from under me as he walks in and smiles. He sees the look on my face, and he knows something's not right. "What's wrong, Paige? You okay? Your face has gone solid white."

I push my computer to the floor and run to the bathroom. I don't make it to the toilet before I start throwing up. I hear him somewhere behind me, but the sounds of my retching are ringing in my ears. I'm sick. I'm physically ill from his betrayal.

He knew. He knew who I was before Miles did. He fucking worked for my father. The man I want dead. He betrayed me like no one ever has, and I loved him. I loved him.

I reach inside the cabinet by the toilet and slip my hand around the cool metal. I twist my body and put my back against the wall, aiming my gun straight at his heart.

He puts his hands up and takes a step back from me. "Paige, what the fuck?" The shock on his face would be comical if I wasn't shattering into a million pieces.

"Get out of my house, you lying bastard. You knew who he was. You even did what he said."

Understanding dawns on him, and he takes a step toward me. "Paige, it's not—"

I point the gun at the wall and fire off a round. The noise silences him, and he takes a step back. I point the gun at his heart, wanting it to break like mine is breaking.

"Get. Out," I grit through clenched teeth, and he nods.

"We are going to talk about this," he says, slowly stepping out of the bathroom.

"There is no *we*. Not ever again."

I keep the gun trained on him as I see hurt slice across his face. Good. He deserves this and so much more. He steps around the corner, his fists clenched at his sides, and I hear him walk through the living room, shutting the front door quietly behind him.

I stay on the floor of the bathroom. I don't know how long I sit there, but every limb in my body falls asleep and my body goes numb. I want to keep throwing up, but there's nothing left. I should probably get in the shower, but I'm starting to shake, and I can't move.

Time passes, and my mind spaces out, like it's unable to wrap around what's happened, so it goes blank. I start to laugh, because this can't be real. I fell in love with the devil. That's when my hysterical laughter turns into sobs. I'm broken like my mother.

TWENTY-FOUR

Ryan

I STARE AT the closed door, my heart pounding out of my chest. My world just crumbled in front of me.

"Fuck."

I punch the wall. My fist easily goes through the Sheetrock. It's no match for my anger. I debate going back inside. It takes everything I have to keep myself in place as an inner battle rages inside me. I want to go back in and make Paige see reason, even if it means facing down a gun. I wouldn't care if she shot me, as long as she heard me out. Right now all she's seeing is betrayal and maybe that's what I've done. I did betray her on some level, but I never meant to hurt her. She laid herself bare to me and told me all her secrets. Yet I still kept mine hidden, because I was afraid of what she'd think when she found out.

I worked for her father's organization for years, and I've been in contact with him over the past five. I fed him bullshit intel so that I could keep tabs on him. I've been trying to get information on him for my handler. I've been undercover digging up dirt on Alexander Owens. To bring him down, as well as his operation.

He's running drugs and weapons in the underbelly of New York, using his companies as fronts. I'd long ago had enough information to take him down, but it wasn't just about him; it was about something bigger. But then Paige walked into my life. She sent everything into a tailspin, and I didn't know what to do. I've been pulled in so many directions over the years. It's a balancing act that I haven't mastered.

It became clear as I stared down the barrel of a gun, with the woman I love most in the world on the other side of it. I know exactly what I need to do. So much pain was on her face. She thought another man in her life failed her, and I never wanted that for her. I will do anything to take that look off her face.

The elevator sounds, and I turn to see Mallory getting off, her panic clear on her face. When she sees me, her expression turns to anger as she heads right toward me. When she lifts her fist to swing at me, I don't bother trying to block it. I even let my head jerk with the punch, giving her the satisfaction she's looking for. The punch hits part of my lip, and I taste blood.

"Holy motherfucker!" she yells. Paige's front door flies open. "Why the hell didn't you ever tell me how much it hurts to punch someone?" Mallory is yelling, but my eyes are on Paige. She still has the gun in her hand, hanging down by her side, her face red and blotchy as tears coat her cheeks.

I take a step toward her, but the look she gives me stops me dead. It's not anger. It's pain now. Deep, gut-wrenching pain that almost brings me to my knees. I put that there.

"Move, asshole." Mallory pushes me, and I step aside, letting her get to Paige. She engulfs her in a hug, and Paige's eyes fall closed as she seeks her friend's comfort. Not mine. I was the one who was supposed to comfort her. Not rip her apart.

Mallory pulls away and pushes Paige back into her apartment. "Leave," Mallory growls at me, before slamming the door, leaving me alone in the hallway all over again.

This ends tonight. I take the stairs down to my apartment and go straight for my safe. After pulling out everything I need, I go over to my computer and reach out to another operative. One I know I can trust to never speak a word of what I'm about to do. He owes me from when I saved his sister and kept my mouth shut. I had him in my back pocket once the man who had hurt her suddenly went missing.

I'm calling in my favor. Fuck everything else. Fuck the job. It stopped being about the job a long time ago. Everything I did always put Paige first, but maybe I should've taken out Alexander sooner. I wasn't sure if that was what she really wanted until they came face-to-face weeks ago. The terror in her eyes was real. He was a monster that haunted her dreams, and only his death would bring peace.

When I held her in my arms while she cried and told me what had happened to her mother, I realized what she truly wanted. I'm going to give it to her. I would have done it years ago if I had known, but I know now. I'll show her that I'll do anything for her. Even if she doesn't want me after. Even if everything blows up in my face, she will have peace of mind.

Strapping on my guns, I take out my cell phone and toss it on the bed, not wanting to be tracked.

I glance around my bedroom, wondering what Paige would think if she saw it. My walls are lined with pictures of her. She coats every inch of space. It's part of my dirty secret, my obsession with her. Hundreds of pictures that I'd collected over the years act as wallpaper.

Maybe I should be embarrassed, but I'm not. Is it crazy? Yes. But it is what it is. She has fueled my life for the past five years. She's been my everything, and I'm going to show her how much she means to me. I'll prove to her that I'll always do what needs to be done for her, and maybe in the end I can have her.

TWENTY-FIVE

Paige

MALLORY WRAPS HER arms around me, holding me tightly as I cry on her shoulder. She lets me get it out until no more tears can break free. I want to pull her closer and push her away at the same time. I don't want to be touched, but I feel like I'm falling apart. My world is slipping away from me.

Maybe this is payback for what I've done. I forgot about my mother and tried to have something for myself. All of that has led to everything around me crumbling. Not all at once, but taking me piece by piece until there's nothing left. It feels like there's no life inside me, only emptiness. I'm left with an empty heart and hollowness in my chest.

"What happened?" she asks, pulling back and looking at me. Her eyes go to the gun in my hand, and they widen before she can hide her reaction.

"Captain." I shake my head. "Ryan," I correct, not wanting to use the silly name we'd given him. "He works for my father." The last of my words are ripped from me. It's like I can't believe them. That they can't be true.

"No." She shakes her head, as much in denial as I am.

I turn from her, gripping the gun tighter. I'm not sure if I can use the thing. I'd shocked myself when I shot the wall. That I actually pulled the trigger. Why does this hurt worse than losing my mother? Because I'm selfish. That's all I've been these past few weeks.

"I saw it. All the emails."

I'd read only a few of them before I pushed the laptop away from me. I didn't want to look at it anymore. I didn't want to believe it. I'm not going to be a fool any longer. I put the gun down and pick up the laptop. Then I start typing away.

"What are you doing? Maybe we should call Miles. Or, fuck, I don't know. Paige, tell me what to do. You're scaring me."

I ignore her rapid firing of questions and keep typing until I find him. "Got you," I whisper to myself, picking up the gun and heading to my bedroom. I pull off my clothes and change into black running pants, a sports bra and black hoodie, then I pull my hair into a ponytail.

"You're doing it, aren't you?" I look over at Mal standing in the doorway of my bedroom, tears sliding down her cheeks. "I know I—I s-said…" She stumbles over her words. "I know I said I wouldn't stand in your way, but…" Her hands go to her mouth like she's trying to calm herself so she can get the words out. "You're my family, and I can't lose you. I know that's selfish, but please just…just…" She repeats the word over and over, like she can't form a sentence or think of how to end it.

I walk over to her and she drops her head, our foreheads coming together. We stand there until she finally looks at me.

"Okay. I know. I know," she finally says, getting herself together. It helps calm me, too, knowing I can't walk out of here with her freaking out. For so long it's been her and me.

"I wish I could come with you."

I shake my head at her words.

"Promise you'll come back. Promise me."

"I'll always be with you, Mal. You're the only person who's never used me. All you cared about was being my friend, and you'll never know what that means to me. The only person who really loved me." Tears stream down her face. "How could I not love you?" I say, grabbing her and hugging her tight, hoping this isn't the last time I see her.

"I know you don't believe it, but you're the strongest person I know, Paige."

God, do I wish I could believe that. I feel like I could fall apart at any moment. I'm terrified at the thought of going through with this. Of holding a gun to my father and pulling the trigger. I don't know if I have that in me, but I'm going to find out.

"Go make him wish he never fucked with you," Mal says, letting me go.

I step back, going to my closet and pulling out my backpack. It's the same one I had when I lived on the streets. This time it's filled a little differently. I could disappear with this if I had to. Fade away. All I have to do is pull the trigger and go. I glance over at Mal, thinking how much it will hurt to never see her again. But how much more would it hurt to come back here? To remember Ryan.

I head to the living room, grab the laptop and shove it into the bag. I look around my apartment, wondering if this is the last time I'll see it.

"You're thinking about running after, aren't you?" she asks.

"You have Miles. You'll be fine." I don't know if I'm reassuring her or myself.

"I know I'll be fine, Paige. That's not the point. Can I live without you? Yes. But the point is, I don't want to. We're a family."

"My only family," I tell her. "No matter what happens tonight, I have to go for a little while. I can't come back here. It's too much," I explain. "It hurts. Everywhere I look, I see him."

"You do what you have to do. Don't worry about me." She walks over to stand in front of me. "You know where to find me. I'll always be here, and I'll always come if you call."

"I love you," I say, feeling the tears rise again.

"I love you, too." She grabs me and pulls me into a hug. We hold tight before I finally let her go. Then I walk away from the only family I've ever known.

TWENTY-SIX

Ryan

"You're sure he's in there?" I ask into my headset, staring at the vacant-looking warehouse that's seen better days. Alexander is scurrying to clean up the mess Miles made of his life, and desperate men do desperate things. Like get sloppy. It doesn't help when the people around you are only there for money, and with how unsteady things have been for him, I'm guessing his security isn't as great as it once was. I'm counting on it.

Alexander's men are bottom-feeders. In all the time I worked with him, never did I meet one worth anything. They'd drop Alexander and be on to the next. Whoever pays the most gets their protection. There is no loyalty, but there never is with men like this.

"If I wasn't the best for this job, I wouldn't be in your ear right now. Yeah, he's in there. There's two at the front and two at the rear entrance. You'll need to go silent once you leave the vehicle. There isn't much traffic down here at the docks, but you never know if a beat cop will make a drive-by."

"Thanks, Kearns. We're even, man."

"Good luck, Justice. Hope I'll see you on the flip side."

I take off the microphone and slip from the vehicle. I'm parked far enough away that I can see the small building, but they won't see me coming. From what I could make out, they've finished packing up a shipment of what I presume is guns on a boat and are about to clear out. I need to strike while they think they've gotten away with it. I shake my head, thinking about how poorly they are protected here and how things have really gone to shit for Alexander. Normally he'd have twenty men watching his products on a job like this. He was also never at the drops and moves. I'm guessing he's trying to offload as much shit as possible as fast as possible, with the Feds crawling through all his business deals now.

Making my way around to the side of the building, I stay in the shadows and don't make a sound. I take out my Beretta and screw the silencer on the end. I want this to go quietly. Just as I finish, I hear someone coming. It's from the back of the building—the two guards in the rear Kearns warned me about.

"Let's load up the truck and get out of here. I'm tired and I'm ready to go fuck that blonde."

"Maybe she likes the both of us."

I hear the two of them talk as they walk within feet of me, and I hold my breath, waiting for my opportunity. I'll have to make it fast so they don't give me away. It takes another ten seconds before I can get a clean shot, and I pause before I step out.

Picking the guy farthest away, I take my aim

straight between eyes and pull the trigger. Not a heartbeat passes before I'm turning to the next, and I take him out, too. They both fall without a single sound, and I tuck back into the shadows, slowing my breathing.

I come around the corner, looking for the two in the front and see them leaning against the building, both smoking. They're armed, but they're distracted, and this will work in my favor. Again, I'll have to be quick so that they don't alert Alexander inside.

Crouching low, I grab a rock and toss it away from me, toward a pile of old metal barrels. Both guys sit up, on alert, and look over, waiting to see if they hear something else.

I fire two silent shots and they drop instantly, never knowing it was coming. Not another sound is made.

Cautiously, I slip down the side and to the entrance, taking care to open the door without a noise. There's a short hallway that leads to an open area in the back, and I pause, listening. When I don't hear anything, I slowly make my way to the room.

The end of the hall is lit by a bare bulb, and as I turn, I see Alexander standing with his back to me. He's leaning over a big table covered with what looks like blueprints and notebooks, and weapons to his right and left. An image of Paige pops into my head, and I grip the gun tighter, thinking that all this is for her. That I wish I'd done this a long time ago.

"Turn around." My voice echoes in the empty room, and I see his jaw twitch, letting me know he heard me.

Slowly, he does as I ask. The initial confusion on his face is replaced by a sneer. "What are you doing?"

I stare into the same blue eyes of the woman I love more than anything. I wonder how she came from this man. She's nothing like him. She thinks they share a darkness, but that couldn't be further from the truth. She is *nothing* like this man. Where he has spent his life ripping people apart to get what he wants, she has spent her life fighting a battle that isn't hers. Fighting for a mother who didn't deserve her loyalty and devotion. A mother who should have saved her, protected her from this man and the scars he left on her.

He says it like he doesn't have time for this. Like my presence is annoying and not threatening. I've got a gun pointed at him, but he has no patience to deal with me. Stupid fucker.

"How the mighty have fallen," I tell him, glancing around the room. There's even a cot in the corner, making me wonder if he's staying here. Surely things can't be that bad. Unless maybe he's not just hiding from the Feds. Maybe some of his own have turned on him. I wouldn't be surprised, with how everything is closing in on him. I'm sure Alexander would be more than willing to cut a deal now to keep his ass out of jail.

He stands a little taller. "All those years next to Miles and you didn't see this coming? What was I fucking paying you for?" He points at me, his face growing redder with each second. For a guy who built an empire, he isn't that smart. Or maybe his balls are that big. I haven't been in contact with Alexander in

over a month. Not since Miles started slipping his
world out from under him. That should have clued
Alexander in. No one goes dark without a reason, and
mine should have been clear. He should have known
I was no longer on his side.

"Let's not beat around this. I never worked for
you." He looks even older than he did the last time
I saw him.

"FBI?" he finally grits out.

I shake my head. He actually sounded a little relieved when asking that question, so it leads me to
think someone bigger might be hunting him. No, if I
was FBI, we would have grabbed him already. That
wasn't what my mission was. I was here for intel. To
find out who Alexander worked for and worked with.
Because with men like Alexander, it doesn't matter
if you take him out. If it did, he'd have been thrown
in jail a long time ago. No, men like Alexander were
a dime a dozen. As soon as you pulled him, another
one like him would pop up like a fucking weed. You
had to get to the root of the problem. You had to take
them all down. Not one man in a group. In order to
make real changes, the whole lot would have to go.

"I'm here for Paige," I throw back at him. Because
that's the truth. This might have started as some job,
but it wasn't that anymore. Not since the first time I'd
seen her picture. Everything changed that day. Before,
I was doing a job, not even one I enjoyed. Over time,
getting dirtier and dirtier, I found the lines between
what was right and what wasn't beginning to blur. It
made me question who I was and what I'd been doing,

and if it had been worth it to crawl around in the filth, never seeming to get anywhere but deeper and deeper undercover. Everyone and everything started to look dirty. Even myself.

Then there she was. I knew in that moment that she was my reason. The path I'd been on was to get to her, and I'd crawl through any filth to reach her. The only reason I was standing here right now was for her and her alone. I don't care about my mission anymore. None of that matters. She's all that matters. Making her nightmares disappear is my only objective. I'll give her that if it's the last thing I ever do.

His face scrunches with disgust. "Just like her mother, I see. Getting men's attention with her pussy. All they're good for." He shrugs one shoulder, as if Paige and her mother are nothing more than trash.

Maybe he really has gone off the deep end. I'm standing here holding a gun to his head and he's done nothing to protect himself. He must feel the shift in the room. The anger pulses off me and fills up the space. The smirk drops from his face.

"You didn't even know who she was until I told you."

"Never said it started with her," I say flatly.

"So you're some kind of cop?"

I don't answer him.

He starts to move, and I take a step closer to him. He holds his hands up. "I've got this. It will make your fucking career." He nods toward a stack of books. "Dirty cops, senators—there are names in there you wouldn't believe."

I keep staring at him, letting him run his mouth.

"You don't want it? Fine. I can get you money. How much do you want?"

"I don't want your money." I enjoy watching him squirm. A dark part of me wants to do other things to him. Make him cry and beg, after all the years he haunted my Paige. Make him pay for all of it. A single shot to the head seems too fair.

"What do you want? I'll get it. I can get you anything." He drops his hands to his sides, his fists clenching. Clearly not a man who likes to beg. Probably never begged for a thing in his life, thinking he was too important to do something like that.

"The only thing I want is you dead."

"Why?" He takes a step back, but there is nowhere to go.

"I told you that already. I'm here for Paige."

He studies me for a second, trying to get a read on me, but I give him nothing. "She hired you?"

"No."

He lets out a humorless laugh. "You love her." His tone suggests it's the stupidest thing in the world. An emotion I'm sure he can't comprehend. "You came here to kill the father of the woman you love? How romantic."

"The only reason I haven't killed you yet is because I thought maybe the plans Miles had for you would be enough. But after hearing her talk about you, the pain I see in her eyes, the anger and fear there... I know only one thing will do. She didn't have to ask me to do it. I wanted to make sure I got to you before she did. I wasn't letting your filth touch her ever again. I won't let anything touch her."

"You think you're any different than me? You kill to get what you want. It's the same. We just want different things."

"Maybe so." I shrug, because on some level this is true. I'd do anything for Paige if it made her smile. "She wants you dead, so be it." With that, I pull the trigger. His body drops to the ground, and I only pray that with this, my kitten finds some peace. I stand there wondering if this will be enough to win her back. I tuck the gun away. I'll find a way or I'll die trying.

I see a movement out of the corner of my eye, and I freeze. Paige is there with a gun in her hand. It's down by her side, and she's looking at me with tears in her eyes. She's seen it all. Heard it all.

I'm angry that she's here and that she's put herself in what could be a harmful situation. She's had to see another one of her parents die. Even if she hated him, I didn't want her to have this memory branded into her brain, too. I didn't want any of this to touch her. Seeing her makes every protective instinct I have push forward. I want to shield her from this dark, ugly world.

"Kitten," I whisper, and I want to run to her and take her in my arms but don't know if she'll let me.

Her father lies dead between us, blood coating the dirty floor, and I don't know if she can look at me after this. It's one thing to want him dead and to wish for it to happen. It's another to see the man you love doing it. That is, if she still loves me.

"Captain."

She runs to me, throwing herself in my arms and sobbing. I can feel her worry and fear melt away with every breath. I hold her tight and carry her out of this place. Away from the darkness and all the evil that can never touch her again.

I take her out to the car and set her down, pulling my gun out and placing it in her lap. "Wait here, kitten. I need to finish this."

Her eyes are wild, but she nods and holds my weapon. She watches me as I go to the trunk and pull out a gas can and walk back to the building. "The books. Get the books," she says, making me turn to look at her. I debate it for a second before setting the can down and running back inside. I grab them off the table. When I get back to the car, I hand them to her. I pick up the gas can again and pour it around the perimeter and then throw the container inside. Standing back, I grab the Zippo out of my back pocket and light it up.

"This is for her, you sorry bastard."

I grab a piece of trash and light it. I look at the flame and make sure it's caught before I throw it onto the waiting gas and watch the building ignite. I turn and walk away. No one will look into this too much, because they were all known criminals. And if anyone does decide to dig, I've still got enough pull to make it go away. Nobody is going to miss that piece of shit, and this world will be a better place without the filth he brought to it.

When I get into the car, I reach over and pull Paige onto my lap. It's dangerous, and probably illegal, but I drive back to our building with her in my arms. I'll be damned if I ever let her go again.

TWENTY-SEVEN

Paige

"WHERE ARE WE GOING?" I ask, burying my face back in his neck when we get in the elevator and he hits the button to the wrong floor. I can't let him go. I never want to let him go again.

"I need to show you something."

It's late, and we've both been through so much. I'm drained. I don't know if I can handle much more, but I'll be strong. For him and for me. For us. And at this point, he could take me anywhere and I would go without a fight. After tonight I'm his.

He carried me from the car and has refused to put me down since. The doors open, and he walks out with me in his arms as he goes to a door. He unlocks it, and once we are inside, he sets me down and closes it behind us.

The place is sparse, but I can tell right away it's his. The smell of rosewood and clean linen makes me smile. This is his home. There's not a lot of furniture and no pictures anywhere, so it doesn't take me long to see everything. I turn to him. It doesn't feel like a home at all.

Captain takes a deep breath and pulls me down the

hallway to a door. He pushes it open and then steps aside, letting me walk in. My hands go to my mouth as I see thousands of pictures of me.

"What is this?" I ask, looking at him and then at the pictures. Some from right before I went to college, around the time Miles found me; some from my college years. I take up every inch of his walls.

"I barely graduated from high school when the CIA got ahold of me. I'd shown interest in going into the marines, and they swooped in and grabbed me. I wasn't with them long when they started pushing me underground. My target—Alexander Owens."

He'd given me a lot when he was talking to Alexander, but now he was giving it all to me.

"I had to play dirty for a few years until I built up a little bit of a name for myself in Owens's crews. Then that day came. I'd actually thought about not going to the meeting. Just thought about getting out. I was having to do things I didn't like, and each time things got dirtier and dirtier. But I went to the meeting to see what he'd say. My handler was pressing me hard. Alexander wanted me to get close to Miles. Keep an eye on him. Thought his son was gunning for him, as you know he was."

I step in a little closer, showing him I want to hear more. That I'm not going anywhere. He's just filling in the details for me. I already knew he'd never betrayed me. Only tried to protect me.

"Then out slipped your picture. All that red hair and fire in your eyes. Hit me like a fucking truck. Knew right then why I was on the path I was on. It was leading me to you, and all the dirtier shit I had to do to get there was worth it. All of it. I knew I had to have you. You were mine. And then once I met you, I couldn't stand not being with you. When I went to Miles, I struck a deal. Told him I was with the CIA, deep undercover. Didn't care that I was breaking so many laws I could end up in a cell and never see light again, but we hatched a plan together. He thought I was working my case. I was working to get you. To do what I had to do to take Alexander down, and in the process keep him the fuck away from you."

He cups my cheek, his thumb rubbing back and forth. I lean into it.

"When Miles and I came up with you watching over Mallory, I hired a private guard to follow you around and take pictures and keep an eye on you. It was all I had for years. I put them in here so that every night I could fall asleep looking at you while I waited for the time when you were close."

I'm shocked and overwhelmed as he sits me on the end of his bed, and he goes to his knees in front of me.

"I've been beyond obsessed with you since I got a glimpse of you. I gave it all up for you, Paige. My mission with the CIA, my plan to take down Alexander. All of that was pushed aside the day I saw you. You came first. I had to protect you, and I knew the only way to do that was to hide you. I knew sending you away was the best bet. Miles and I had a common goal. Take Alexander down. I made him keep you in school and isolated from everyone. God help me, I wanted to put you in a tower and throw away the key, and this was as close as I could get."

He drops his head to my lap, and I don't know what to say. All of this is hitting me like a ton of bricks.

"I made sure you were alone, with no one else to lean on besides Mallory and myself. I'm not the good and perfect man you think I am, but I can't say I'm sorry for it." He lifts his head, and his dark green eyes are pleading. "I would do everything all over again to have you end up in my arms. I love you, Paige. I love you more than my own life. I would set fire to the world to make you smile. With one word from you, I would turn it into ash. You are the beginning and end of my life. Don't make me live a life without you. Because I won't survive. Without you there is no me. You have been my everything and I swear you're all I know anymore."

Tears fall down my cheeks, and I wonder how my body has any left to shed.

"All these years I felt like the only thing I've ever wanted was revenge," I tell him. "That's it. It was all I could see. But then today I thought I'd lost you, and my world crashed. That was the worst pain I'd ever felt. Worse than losing my mom. You know why?"

Captain leans in, kissing one of my tears. "No, kitten. Why?"

"'Cause I was happy. I don't think I've truly been happy until I was with you. You made me light up inside. Made the real me come out. No walls or mask. I could just be me, and I knew you loved the real me. Faults and all. I'd never had that before. Someone who would do anything for me without a thought for themselves, and then I thought it was gone. All a lie."

"Kitten." The word comes out pained.

"But I saw you tonight. Heard the words you said to my father. You said you'd do anything for me. I'd do anything for you, too. I love you more than anything. I don't think I can breathe without you," I admit. When he was gone, the walls had started to close in.

"No more secrets, no more lies," he says. Everything is out in the open now. All of it.

I throw myself into his arms so hard that it topples him onto the floor. His lips connect with mine as he rolls us over so that I'm under him. He puts his weight on me, and it's a welcome pressure. The knowledge that he's here with me and that I'm safe allows all the years of worry and sadness to leave me. It's like he's chased away all my demons and I have a new beginning.

His lips are fierce and demanding as I give him what he wants. The kiss is desperate, and we cling together as if it's been years since we've held each other.

"I love you," I whisper through kisses, and his mouth echoes the same. The three words are repeated like a chant over and over in the space that separates our lips. With every syllable, we are one step closer to leaving our ghosts behind and righting the wrongs between us.

TWENTY-EIGHT

Ryan

"NAKED. NOW," I GROWL against her mouth, and start tearing at her clothes. I hear the sound of cloth ripping, but I can't be bothered to slow down and check.

Everything is in the open, and we've both come clean. Now I need to bind us together to seal this deal. I want inside of her more than I want air in my lungs. She fists my shirt, and I lean back to let her pull it off me. I've pushed her hoodie off her and torn her sports bra away. She kicks off her leggings, and I open the front of my pants, pulling out my steel-hard cock, throbbing with need. She looks down at it and widens her thighs for me, moving her ankles around my waist. The aggressive look in her eyes has me wild with lust. In a flip of a switch, she's gone from tender, sweet kissing to wild passion, and I'm right there with her. We've made sweet love, and it's earth-shatteringly beautiful. But right now we need to reconnect, and our primal needs are the loudest voices in the room.

There's a perfectly good bed right beside us, but we don't have time for that.

I push her legs off my hips and move quickly down

to her pussy. I give her one long lick before moving back and lining up my cock with her opening. I want the smell and taste of her on me as I take her. I thrust fully into her in one hard stroke, and her nails dig into my shoulders as she cries out in pleasure.

I blanket my body over hers, giving her some of my weight. The flavor of her pussy on my tongue makes me act savage as I grunt on top of her. Her hips move in time with mine, our wild lust fueling the need. She moans my name, and she doesn't take her gaze from mine as she rakes her nails down my back.

Taking her mouth, I let the flavor of her desire pass between us, and it ratchets up my need for her. I slip my arms around her back and hold her closer to me as I thrust. With Paige, it's always like the first time, given how perfect she feels. I can't ever get close enough, but I keep trying. Moving inside her deeper and harder, feeling her clench around me. Our passion is building and it's going to break me in two when we finally explode.

I've waited so long to have her like this. To have no secrets and both of us truly exposed. It makes every kiss sweeter, every touch more tender and my want for her that much stronger. Everything that happened led us to this, and I wouldn't change a thing. The feel of her under me is raw and real. I've never experienced a connection so strong that it literally brought me to my knees. But Paige does that to me. She has me wrapped around her finger, and one look can bend me to her will. One day she will understand the power she holds over me, but until then, I'll try every day to show her. To let her see what she does to me, and that I will never, ever stop fighting for her.

"Ryan," she breathes against my lips, and I feel her shudder under me.

I move my mouth down her neck and to her breasts, taking one nipple in my mouth and then the other. I hold her body up slightly off the floor, bringing her chest to my mouth as I thrust into her. I alternate kisses and nibbles on each breast as I keep a steady tempo between her legs. She clenches around me, and I hear her cries become louder as she nears her orgasm.

"Tell me you love me when you come, kitten. I want to hear your pleasure wrapped in it."

She clenches hard on my cock one more time as I suck her nipple into my mouth. Her back arches and she shouts the words I want to hear as her body peaks under me. Waves of her release pulse on my cock, and I have no choice but to join her. I hold myself inside her as deep as I can go and release all that I have into her.

Hearing her chant my name with whispers of love as she climaxes is heaven on earth. I hold her close to me as we catch our breath and come back to reality. It takes all the strength in me to pull out, but I do. I scoop up her boneless body and lay her on my bed. I finish kicking off my boots and pants so I'm completely naked before I climb in next to her.

She's on her side facing me, and my eyes roam her beautiful curves. I stretch my hand out and pet her from her shoulder down to her thigh, unable to stop myself from tracing her lines. Her eyes are heavy with sleep and lust, and I want her again so badly. I had her seconds ago and it already feels like an eternity.

"Do you remember the first time we met?" I ask, and she rolls her eyes, smirking at me.

"Of course I do."

"I was so nervous that day. I couldn't sleep the night before because I knew you were coming in. Miles had already talked to you and convinced you to work for him. You were to come meet me, since I would be your contact person for the duration of your job."

"Why were you nervous?" She reaches out, running her fingers through my chest hair.

"Because I knew you were the one." I shrug like it's obvious. "I was meeting my future that day, and it was so exciting and scary. But the second you walked in the door, I felt a calm fall on me."

I place my hand over hers and press her palm flat over my heart.

"You wore jeans and a dark blue sweatshirt that made your eyes look like brilliant stones. Your hair was pulled up, and you came in with a scowl on your face. You had the biggest chip on your shoulder, and all it did was make me want you more."

"God, I was so pissed that day. I didn't want to have to report to you. I just wanted to do my job watching Mallory and be done with it. I hated the thought of having someone keeping tabs on my every move." She smiles and shakes her head. "You were such a pain in the ass."

"I was," I agree, smiling at her. "I wanted to get your attention, and the only thing that seemed to do it was when you were trying to tell me off. That auburn ponytail was swishing back and forth as I was going over what I wanted from you. You gave me so much attitude I could only smile the whole time."

"You did it on purpose."

"Most of it, yes. I wanted to see you riled up. To see if I could pull out of you even a tenth of the passion I had. You were so tough that day. But I could see past that concrete wall you had in front of you. I saw that there was something special underneath. That behind the tough exterior was a tender woman who was afraid to let someone love her."

She nods, and I bring her hand up to my mouth, kissing her wrist.

"That day changed my life, Paige. Seeing you there was incredible, but before I handed you the paperwork and you left, we had that moment."

She looks at me and nods, remembering it, too.

"I held on to it, not wanting you to leave. I knew once you had the information, you'd be gone, and I didn't know when I'd see you again."

"I had that feeling, too," she confesses.

"I had to let you go, and it was the hardest thing I'd ever done. But when I reached out and touched your cheek, I knew you were the one. I couldn't let you go without that one touch, because I had to have something. I knew when I saw your picture you were it for me, but having you in front of me and being able to connect made it real."

I reach over her to a bedside table and pull out a small box. I lean back and place it between us, letting her look at it.

"That day after you left I bought this. Because I knew that it was yours, and no matter what you chose, this would always belong to you. I would never have another woman in my life if you wouldn't have me, so I waited until you couldn't turn me away."

"Ryan," she whispers, but doesn't move.

"I've already called you my fiancée, and in truth you have been since that first day we met. You just didn't know it." She laughs as the tears start to fall, and I kiss her wrist again. "I married you in my heart the night we first made love. One day, I want to make it legal, but in my soul, I'm already there."

"You really are a caveman," she says, and I laugh with her. She's definitely not wrong.

"I should get on one knee and ask you in a field of butterflies or something." She smiles and shakes her head like I'm ridiculous, but I know she loves it. "But I can't take the chance of you not saying yes. So you'll marry me, Paige. You and I will be together until the end of time. We'll make babies, have fights, make up, laugh, cry and spend every moment of every day as one."

"Oh God," she says, and closes her eyes.

"I promise to give you the family you deserve and the one you've always wanted, deep down. I promise to give you a hard time and be a pain in your ass, because you really do love it."

She tries to smack my chest, but I tighten my grip

on her wrist with one hand and open the ring box with the other. I take out the simple band with the solitaire stone and place it on her ring finger. Once it's there, I kiss it and look into her eyes.

"I promise to love you without hesitation, without exceptions and without a single doubt. You are mine until the earth stands still and there's not a breath left in me."

She looks down at the three-carat ruby, and shock is clear on her face. It's the one she saw the day we first met. There was a jewelry store right outside, and I watched as she left the building and stopped in front of the window. She stood and stared at it for a moment, but I could see something in her eyes. I found out later what it truly was. I saw all the hopes and dreams she'd ever had placed on that stone. She walked away that day dismissing its possibilities, but I saw more. And I was going to do everything I could to give it to her.

She nods, not saying a word. She doesn't need to speak, because there's nothing to say. My heart belongs to her, and hers to me.

I roll her on her back and move on top of her. My lips connect with hers, softly this time, more tender than when we made love on the floor. This time it's slow and sweet, and I spend hours worshipping every inch of her body. When we find release, it's more passionate than anything I'd ever dreamed possible.

Afterward I hold her, and I know what true love is.

TWENTY-NINE
Paige

"OH MY GOD, we're moving out of this building," I moan, trying to crawl from the bed. Can I not go one day without someone banging on a door and waking me up? I don't make it one step and Captain is pulling me back onto the bed and caging my body with his. He's giving me his wide morning smile. We're going to have to work on this perky morning thing he's got going on.

"I'll get it," he says, before taking my mouth in a soft, lazy kiss, making me melt back into the bed. I don't care that someone is banging on his front door at God knows what time. He pulls his body from mine, and I make to grab at him, but he keeps moving as I latch around his back and he stands.

"Kitten, I love you hanging on to me, but I'm not answering the door with you naked unless you have a death wish for whoever's on the other side."

I smile, nipping at his neck before I drop my feet to the floor and let him go.

He grabs a pair of boxer briefs from his dresser, cursing when the banging on the front door comes again.

"Jesus. It's not even morning," I growl.

"It's almost noon," Captain corrects. I glance over at the clock on his nightstand. Wow. He must have really gone at me last night. When I look back at him, I can see him thinking the same thing with a smirk on his face. His eyes roam over my naked body, clearly ready to do it all over again.

I bend down, picking up his shirt and handing it to him.

"You put this on unless you want me to claw someone's eyes out." He smiles even bigger as he takes the shirt from me and slides it over his head. I start digging for some gym shorts. Captain has a great chest, but his legs are my weakness. His thick thighs might be the hottest thing about him.

"Why the fuck does it turn me on when you get jealous?" he asks as I find the shorts and hand them to him. I roll my eyes.

The banging is louder this time.

"Open the fucking door!" I hear Miles bellow, surprising us both. Captain heads out of the room, and I search for something to wear, opting for one of his shirts. I slip it on, and it falls all the way to my knees and hangs off one shoulder. Jesus, he's huge.

"She's naked. Don't go back there," I hear Captain say, and that's followed by a curse from Miles. The door swings open; Mallory barrels in, throwing herself at me. I fall back, both of us hitting the bed, with her landing on top of me. She starts sobbing, and I wrap my arms around her.

"I'm fine," I whisper to her. Then she's being

pulled from me. Miles picks her up and puts her on her feet. Then he's pulling me from the bed, too. Shock hits me when his arms wrap around me, the hug so hard and tight I almost can't breathe.

"I want to fucking beat your ass," he grits out between clenched teeth. When I pull back to look up at him, I can see relief on his face. "I told you I would help you. You don't fucking run off like that alone. You hear me? I'm your brother. I would have gone with you. If something happened to you…" He shakes his head. "Fuck!" he barks again, pulling me in for another hug as tight as the last. "I should have protected you. Not pulled you into my plans. Got you wrapped up in our father's mess. I did this all wrong. I'm sorry, Paige. I should be taking care of you."

I hug him back, holding him tight. It's a comfort I didn't know I needed until this moment, having my brother hold me and tell me it's going to be okay.

"I get it. If anyone gets wanting to go after him, I do," I tell him. I would have done anything to go after my father. I never felt used by Miles. The only thing I ever felt was that I was cheated out of having some kind of relationship with my brother, but I never thought he wanted that.

"We are changing this. Starting new. Having a different kind of family." He demands it, like he does most things.

"I like the sound of that," I agree.

"Alexander can—"

"He's dead," Captain says, cutting off Miles's words. Miles slowly lets me go, glancing between

Captain and me. The question is clear, but I really don't want to go over all of it again. He and Captain can have that conversation. I'm done with my father. Done with living in the past. Done with not living at all. My life is mine now. Nothing's hanging over my head. I'm free.

"Good," Mal says, her voice filled with tears, clearly not caring that one of us killed someone last night. "You two are so adorable," she adds, looking from Miles to me before walking over and trying to wrap her arms around both of us. "These pregnancy hormones are the worst," she exclaims into a group hug of her making. She gives a little hiccup. I laugh.

"You're crazy," I tell her.

I step back from the hug, and Miles pulls Mal into him, comforting her.

"She was like this most of the night. I couldn't get it out of her for the longest time. Finally, I got her to crack."

"Sorry," she says, pulling her face out of Miles's chest. "I know you didn't want me to tell him, but…" She hiccups again.

Captain comes up behind me, his front to my back as he wraps one arm around me, locking me to him.

"It's fine," I tell her.

"It's not fine." Miles shakes his head. "I'm glad he's gone. The world is a better place without him," he admits. "But I should have been better with you. I should have known everything. Fuck, I should have put the pieces together. Not asked my seventeen-year-old sister to plot revenge with me."

I'm not sure Miles would have ever been down with killing Alexander. He wanted to make him suffer. That was his revenge. To make Alexander feel pain like he'd made Miles's mother feel. In that way we are alike. We both wanted to do to him what he'd done to our mothers.

"You didn't really, Miles. I mean, all you ever did was send me to college. Make sure I was taken care of. You never promised me anything about our father except that you'd make him pay." He'd shielded me from it, even if he hadn't realized he had.

We might not have been close at the time, but he pulled me off the streets and gave me a purpose. Gave me a life and a goal to work toward. In the end, I got a family. I wouldn't be standing here without him.

"It's over," Captain says from behind me, placing a kiss on the top of my head. I bring my hands up, holding the arm that's holding me.

"We can move on," I confirm.

"Did you…" Mal asks. I shake my head, understanding that she's asking if I'm the one who did it. She looks at Captain and smiles up at him.

"Sorry I punched you," she says sheepishly. Miles picks up her hand and kisses it. "Miles told me everything. That you've been working with him since Alexander tried to use you to get close to Miles."

"Though it took me a minute to realize it wasn't so much me he was interested in." Miles glances around the room, and my face turns red.

I look at Captain, but he doesn't seem to care that

everyone can see his crazy little picture collage of me. He absolutely doesn't give a shit what anyone thinks.

"Oh. My. God," Mal says, noticing the pictures for the first time. "Are you sure Captain and Oz aren't related? Because they're definitely both stalkers."

I can't help but giggle again. I like that Captain is a little crazy. That his walls are covered in me. Mal squeals, making us all jump.

"Your finger!" She breaks from Miles's hold and grabs my hand. "It's perfect. It's so you." Her eyes start to water all over again.

"You have got to get this crying thing under control," I tell her.

"Totally fine," she sniffles as Miles pulls her to him again. I'm not sure why she even tries to leave his reach. It's pointless. I laugh as she sneakily wipes her nose on his thousand-dollar shirt.

"This has been great and all," Captain says, clearly wanting everyone out of his bedroom. We'd made plans to not leave the bed all day.

"That's sweet, but I'm not going anywhere," Mal tells him, grabbing me by the hand. Captain lets me go as she pulls me from his room and down the hallway to the kitchen.

"You can't live here. There's no food in here," Mallory says, opening all the cabinets and looking around. "Captain, you know you're marrying Paige, right? Wait." She stops moving around the kitchen. "Where will you live? Are you leaving? Does Captain still work for Oz now that this whole Alexander thing is over?" She lets out a little gasp. "Are you still with the CIA?"

She whispers the last question, like she hasn't been asking the room questions all at once. We let her get all of them out before I answer.

"He will no longer be with the CIA, we are both staying at Osbourne Corp, we will live in my place because it's bigger," I tell her. "But we'll have to move the Paige shrine because that's obviously coming with us. And never once has my man let me go hungry."

Captain rounds the kitchen island, picking me up by my hips and sitting me on it, then places a deep kiss on me. "What do you want, kitten?"

"The bakery."

"I'll be right back."

"Oz is going with you," Mal adds. She walks over and gives Miles a kiss before pushing him out the door with Captain. I sit on the island, watching her rush them out.

"This is crazy," she finally says, when the door closes. "What happened last night? I really am sorry I broke down and told Oz. He was so worried about you. You should have seen him."

Her words warm me deep inside, knowing how much Miles actually cares about me. After the past week, I think he always has. He just hasn't known how to show his feelings. That is, until Mal ripped them open, and now they seem to be pouring out.

"He killed him for me." I lick my suddenly dry lips.

"The oh-so-perfect Captain isn't so perfect, after

all. Guess you don't have an excuse now," Mal says, hopping up on the kitchen island with me.

"No, he is. Perfect for me." I look over at her, and her whole face lights up with a smile.

"That's the cheesiest thing I've ever heard you say."

"I know. You three must be rubbing off on me."

"Oh, I think someone has been rubbing on you." She wiggles her eyebrows.

"I thought when I lost him yesterday I'd never pull through. It hurt so bad. Worse than anything."

"I knew something wasn't right. I mean, I see the way he looks at you. I see the same look when Miles looks at me. Captain's so in love with you. He's been giving you that look from the first time I saw the two of you together."

We sit in silence for a moment. She reaches over and grabs my hand.

"How do you feel today, now that it's over?"

"All I feel is happy." I squeeze her hand. "And I don't think the happy comes from him being gone. I know I've wanted that for so long, but last night gave me Ryan. That man would do anything in the whole world for me. I have no doubt of that. I am the single most important person in the world to him. That's not something I've ever felt before. To be someone's whole world."

"I get that," Mal agrees, and I know she understands. She never had a family of her own, and she has a man who would do anything for her, too. It's empowering.

"So you need that pink wedding dress?" She bumps my shoulder with hers.

"You know, I think I'd wear anything as long as I got to marry that man."

"You going to be this cheesy all the time now?"

"Are you going to keep bringing up cheese when you know I'm hungry?"

"Hey, I'm the pregnant one." Mal jumps off the island suddenly. "I am the only pregnant one, right? Are you and the Captain wrapping it up?"

I bite my lip, not sure what to say because I have no idea if I am or not. I hadn't given it much thought before now. I can't really think at all when Captain gets his hands on me.

Mal starts jumping around excitedly, and I can't help but join in.

THIRTY

Paige

STANDING IN FRONT of the long mirror, I look myself over. My auburn hair is swept to the side and pinned with wavy curls over one shoulder. Mallory chose a deep blue color for me to wear as a bridesmaid because she said it matches my eyes perfectly. She's right, of course, and I look amazing. The halter neckline is silky, with a dark blue lace trim. The dress is fitted until it gets to my knees, flowing out slightly in a mermaid style. I look like I'm about to walk a red carpet, not walk down the aisle to watch my best friend get married.

"Perfect," I hear Mallory say from behind me, and I turn to look at her.

"I could say the same thing." I take in her white dress and love how amazing she looks.

Her dress is off the shoulder, with long lace sleeves. Her dark hair is up, exposing her beautiful neck and collarbone. Her dress is fitted to the waist and then flares out a little. The bottom of it is lace, and when she takes a step, her pink glittery heels peek out.

"You just had to have the pink, didn't you?" I ask, laughing.

She shrugs a shoulder, like of course she did, and comes to the mirror beside me. "We look amazing," she says excitedly. "I can't believe we pulled this off in a month."

Oz wanted Mallory to have everything she ever dreamed of, and with enough money, you can have that in four weeks or less.

She rubs her belly. She doesn't look pregnant, but I think she keeps sticking it out deliberately, trying to give the appearance.

I twist a piece of my hair so it's perfect and check my dress again. I can't wait for Captain to see me in this thing. He's probably going to want to rip it off me the second he does, but I'll enjoy teasing him in the meantime.

"So. There's something I've been meaning to tell you," Mallory says, turning to me.

"What? There better be crab cakes at this reception. You promised." I put my hand on my hips, getting fired up again. She said I could pick what I wanted, without argument.

She smiles at me, and it's a little wicked. Suddenly I'm wary.

"So today isn't just my wedding day." She grabs a bouquet of bloodred roses from the side table and hands it to me. "It's our wedding day."

I take the flowers and look at her quizzically. "You mean *ours* as in you and Miles?"

"No. Ours as in you and me are the brides, and we are both marrying our men today. Surprise, Paige! It's a double wedding!"

She sings the word *wedding* like somehow it will soften the blow.

"What?" I say, dropping my voice. "I didn't agree to this. Captain and I said we were going to work it out after yours. That we didn't need to plan some big…some big thing!" I half shout, and Mallory only smiles more.

"It's cute you think I haven't been planning this with Captain since the beginning. Why else do you think he went to see the wedding planner with me every time I went?" She grabs my upper arms and leans in. "Remember that time you lied to me for four years and pretended to be my friend? Payback is a bitch, Paige, and you owe me. Big-time."

She steps back, and I stare at her in utter shock. What the fuck just happened? I'm getting married?

"Captain and I knew you needed a little push, so here you go. You can thank me later for doing all the work for you." She winks and turns, grabbing her own pink bouquet. Then she puts her arm in mine and leads me out of the room.

"Mallory, I can't do this." I tug on her, but somehow she's got a superhuman grip on my arm. "Let me go."

"What are you afraid of, Paige?" She looks in my eyes, and I can see she doesn't have a hint of worry or doubt. She's calm and smiling, like it's her wedding day and nothing can go wrong. "On the other side of those doors is the man you love, waiting to make you his forever. Think about that for a second."

She's right, and I don't know why I'm freaking out.

Maybe it's because I wasn't expecting this, and Captain and I haven't really discussed details. I knew that in his heart we were already joined, so this is just a formality. Nothing in the world could break us apart. Having a wedding wasn't something I dreamed of, and maybe it's another thing I didn't allow myself to hope for. But here it is, laid out for the taking, and I want to run.

No. Not ever again. The only running I'm doing is straight into Captain's arms.

"There you go," she says, seeing the change in my eyes. "Took you a second, but you got there. Now let's go get married to our men."

"Holy shit," I breathe as the double doors open.

"I SHOULD HAVE known better than to leave you two alone," I say, looking between Captain and Mallory.

I'm sitting on Captain's lap, and his arms tighten around my waist. He kisses my shoulder, and I can feel him smile against it. I pick up the champagne bottle, drinking straight from it, and Mallory laughs.

The party went late into the night, and our guests have left. We didn't have a big wedding, considering all the people Miles knows. Captain invited his family, and I was happy to meet them. They were all very nice, and we made plans to maybe visit during Christmas, and that seemed to suit everyone. Captain even invited Patrick and his husband, Amos, which I thought was a sweet gesture. It's been nice seeing Patrick from time to time. He's a reminder that not everything in my past was horrible. There were sweet points in my life, and it's not so bad revisiting them.

Mallory had a couple people from work, but other than that she and I didn't have any guests. I kind of liked it that way, because we have each other. And that's more than enough.

The band is still playing softly in the background, and I lean back against Captain, closing my eyes. It's been the most perfect day ever. Mallory and I walked hand in hand through the doors and to our future. When I looked up and saw those dark green eyes waiting on me, every thought I had went out the window. Mallory had to tug my hand a couple times to keep me from running down to him. I didn't realize how much I wanted a wedding until that moment, something to celebrate us becoming one and to let the world know I belong to him.

The ceremony was mercifully quick, and I didn't have to stand in front of the crowd too long. We said traditional vows, except Captain had asked the minister to take out *obey* and replace it with *feed*. God, I love that man.

After it was over, the four of us came to the garden for our reception. It's the place Miles built for Mallory, but I feel like it's a part of me, too. Their story is so much a part of mine and Captain's that it made sense for us to have a double wedding. There are twinkling lights strung everywhere, and the garden looks so beautiful. It's peaceful here, with the music and the waterfall, and I don't know if I want the night to end.

Mallory is sitting in Miles's lap across from us, and I reach out, grabbing her hand and squeezing it. "Thank you," I say to her, and I see little tears form in her eyes.

"I think it's time we head out. We're wheels up in an hour," Miles says, and picks Mallory up.

I stand, taking Captain's hand, and we make our way out behind them. He wraps his arm around me, and we exit the front of Osbourne Corp. The limo is waiting on them, and I see Mal wiggle in Miles's arms before he puts her down. She runs over to me, wrapping me in a huge hug before kissing me on the cheek.

"I love you so much, Paige," she says, and then pulls away, getting into the back of the limo.

Miles comes over, kissing me on the cheek and shaking Captain's hand. "We'll see you guys in two weeks. Have fun." He winks at Captain and then joins his bride. The limo pulls away from the curb.

I turn to Captain, feeling a little bummed that the night is over. "Think there's any crab cakes left?" I ask, looking back at the building longingly.

"I think they were all gone when you made the caterer cry, kitten." He pulls me into a hug and kisses the top of my head. "Besides, we don't really have the time."

Just then another limo pulls up, and Captain opens the back door.

"What's going on?" I ask, excitement bubbling up inside me.

"Get in, kitten. We've got a honeymoon to catch."

I beam at him, thinking this is the kind of surprise

I could get used to. I'm not one for having everyone look at me, but I'll take a vacation any day of the week. I climb in and I'm bouncing in my seat as he comes in after me. The car pulls away, and I look at him, suddenly feeling wide-awake.

"Where are we going? I didn't pack a suitcase. How did you do this? I'm so excited."

Leaning forward, I plant a kiss on his lips, and he laughs as he takes over. My back hits the seat of the limo as he covers me with his body.

"It's a surprise, and I packed your suitcase. Some things are worth waiting for, Paige. And you were worth every second." His mouth moves down my neck, and I feel the slick heat of his tongue between my breasts. "My God, I know I've told you seven thousand times today, but you look so beautiful. The most beautiful woman I've ever seen."

I wrap my legs around his waist, and I feel the limo hum beneath us. The vibrations along with Captain's mouth have me all too ready for him. The whole night has been full of sneaky touches and soft kisses, both of us knowing what was to come. That tonight we would make love as husband and wife, and though it would be the same as before, it would be something new. I can't keep my hands off him as I run them up his dress shirt and under his suit jacket. I want him naked and grunting on top of me, but this limo seat isn't big enough for that. It's barely able to hold me, and Captain has his knees on the floor.

"How long do we have?" I ask, panting with need.

"Forever," Captain says, pulling one of my nipples free and latching on to it.

"Ryan!" I cry out as the pain turns to pleasure. "I meant to where we're going."

He releases my breast and looks up at me with a wicked grin. The limo comes to a stop, and I want to curse. He moves my dress back in place and gives me a soft kiss before sitting up and adjusting himself. Once we're both decent for the public, he opens the back door and helps me out. Our driver holds the door as someone takes our luggage out of the trunk and wheels it away. We're on tarmac, and I see a plane a few feet away.

"Is that us?" I ask, looking over at my new husband.

"It is, Mrs. Justice."

I love him calling me that, and I wrap my arms around him. "That thing have a bed?" I ask, wiggling my eyebrows.

"It does, Mrs. Justice."

"Looks like you get to fuck me in the air. You really are a superhero," I say, giving him a quick kiss.

He scoops me up, causing me to squeal out in surprise as he walks us to the plane. "You seem to have forgotten that. So I suppose I'll have to show you. But I plan on making love first. Then fucking you."

Captain carries me onto the plane and then buckles me up. I look around and see the thing is bigger than I expected, with bench seating on one side and a table and chairs on the other. There's a door in the back that I assume leads to the bed, and I look at it and then at Captain, giving him a wink. He sits beside me and buckles up as the plane gets ready for takeoff.

"Are you sure you won't tell me where we're going?" I ask, giving him my best soft pouty face.

"Hmm," he says thoughtfully, like he's seriously thinking it over. "Tell you what. If I can get you off ten times before we land, I'll tell you."

"Ten!" I shout, and one of the crew turns to look at me. "Sorry," I mumble, and look back at Captain. I lower my voice this time, not wanting anyone to hear us. "That's impossible."

"Oh, sweet kitten," he says, taking my chin. "You forgot you're married to me."

THIRTY-ONE

Ryan

I STARE DOWN at my wife, her auburn hair spread out all over the white sheets of our bed. I've said the word over and over again and I still can't wrap my mind around the fact that she's really mine now. *Wife.*

She hasn't stirred in hours. Not since I pulled her from the plane. She barely even opened her eyes. Not that I blame her. I hardly left her alone the whole flight and I knew she was exhausted.

Her body looks so soft and welcoming. After I ruined her wedding dress, I had to give her my button-up shirt. I'd carried her from the plane into the car and right into our little hut over the water. As I stripped her bare and put her into bed, she didn't make a sound. She didn't wake for any of it. If she hadn't placed a few sleepy kisses on my neck throughout the night, I would have been worried.

She rolls over, her legs dropping open and showing the evidence of all the orgasms I'd given her on the plane. My stubble left little marks on the inside of her thighs. I told her I'd tell her where we were going once I got her to ten orgasms, but my kitten passed out around number seven.

I trail my hand up her silky skin, cupping her pussy in a possessive hold. I never thought this day would come. Having Paige in my bed all spread out before me. The evidence of her belonging to me all over her body. You can't look at any part of her and think she doesn't belong to someone. It might be barbaric, but I don't care. I want her to always look like that. Too many years spent away from her makes me a little inhuman when it comes to her.

She makes me feel whole. Washes away all the dirt that collected on me over the years doing undercover work. Makes me feel clean again. Makes me want to live up to this perfect picture she made of me. Just for her.

Her eyes slowly flutter open, a sexy smile spreading on her face. The sun shines in the window, making the little freckles on her nose show even more. "I think you killed me." The words are filled with a lazy pleasure.

I lick my lips, thinking about killing her all over again. I could spend this whole honeymoon doing nothing but feasting on her pussy if she'd let me.

"None of that. I think you've had your fill. I don't even know what country we're in." She laughs, sitting up and going straight for my mouth, despite what she said. She wastes no time climbing into my lap. Fuck, I love that she can't seem to get enough of me, either. Her sassy mouth is always saying one thing, but her body does another.

"I need to feed you, kitten," I tell her, when she finally lets my mouth go.

"You need to tell me where we are," she says, and tilts her head to the side, making me smile because I know what she wants when she does that. I grip both her hips in my hands, pulling her closer and nibbling at her neck until she wiggles in my lap.

I release one hip and grip her hair in my fist, making her give me even more of her neck. I suck hard with every intention of leaving a mark on her.

"Do it," she says feverishly, grabbing on to me, her fingers digging in. "Mark me. I love seeing you on me when I look in the mirror. Turns me on."

I suck on her harder as she moves against me, dragging her bare pussy along my cock. Come leaks out of me, her words alone making me lose control.

"That's it. Oh God. Mark me." Her words come out breathy, and I know she's already close. She knows just what to say to get me off, sinking her claws into the possessiveness I have for her.

"Show everyone I belong to you." I feel the muscles in her body lock up. "Oh God. I'm yours, Ryan." She yells out the last part, making me come against her. I hump her pussy and come like a teenager who saw his first *Playboy*. My come spreads across her pussy, ass and thighs, marking her even more. I keep moving against her as her own orgasm explodes through her.

I lean back and watch her ride out the wave. Her eyes fall closed, and her body jerks against mine. The sign of her pleasure makes my cock come back to life, as if I hadn't released all over her.

Her head falls forward, her dark red waves brushing

over the both of us. A lazy smile spreads on her full lips, which still show signs of our make-out session. When her blue eyes open and lock on me, I can't stop myself from kissing her all over again.

"I can't believe I get to wake up like this every day for the rest of my life," she says against my mouth. "You make everything else fade away. You know you did that, right? Filled me up with so much happiness I can't remember anything else."

A lump forms in my throat. I have to fight it down. "You don't know what it means to me to know I did that for you. It's all I ever wanted. To make you happy. Take away that sadness I saw in your eyes the first time I ever saw you."

"Well, Captain, I promise you've done that and more." She wraps her arms around my neck. "It's all behind us, right?" she asks, and I know what she's talking about. There's still a trace of fear that lingers there. That we could be caught for what we did. I can see it in her eyes, but I know we're in the clear. I would have let her know if I thought there was even a question of getting caught. I made sure we wouldn't. Plus, I had a plan for if we weren't safe. In fact, we're sitting in my plan right now, but for a different reason.

"I turned it all in." I'd grabbed the information because she told me to. I hadn't even thought about it. My only focus had been on her and getting her out of the warehouse. If the CIA wanted to thank anyone, it should be her. "They got what they wanted and I'm done with all that. Nothing from that life will ever touch us."

I had been out of the CIA for a while already, working only for Miles toward the end. My old handler was shocked to see me when I showed up with the evidence. I let him know he needed to make sure a burned-down warehouse could never be traced back to me. That nothing about the CIA or my work with them would ever surface. That life was behind me, and I wanted none of it creeping back up. Ever.

"How long until I have your job?" Paige asks, crawling from my lap and changing the subject. She lets it all go, leaving it in the past where it belongs. Moving toward our future.

"You after my job, kitten?" I lean back on the bed and watch her look around the little hut. She still has no idea where we are.

"It would be fun to boss you around from time to time," she says, like she doesn't already do it. She creeps toward one of the windows before a gasp leaves her lips.

"Are we over the water?"

"Yes."

"Where are we?"

For some reason I don't want to tell her. I like the idea of her being lost, with only me to hold on to. I don't care if that idea is a little fucked up.

I get up from the bed and walk over toward her, wrapping my arms around her from behind and looking out into the clear blue ocean with her.

"You're with me," I finally tell her, making her shake her head and giggle.

"Then I think you picked the perfect place for our

honeymoon, because there isn't anywhere else in the whole world I'd rather be."

"Good, because it's ours."

She turns, looking up at me. "What do you mean, it's ours?"

"I own it."

"You own this hut?"

"Yes. And the whole island it sits on."

Her eyes widen, like she doesn't quite believe me. The island isn't giant, but it's a nice size.

"Miles pays good, but not that good," she counters. I smile. Miles pays more than good, actually.

"I was smart with my money." I invested in almost everything Miles told me to, and it paid. Big-time. "I made sure I put it in the right places and I don't spend much. Unless you count this little island."

"Little island." She laughs. "That's fine, Captain, because I love shoes and I'll spend the shit out of your money for you."

"As long as I get to fuck you while you wear them, you'll never hear me complain. Besides, it's half yours now." Hell, it's all hers if you ask me. The only reason I ever invested money was because I had an endgame to make her mine, and I knew families cost money. I needed to build a life for us. Make sure I could give her anything and everything she dreamed of.

"Hmm." She wiggles her eyebrows. "How about nothing at all?" She rubs her naked body against mine. "If you own this island, does that mean I can jump in like this?" She breaks from my grasp, walking toward the sliding doors. I watch her as she pulls them open and steps out onto the deck and into the sunshine.

I let her, knowing there isn't anyone else on the island. There won't be for the next two weeks. It will be only her and me.

"Oh, there's a boat." She lifts her hand to wave, and I'm on her in the blink of an eye, pulling her back into the hut.

She breaks out in a fit of giggles, and I quickly realize she was fucking with me. There's no boat. I growl. I throw her over my shoulder, carry her over to the bed and toss her onto it.

The laughing stops, and a look of lust crosses her face. She crawls backward on the bed, licking her lips. When she gets to the headboard, she lets her legs drop open, my come still coating her, tempting me with her pussy, making my mouth water. I want her taste all over me again. It's been too long since I've had my mouth between her legs.

"You like to get me worked up?" I ask. I already know the answer. She gets off on this shit. It's a good thing my jealousy and caveman tendencies make her wet, or we could have problems. I'm not sure they are something I can control. Not with her.

I put one hand on the bed and watch her breathing pick up. I reach out, grabbing her ankle, pulling her down and back to me. When I get her where I want her, I flip her over, landing one smack to her ass. She moans, sticking her ass even more into the air. And as if overcome with need, she parts her legs a little more.

She looks over her shoulder at me, and I wrap my

hand around my cock. I pump my fist up and down it, and she licks her lips. She pushes her ass back even more, wanting it, wanting me.

"I missed a spot," I tell her. I didn't mark her ass well enough. "If you're going to try to get me worked up, then I'm going to have to coat you with me. I won't have to worry if I've marked every inch of you." That's a lie. I'll always worry about someone trying to take her from me. Who wouldn't try to take her? She's fucking perfect in every way.

"Maybe you should mark me on the inside." She pushes her ass out even more, and I have to bite back a smile. I keep stroking myself, and she narrows her eyes on my hand. A flash of jealousy flares as she watches me pleasure myself. She doesn't like that my hand is getting to do the work.

I should keep going, teasing her. But the truth is, I want to give her everything. I kneel on the bed, dropping over her. I plant my fists on either side of her and then slide my cock right into her. We both moan together. I put my mouth on her neck, sucking and licking just like she likes. I don't stop making love to her until every part of her has been marked by me.

THIRTY-TWO
Paige

Three months later...

THERE'S A SMALL knock on the door, and I open my eyes to see Vivien, Miles's mother, coming into the living room. I've been so sick the past two days that I've stayed on the couch, and now I look around at the mess I've made and feel embarrassed.

"You look like shit," she says, and I laugh. I make a move to get up, but she holds out her arms to stop me. "Don't get up. I simply wanted to come by and check on you."

"I'm going to get you sick," I say as I watch her walk over to me and sit down on the coffee table.

She reaches out and brushes a strand of hair out of my eyes. "Miles told me you were home sick, so I thought I'd see if there was anything you needed. He said you made Ryan go to work." She smiles, and it fills my heart up with warmth.

Last week Captain got sick with a stomach flu, and he was down for the count for a couple days. I, being the incredible wife I am, nursed him back to health. But then the bastard gave it to me. I was in bed for a couple days, wearing a path to the bathroom. But even after the worst was over, the sickness is lingering and keeping me down.

"He keeps hovering while I lie here and die. I want to do it in peace," I joke, rolling onto my side.

The past few months of married life have been wonderful. Captain and I have not only bonded unlike anything I ever knew possible, but I've gained a whole family along with it. We have dinners during the week with Miles and Mallory, and Vivien always invites us over for Sunday brunch. She knows the key to my heart is in my belly. Vivien has opened up to me, and it's been the kind of relationship I always dreamed of. She was nice to me before, but I had my defenses up. But since Captain tore down my walls, I've been unable to put any back. And Vivien slipped in. She gives me the tender mothering that I never had, even from my own mother. Sometimes I feel guilty about how much I enjoy it, but I know that deep down my mother would want me to have this. To have someone give me what she wasn't able to.

Vivien stopping by today is another reason why having her in my life is truly a blessing. Because there's nobody like a mom when you're sick.

"Well, I thought I'd bring you by something to make you feel better."

"I don't know that I've ever uttered these words, but I don't think I can eat."

Vivien laughs and shakes her head, reaching in her bag and pulling out a package. She hands it to me and I take it.

I look at the box and feel a shot of anger. "I'm not pregnant," I say, handing the box back to her. I'm annoyed at the woman on the front of the box, thinking how much I hate her.

My periods have always been irregular, but I never worried about it before. Captain and I got back from our honeymoon and went at it like horny bunnies. Thinking that any day now I'd be knocked up. After a month of trying, I went to the doctor, and they ran some tests. He said there was just a very slim chance, with my history and body size, that I'd be able to conceive. Or carry a baby full-term, especially with Captain's size and knowing how big a baby of his might be.

It was a devastating blow, and one I hadn't told Captain about. He knew I went to the doctor, but he didn't push when I wouldn't explain. I knew that eventually we'd have to have that talk, but I've been putting it off, unable to voice it out loud.

Vivien reaches out and squeezes my shoulder. "Get up and take the test." Her voice is stern, and I have a glimpse of what it was like for Miles growing up when his mother told him to do something.

There's no room for argument in her tone, and I get up, taking the box to the bathroom with me. I figure if anything, I'll indulge her and get it over with. She doesn't know about my body, or the fact that I can't get pregnant. But I don't say any of that.

When I'm finished peeing on the stick and cleaning up afterward. I open the bathroom door to find Vivien on the other side, waiting.

She follows me back to the living room, where I fall back down on the covers and she buzzes around the place, cleaning up. I tell her not to, but she shrugs it off and goes back to clearing up my tissues and the blankets that are scattered about.

It feels good having someone else there to take care of me. Captain does a great job, but he hovers over me like I'm going to break out with a deadly case of malaria any second. His worry only makes me worry, and it does me no good. But it feels like Vivien's got this under control.

At some point I close my eyes, and a little while later wake to the scent of chicken soup, and my stomach growls.

Vivien walks over with a tray, and I sit up on the couch as she puts it in my lap. There's a cup of chicken broth on there, with two ginger cookies and a mug of something that smells hot and sweet.

"Thank you. I think I'm actually hungry now. You must have the magic touch," I say, reaching for a cookie.

"You're welcome. When I was pregnant with Miles, I was so sick. I thought I had a stomach flu, too. The only things I could keep down were ginger cookies and chicken broth."

She looks at me sweetly, and I roll my eyes. I let out a sigh and try not to sound like an asshole.

"I can't get pregnant. The doctor said it would be almost impossible." I shrug, eating the second cookie. Damn, these things are good.

She nods but keeps smiling and watches me eat.

When I've finished, she hands me the hot tea, telling me to sip it. It warms my belly as it goes down, and I feel a thousand times better after the small meal.

I watch as Vivien grabs her bag and sets a small box of cookies in front of me. "You might want to hang on to these," she says, placing the pregnancy test on top of them. Then she leans forward, presses a kiss on the top of my head and walks out the front door.

Excitement creeps in as I set down my mug of tea and hesitantly glance at the test. Then my nose burns as tears start to pool in my eyes and my vision blurs.

THIRTY-THREE

Ryan

I WALK THROUGH the lobby of our apartment building, waving at Chuck at the front desk. I left work early even though I know Paige will probably be pissed about me coming to check on her, but I'm worried.

"Hello, Ryan."

I hear Vivien's voice and turn my head to see her exit the elevator. Her boyfriend, Tom, gets up from a lobby chair and walks over to join her. She and Tom started dating right after Mallory and Miles got engaged. Mallory likes to tell anyone who will listen that it was all her doing.

I smile at them, walking over and shaking hands with Tom. Vivien gives me a kiss on the cheek. I look out front to see her security waiting. I assumed when I saw them that she was here to see Miles or Mallory. It's strange she's coming during the day, though.

"What brings you here?" I ask.

"I had to stop by to drop something off. I heard Paige was sick, so I wanted to check on her."

It makes me happy that she and Paige have been able to form a bond, and I think it gives them each something they were missing. Peace and comfort.

"We need to hurry if we're going to make that lesson," Tom says, placing his hand on Vivien's lower back.

"Hope you've got on your dancing shoes," she says, winking at him. "Tonight's class is the samba." She wiggles her shoulders and leans into him as we say our goodbyes.

I walk over and hit the button for the elevator, waiting to go up and see my wife. I'm glad Vivien was able to check on her, but I need to see her for myself. She's had this virus for a lot longer than I did, so maybe it's time to go to the doctor. I'm hoping if I can get to her early enough, we can get her in today before they close. I know that's what's been wrong with her the past few days, but I can tell something else is bothering her, too.

A few weeks ago she went to the doctor, but she won't tell me what's wrong. I know she's disappointed we didn't get pregnant right away, but sometimes it takes a while. And so what if we don't have kids? I want to be with her forever, and having children or not having them doesn't change that. If she wants them bad enough, I'll make it happen. We'll adopt or have a surrogate. Whatever she wants is what I'll give her. End of discussion.

I don't know if that's what her doctor's appointment was about, but I know Paige. Something is bugging her, but I know I can't push her. She'll tell me when she's ready, and when she is, we'll work through it. Together.

I ride the elevator up to our floor. We moved all

my stuff up here, including the Paige Shrine, as she likes to refer to it, as soon as we got home from our honeymoon. I open the door and see Paige sitting in the living room with her head in her hands, sobbing.

I run over to her and kneel at her side, rubbing her back. "Kitten, what is it? Tell me what's wrong. Do I need to take you to the hospital?"

She pulls back her hands, and I see her smiling from ear to ear, tears rolling down her face. "I'm not sick. I'm pregnant."

I look to her lap and see the pregnancy test there, two bright blue lines staring back at me. Suddenly I'm pulling Paige into my arms and kissing her so fiercely that it's almost like the first time.

"I'm so happy. I love you so much," I say, when I finally break from her lips, moving my mouth down her neck. Turning her, I lay her down on the couch and push her shirt up, kissing her belly. "And I love you, too, baby."

Paige laughs and clings to me, and I kiss her all over this time. Her belly, her arms, her legs. Anywhere I can get my mouth on her. I'm relieved she doesn't have a life-threatening virus, and that she's been sick because she's having our baby.

"Why didn't you tell me?" I ask, looking into her dark blue eyes.

"I just found out," she says, smiling at me. When I shake my head and she sees my meaning, I'm disappointed, because I know there's more to this than she's letting on. I can read Paige easily. She shrugs. "I was scared we might not ever be able to have kids.

I didn't want to say it out loud because that meant it was real. I didn't want to worry you."

"Paige, I love you. My life is with you. In good times and in bad. We share all the burdens together. Right?"

"Right," she says, and wraps her arms around my neck.

I can't stop myself from kissing her as I pick her up in my arms and carry her to bed. "This calls for celebration sex," I say, and she laughs.

When we make love, it's soft and sweet, and we both smile while we kiss. It's like we can't believe that we've gotten to this next step, and it's both exciting and scary. Afterward, when we've each exhausted the other, I hold her and we talk about the future. Our future. A life before us with all the possibilities we ever dreamed of. A world where our love is all that matters. It's paradise, and I plan on giving it all to her. Because she's mine and mine alone.

EPILOGUE

Paige

Four months later...

"GOD, THIS LITTLE boy is going to be a giant," Mal says, rubbing her hand over my belly as she stands to the side of the exam table. Captain stands at the other side, one hand locked with mine, his thumb rubbing my wrist. I bite my lip to keep from smiling. Today we find out the sex, and both Captain and Mal think it's a boy, and maybe it is, but what they don't know is that there are two babies.

I'd worried about telling anyone that I was having twins. I was already told I was unlikely to get pregnant. They worried about Captain's size compared to mine, and my small body carrying his baby. I was scared, and I knew everyone else would be, too. But the doctor told me if I could get to the second trimester, then everything should be smooth sailing. I've passed the mark and now I'm nearing the third. I can't believe how fast it's flown by. Everything's looking great, and I'm ready to tell them my little surprise. I'm nearly bursting with it.

"You're almost as big as me and I'm months ahead

of you." Mal looks down at her own baby belly. She's having a little boy. We thought it would be nice to have two boys who could play together, but Captain's always wandering toward the little girls' stuff when we go into the baby sections. I know he secretly wants a little girl, but he won't say it. I'm not sure I'll know how to handle a girl, but seeing how much he wants one makes me want one, too.

"It could be a girl," Captain counters. His free hand slides into my hair. "Your eyes and hair. She'd be my little angel. Daddy's little girl." I can see him playing it out in his head. She would definitely be spoiled. Captain would be so fucked. She'd have him so wrapped around her finger.

"Then she better have your personality, because I'm no angel," I tease him. It would be cute to see a little girl like him.

"She's too big for it to be a girl. It has to be a boy, and he's clearly going to be a giant like his father." Mal nods like her words are facts that can't be argued. I am gigantic, but I've been trying to stay on top of it. Eating right and walking now that I'm too big to run. I've even started doing some yoga. I'll do anything to make sure this pregnancy goes right.

The doctor steps into the room at that moment, a bright smile on her face. She's been just as excited to tell everyone it's twins. Only she and I know.

"How is our mom-to-be doing?" she asks, heading over to the sink to wash her hands.

"We're good." Mal answers for both of us, making the ob-gyn laugh. She happens to be her doctor, as well. She demanded we go to the same one, not giving me a choice. Not that I put up a fight when the doctor is the best in New York. I knew I was high risk, so I wasn't playing around. "Come tell Paige she's having a baby boy already so we can go."

I shake my head at her. "Yes, please tell me what I'm having so I can get some lunch. These two are killing me. They haven't fed me all day," I lie. I literally just ate breakfast, but I'm eating for five. Well, it feels like I'm eating for five, anyway.

"You're hungry?" Captains asks. He stops playing with my hair, and a concerned look crosses his face.

"I'm always hungry. Keep petting me," I snap. "Sorry," I add, and he laughs. I get snippy when I'm hungry. I also cry all the time for no good reason whatsoever. I'm turning into Mallory.

"All right. Let's see what we've got here." The doctor walks over to Mal's side of the bed, and Mal reluctantly moves out of her way, coming to stand by my head while the doctor opens my gown and starts putting the gel on me.

When the monitor touches my belly, the whole room goes quiet as their heartbeats fill the room.

"Oh my God," Mal says, and I know she sees it. I can hear it in her voice, and I know she's crying.

I stare at Captain's face. He's looking at me until Mal sniffs, then his eyes snap to the screen. "Is something wrong?" I can hear the panic in his voice, and I grip his hand a little tighter. I don't like that he's scared. Captain is never scared.

"No, big guy. There's just two of them," I tell him.

His eyes come back to me, but the panic doesn't disappear. He's been so worried about me and the baby, and now there are two to fret over. One more person for him to be concerned about.

"Is she okay? I thought... Fuck, can she handle two?" His voice is filled with both fear and awe. He wants this, but not at the cost of hurting me.

"Everything looks fine," the doctor declares. "Both these baby girls are right on track, and the tests I've gotten back show Paige is doing better than fine. She's in great shape, and she's keeping herself and the babies healthy. She's not the first tiny woman to carry twins," she assures him.

"Two little girls," Captain says, staring at the screen now. Then his eyes come back to mine again, and I can see they're filled with tears.

"Let's give them a moment," I hear the doctor say as she wipes the gel from my stomach. I can't take my eyes off Captain. Watching everything pass over his face is beautiful.

He leans down, putting his forehead to mine. "You're giving me two little girls?" He says it again, like he can't believe that I would grant him this wish. I would give this man anything I could. Anything in my power, and maybe even beyond. He makes me whole and happier than I ever thought I could be. I want to do the same for him.

"You put them there." I smile up at him, feeling my own tears form.

"I'm going to be so good to you and our family. I promise, Paige." There is so much determination behind his words, and I know he means it. He will be an incredible father.

"Ryan." I sink my fingers into his hair. "You're already so good to me and these girls." He is. This man would do anything for me and our babies. It shows in everything he does. "I've never doubted you would be the perfect father and husband. That's why I was so sad when I thought we couldn't have babies. Because I know how good you will be at it. I also know these girls will come into this world knowing what a man should be like. I don't know how they will ever find husbands of their own with a father as perfect as you."

"They aren't having husbands," he growls, before taking my lips in a kiss. His tongue slides into my mouth, lazy and sweet, and I know when we get home I'm going to attack him. He lets go of my hand and slides his palm over my belly. I feel one of the girls give a little kick. I debate if I want to get lunch first or just eat him. When he deepens the kiss, I know my answer. I'm definitely going to have him.

"It's twins! Two little girls!" I hear screaming outside the room, and I know Mal is losing it on Miles, who's been out in the waiting room. I can picture her trying to jump up and down and Miles freaking out and trying to get her to sit down.

I start laughing, breaking the kiss.

"You think I was bad before? I'm not sure I'm going to let you out of our bed now," Captain says, and I know he's talking about bed rest. But if he's in the bed with me, I won't be able to resist. I rub his hard cock through his jeans. I wonder if it's from the kiss or my belly being out. Something about seeing me pregnant gets my caveman all worked up.

"Sounds good to me."

EPILOGUE

Ryan

Five years later...

"*Ninja Turtles.*"

"*Princess and Her Fairies.*"

"*Ninja Turtles.*"

"*Princess and Her Fairies,* and you pick the snacks!" Penelope says to Pandora.

Pandora narrows her eyes like she's thinking it over, but we all know she's going to pick the snacks option. She tucks one of her red curls behind her ear, and she's never looked more like her mother.

"Deal," Pandora agrees.

Penelope scrunches her little freckled button nose in a happy smile, then winks one of her deep green eyes at me. The girls look almost identical, but Pandora has Paige's eyes, whereas Penelope has mine. Their eyes and attitude are the only real way to tell them apart. Pandora is her mother through and through. Penelope is more girl than any of us can handle, but she seems to be able to manage us all too well.

Just then Paige comes strolling into the room. It takes everything I have in me to keep my ass planted on the sofa between my girls. She's got on some denim-looking thing that could be a short dress or a long shirt. I don't know which it is, but it's too fucking short. It looks almost indecent with her boots that go up over her knees. Her lips are painted a deep red, and all her hair is piled on top of her head, showing off her fucking neck. I want to growl at all the skin showing. She needs to put on a turtleneck and some jeans or something. Ever since she's had our girls, she's been dressing up a little more here and there. And the pregnancy only made her hotter. Her hips are a little wider now, and her breasts a little fuller.

"You look pretty, Mommy," Penelope says.

"Thank you, sweetheart," she says in return, her gaze coming to me. She is not fucking going out in that. I don't give two fucks if it's girls' night and she and Mal will have two guards on them.

"What the—" I stop myself before I can finish my sentence.

"What the what, Daddy?" Pandora pushes, giving me a smirk. Little troublemaker. Paige walks over to the sofa and leans down to kiss Penelope on the head, and Pandora just giggles.

"I love your shoes, Mommy," Penelope adds.

She can spend hours in Paige's closet, trying on her heels. Sometimes she makes me sit in there while she does it. She's going to keep me on my toes. Luckily, I have Pandora to keep an eye on her. And I've got Henry, Miles and Mallory's little boy, as backup. He already gives the boys at the playground shit when they try to talk to my girls.

"Well, I think your dress is just perfect, my little princess," Paige tells her.

Penelope smooths down her oversize dress. I think she might have more dress-up clothes than anyone has actual clothes around here.

"Blue really is my color," she tells Paige, making me laugh.

Pandora just rolls her eyes, then looks at Penelope. "You better go change 'cause Daddy is taking us out."

Paige raises her eyebrows in question.

"Oh!" Penelope claps excitedly. "Another secret mission!"

"Secret mission?" Paige asks, taking a seat on the coffee table in front of us. My eyes go to her legs, unable to stop myself. Yeah, she's not going fucking anywhere in that dress shirt or whatever the fuck you call it.

"Yeah, when you dress all pretty and go out with Aunt Mal, Daddy turns us into secret spies and we follow you around. Sometimes—" My hand flies over Pandora's mouth.

"I have the cutest spy outfit, Mommy. Do you wanna see it?" Penelope jumps up from the sofa, ready for a wardrobe change.

Paige narrows her eyes on me. I just shrug and let go of Pandora, who's giggling behind my hand, knowing full well what she's up to. That will teach me for not letting her have seconds of dessert.

"Girls, why don't you give Mommy a kiss and go get your pajamas on before you start movie night?"

Both girls do as Paige says, moving in for kisses and hugs.

"I'll make pancakes in the morning," she tells them.

"And bacon," Pandora adds.

"That's cute you think there wasn't going to be bacon," Paige tell her.

"I'm just double-checking." Pandora puts her hand on her hip, and I shake my head. Paige grabs her, pulling her toward her, and starts to tickle her. Penelope steps back like she doesn't want to get involved and chance wrinkling her dress.

"All right. Go change," Paige tells them, sending them off down the hallway. Her eyes narrow on me again. "Something you want to tell me?"

She barely finishes the sentence and I'm on her, picking her up and throwing her over my shoulder, turning to head down the other hallway that leads to our room. When we got a new place, I made sure the kids' rooms were on the other side of the house. My woman can get loud.

"Put me down, you caveman!" Her little fist bangs on my back.

"I have a feeling you wanted me to go caveman or you wouldn't be trying to leave the house like this." I smack her ass, then slide my hand up under the dress, feeling that she's got only a thong on.

She moans, proving my point. She wanted this reaction, and she's going to have to deal with it now.

When we get to our room, I kick the door shut, flipping the lock. I toss her on the bed and her legs fall open in invitation. I stare down at her. Fuck, how does she keep getting more beautiful? She's so fucking perfect it hurts to look at her sometimes.

"As I see it, you have two options," I tell her as I start unbuckling my belt and pulling it from my pants. "You can either let me mark your pussy and you'll wear my come all night, or you can change your outfit."

"Mark me," she says without any hesitation.

Her words come out breathy as I unbutton my pants. I pull my cock out, not bothering to take off my pants. I crawl over her and grab the front of the dress and pull. A ripping sound fills the room, and I give her an evil grin. The dress is destroyed. She gasps as she looks down at it.

"Oops. Guess you'll have to change, too," I say without a hint of guilt.

"You—"

I cut her off, taking her mouth in a deep kiss. I reach down and pull off her thong, the material no match for me. I want to get into her, and I'll destroy anything in my way. My cock easily finds her drenched opening, sliding right in. Her body arches into mine, and her moans of pleasure pour into my mouth as I thrust into her. Hard.

By the time I'm done with her, she'll be feeling me with every move she makes, and there won't be a part of her that doesn't smell like me.

EPILOGUE

Paige

Another thirteen years later...

"I DON'T LIKE IT, Paige. Not one goddamn bit."

Captain paces back and forth as I sip my latte and try not to smile. It's late morning and the girls have just left to get their nails and hair done for the prom tonight. I'm watching him wear a hole in the wooden floor when I hear Miles come in.

"What's he all worked up about?" Miles asks, leaning over and giving me a kiss on my cheek. He walks over to the coffeemaker, pours himself a mug and sits down beside me.

It's a bit comical, us sitting here watching Captain pace as we sip our coffees.

"Prom," I say by way of explanation.

"Ahh. I suppose Henry will be here tonight, too?"

At the mention of this, Captain stops and glares at Miles, but then goes back to pacing. I have to bite my lip to keep from laughing. He's so pissed Miles doesn't have to worry about having a girl and dealing with boys coming around.

The girls are so excited about tonight, but the three

of us have kept it kind of a secret from their dad. It's not that we didn't want to tell him, it's just that we were avoiding the inevitable fit he would throw. So this morning I gave the girls some money and sent them with their aunt Mallory for a day of beauty. I told them I would tell Captain while they were out and take one for the team.

"Yes, Mallory said he's coming over for pictures, and he's bringing a date."

Captain stops abruptly and turns to me. "Do the girls have dates?"

"Yes, Captain. I'm sorry, but they do." I can almost see the words hit him like a physical blow, and I don't know why, but I find it funny. "Pandora is taking Skyler and Jamie's son, Zion, and Penelope is taking Ethan from down the street."

"I knew that little fucker had been hanging around too much." Captain scowls.

"Well, he does cut your grass, right?" Miles asks, and I elbow him. He's stirring the pot and he knows it.

"That's not the point. And what about Zion? Who the hell said Pandora could date him?"

I get up and walk over to him, wrapping my arms around his waist. "You're so cute when you're angry, but it's their prom. You're going to have to give in, okay?"

"No. I don't have to do anything," Captain says, and I rest my head on his chest. After a moment, he wraps his arms around me and lets out a deep breath. "They're still so little."

"They're eighteen. And they'll both be off to college

in the fall. We have to learn to let go," I say, looking up at him. "And by 'we,' I mean you."

He growls, and it vibrates against me. I go up on my tiptoes and kiss him on the chin. But it does nothing to cheer him up.

"Come on, Captain. I'll take you out for ice cream after they leave."

"You're only saying that because you want it," he mumbles, and it's adorable how much he's pouting.

"You're right. But you like to give me what I want. And what I want is for the girls to go to prom with their dates and have a good time. I want them to have the experience without you coming in and taking over, or worse, sulking in the corner all night."

"Well, I feel bad for them," he says.

"Why?"

"Because they're going to be mad when I have to stand between them and their dates in all the pictures. Maybe I should change my shirt." He looks down at what he has on like he's seriously considering changing to be in their prom photos. "You know, I could actually take them. That way they won't have to have dates."

"Ryan," Miles says, and Captain looks over at him. "Remember, buddy, it's all about what we make them believe. Let them think they're going to have their fun tonight. I've got the car loaded up."

I look between the two of them, not understanding. But the smile that spreads across Captain's face is anything but innocent. Then it hits me. They're planning on sneaking out and following them. God help those poor girls tonight. And those boys if they lay a hand on them.

EPILOGUE

Ryan

Ten years after that...

"Paige, where are you?" I walk through the house trying to find her, but she's not answering. I checked the tracker on her phone on my way home and saw she was here. I walk back to the living room and then out to the back patio, thinking maybe she came outside. The sun has just set and we have reservations for dinner in an hour.

"Kitten? You out here?" I call.

I hear a splash and look over, seeing waves in the pool. Walking over to it, I get close to the edge, and then I see her. Right before I'm about to ask her what she's doing, she splashes me and starts laughing.

"You did not just do that," I say, looking down at her.

"Oh, I think I did. And what are you going to do about it?" She puts her arms on the edge of the pool and gives me a sassy grin.

"We've got dinner in an hour, kitten. Or did you want me to come in there and drag you out?"

She pushes away from the edge, and it's then I see

she's completely naked. The light in the bottom of the pool creates an aura around her. I feel myself harden, and I fist my hands at my sides.

"You gonna stand there like a goody-goody all night, Captain America? Or are you going to come get me?"

I see the way her breasts bounce in the water, her hard nipples begging for my mouth. She goes to the other side of the pool and grips the edge, arching her back. She's teasing me and she knows it.

"Be careful what you wish for, kitten," I tell her. I don't know why she thinks she has to bait me. She wants me somewhere, I'm fucking there. No matter where that is.

Keeping my eyes on her, I undo my belt, pushing my jeans down my thighs. She licks her lips, and I take my time, pulling off my shirt and then my boxer briefs. I go slow, letting her eyes roam all over me, seeing how hard I am for her, and letting her think of all the things this cock can do to her. All the possibilities I can offer. How I'll use it to pleasure her until she can no longer walk, and I have to carry her from the pool.

Walking to the steps, I move slowly and let the anticipation build. When I get to them, I take one step down and then sit on the edge. The dry stone is under my ass while my legs are stretched out in the water in front of me. There are three more shallow steps into the pool, but this seat is perfect right now.

"Get over here," I say, leaving no room for misinterpretation.

For a moment I think she's going to give me back a sassy response. Or maybe even refuse. But she looks at me, and I can see the want in her eyes. The need. Paige has always liked to play that she doesn't like to be told what to do, but when it comes to sex, I always lay the path, and that gets her off. We both know it.

We've been together so long that I know every thought that passes through her mind. The twins are all grown up and out of college. They've made good lives for themselves, and we don't have to worry. Well, worry as much. I think there's always a little of that in the back of any parent's mind. But Paige and I have stopped working, and we visit our island as often as we can. We spend most of our time traveling between there and home, and then to see the girls. Giving Paige the family she always wanted, giving me the one I never knew I wanted until her. I can't think of a better way to live my life than being with Paige. Our lives are slow, and we savor all the little things, but she loves to throw in some spice every now and then to keep me on my toes. I'd be lying if I said I didn't like it just as much as she does. She brings all the laughter to this family. The heart of us all.

She slowly swims over, putting on a little show of her own, baiting me as well, and when she gets to me, she looks down at my lap and then back up to my eyes.

"That's right, kitten. You're going to take care of it. Now come over here and climb on top."

"Maybe I want something else first." She licks her lips, and my cock throbs.

I grit my teeth as she slowly crawls up the steps. She exaggerates her movements and looks like a fucking sultry goddess coming to greet me. I'm only so strong, and I don't know how long I can keep from reaching out and grabbing her.

She runs her hands up my legs and to the tops of my thighs as she pushes them open and then kneels in the water in front of me. She looks like a seductress with sun lighting up her hair. She doesn't break eye contact as she leans down and opens her mouth, licking my cock from root to tip.

"Fuck…!" I hiss through clenched teeth and reach out, fisting her hair in one hand. "You've got thirty seconds before I pick you up and slam you down on my dick."

"Then I've got time," she teases, winking at me and then taking my cock into her mouth and to the back of her throat. The pure pleasure of it rocks through my body.

I moan at the feeling of her hot mouth on my cock, and I nearly come. I have to try to think of everything I can besides Paige on her knees in front of me, sucking me off and giving me pleasure.

"Twenty-two, twenty-three, twenty-four." I start counting because I don't know what else to do. I'm dying as the slick heat of her tongue works around my thick cock. Then she sucks the pearl of come at the end, and I die.

"That's it! Time's up!" I half shout as I pull her from her knees and onto my lap. Needing to be inside her. I want to come in her pussy, not her mouth.

I've got her legs spread, and I thrust my cock into her warm channel before she can even begin to protest. I hold her neck as I kiss her, tasting some of my prerelease on her. The flavor of her makes me moan, and I use my free hand to grip her hip.

I hold her steady as I move her on top of me, making her pussy milk my cock.

"Fuck, you know how to push my buttons," I say, thrusting in and out of her.

"I like when you push mine," she moans, pressing her hard nipples into my chest.

I let go of her neck and move my hand between us and pet her clit. I know exactly how she likes it, and I don't play with giving her what she wants. I'm already so close to the edge I could go off any second, and I need her with me.

"You're out here swimming naked by yourself because you know that pisses me off. Then you splash me and pretend to try to get away." She lets out a cry of pleasure as I pinch her clit. "You sucked my cock when you know exactly what that does to me. You pushed me, kitten, and now you're going to come all over me. I want your pussy to get me off." I lean forward and lick her neck, then suck the tender place just below her ear. I want to leave a mark on her because I know she'll love it tomorrow.

"Ryan. Fuck, that's it."

Her pussy contracts around my cock as her orgasm rolls through her. Her legs tense on either side of me, and I hold her in place as she tries to fight it. I don't stop rubbing her clit as she screams out my name and the wave of pleasure hits her hard and fast.

My cock throbs inside her, and I release, giving her exactly what she was after tonight. She wanted me to mark her and make her mine, no matter how she tries to deny it.

When we're both coming down and catching our breath, I rest my forehead against hers and smile. "I'm guessing we're skipping the dinner reservations tonight?"

She looks up at me and gives me a wicked smile. "Guess you'll just have to give me something else to eat."

I pick her up and carry her into the pool, kissing her neck and breasts. She's my strong, sassy woman, but she melts into a puddle of molten sugar every time I hold her. Later, when we finally get out of the pool and I've fed her, we make slow, sweet love. She promises never to go skinny-dipping without me again, but we both know that's a lie.

And we are both okay with that.

* * * * *

BONUS CHAPTER

Ryan

When Ryan meets Paige...

I RUN MY hands through my short hair, grabbing a fistful of it and giving it a little pull. I'm trying to get myself under control. I've been waiting for this moment for what feels like an eternity. Fuck, maybe my whole life. It's been weeks since I first saw her picture, weeks before I could finally track her down. And days since she spoke to Miles, agreeing to take the job of watching over Mallory.

I don't know if I should be proud of myself for coming up with the plan for her to cover Mallory, or pissed. She'd be away from her father, no longer jumping from shelter to shelter. She'd be put up somewhere where she could grow safely, but so far from me. Not easily within my grasp.

Thinking about the shelters makes me clench my jaw. The first night I'd finally found her, she was walking into one. Hoodie pulled over her head, hiding all that auburn hair. Her backpack strapped tight to her, holding everything she owned. She looked so young, but she carried herself with strength. Some little punk tried to grab a hold of her, and she punched him right in the mouth. I smiled at that show of fire. It was nothing compared to what I did to the little prick after she disappeared inside. It was safe to say he wouldn't be fucking with her again. No, no one would. She was going to be sent to a safe haven away from the dirt Miles and I were about to crawl through.

My phone goes off, breaking me from my thoughts. I pull it out and read the message.

She's coming up

I let out a breath of relief that she's here. Fucking hell, I was still scared she might make a run for it. That she might change her mind about taking Miles's deal to watch over Mallory, and I wouldn't be there to stop her.

Normally I tail her. Have been doing it for weeks, but sometimes I have to meet with Miles. Or like now, I have to be in my office. So I had to put someone on her when I couldn't be there. The same guy I planned to send with her to school. There was no way I could make it without eyes on her constantly. If it was up to me, I'd change my mind and drag her away from all of it instead of doing what needs to do be done for everyone. But if I know one thing, it's that Paige hates her father and she wants to make him pay. I want to give her that, and it means helping Miles and making sure Paige isn't around to get any of her father's wrath when we start to make his world crumble around him.

The door swings open as she walks in. She doesn't even bother to knock as the door hits the wall. I'm on my feet instantly as she strolls into the room. Her shoulders are back like she's ready for a fight, and a smile pulls at the corners of my lips.

She's wearing a sweater today, with no hood hiding her. Instead, every part of her softness is revealed to me. No matter how hard she tries to hide it, it's right there in her face. Her creamy skin highlighting the little freckles on her upturned nose. Her bright blue eyes shining even brighter against her cool skin.

"I'm here. Let's do this thing." She puts her hands on her hips, not coming any closer to my desk, but standing in the middle of the room. This is the nearest I've ever been to her. I need more. I want to know what she smells like. Brand it into my brain before she's once again too far away from me.

I give her a smile, trying to hide the fact that I want to leap over my desk and drag her to the floor. That I want to do all the things I've been thinking about doing to her for the past few weeks. It would take me months to get to every one of my fantasies, and by then I'd have created new ones.

"Have a seat." I wave to the chair in front of my desk.

"No, I'm good," she shoots back, making no move to come forward. I take a calm breath and move around the desk myself. I can tell she wants to take a step back.

"Ryan." I reach my hand out. I should probably tell

her to call me Justice. Everyone on Miles's staff does, but I want to hear my name on her lips.

"Ryan," she says, narrowing her eyes at my hand. "I'm Paige."

Her palm meets mine, and I wrap my fingers around hers, feeling her soft, delicate skin. She gives a hard squeeze, trying to assert her power, and I have to fight another smile. This little kitten has claws. I like that. I let my finger run along her wrist and soothe the sparks in her eyes.

She pulls her hand from mine. "So," she snaps.

I go back to my desk and grab the folder. "You will check in with me twice a day with full reports on your and Mallory's activities."

"Mine?" Her face scrunches, like she doesn't get why I need to know what she's doing every day.

I want to tell her, *Because I don't think I can breathe without knowing.*

"Yes, yours, too." She opens her mouth to say something else, but I cut her off. "It's not open to negotiation."

Her mouth slams shut, and she shoots me a look that I'm sure would kill lesser men. But I'm not a lesser man. I'm her man, and all it does is make my cock even harder than it was when she walked into the room.

"Sometimes by telephone, and on occasion we can FaceTime." I reach into my pocket, pulling out the phone. "This will be on you at all times. There is no exception. I text or call you, you always respond or answer."

"What if I'm in class? What if—"

"I'll know your schedule. I won't call then," I tell her.

I watch her jaw clench, but she doesn't say anything. I hand her the file.

"Everything you need is in here. You leave today." I have to force the words out of my mouth.

She grabs the folder, and I don't want to let it go. Her eyes meet mine. Fuck. I can't do this. Something inside me is shaking, trying to break free.

I keep chanting to myself that this is what is best for her, that I have to let her go. This is the only way to free her from her father. I have to so that I can have her. I have to prove I'm worthy of her. She's full of so much fire and passion, but also a sadness she tries to hide with anger.

I release the folder, and she pulls it to her chest, still staring into my eyes. I wonder if she knows she belongs to me. That I belong to her. I can't help myself, and I reach out, touching her cheek softly. There's only a heartbeat of a moment between us, but in that time it's enough. Enough to last me until I can see her again. I expect her to recoil, or to have a sharp comeback. But instead she blinks away our connection as if it never happened. I drop my hand, yet it's still tingling like I placed it on a hot stove.

Then she turns and leaves without so much as a goodbye. I follow her out of my office and watch her get on the elevator. When she's inside, I turn, running toward the stairs, taking them as fast as I can. When I fly out at the bottom, I see her leaving the building. I quietly trail her until she stops, looking in a window at something. She stands there for a long moment, longer than I expect her to, before shaking her head and moving down the street. I carefully trail behind her until I see my guy at the crosswalk up ahead. He nods at me before following her, taking over his job as her secret guard.

I watch her go until I can no longer see even the blurry shape of her silhouette. The longing in my chest is a hollow ache.

When I can't stand there any longer, I turn back and go to where she stopped, curiosity getting the best of me. When I look up at the sign, I see it's a jewelry store, and I glance at the display window. My eyes scan the items and stop when I see it. There, nestled in velvet, is a ruby ring almost as beautiful as she is. I take one look, and I know that's it. That's the ring I'm going to put on her finger, or die trying.

ACKNOWLEDGMENTS

ONCE AGAIN, THANK YOU to Carina Press for taking a chance on the hot mess that is Alexa Riley…. Especially the ladies in the marketing department! You guys always made us feel like celebrities! Big hugs to our editor Angela James! You pushed us to be our best, and although we complained, we secretly love you for it. Thank you to our agent Laura Bradford for always making us laugh…and for all the food pics you post on Twitter. They give us life. Thank you to our publicist Neda Amini at Ardent Prose for always getting our name out there, and telling everyone how great we are.

Huge thank-you to our beta readers, Gia Paar and Polly Matthews. Your words of encouragement and excitement helped so much…but pointing out errors gets you the non-sprinkled doughnuts.

To our powerhouse entourage, Jeanette, Jen and Eagle, we couldn't live without you guys and we owe you our firstborn. Literally, take them. J. Peanut Butter Shawty, you make us shine like the dime pieces we are, and we will literally never do a signing without you. We love you as much as you love your hoops. Jen, you've been a devoted mentor and friend for reasons we still can't understand. Seriously, why do you hang out with us? Thank you for giving us the vault and pretty face creams. Eagle, you've been the backbone of AR since way before day one. You're our number one ride or die OG, and you can never leave us. No matter how hard you try. Thank you for believing in us.

And as always, thank you to our husbands. You've watched us work, worry, and whine and most of the time you've been okay with it. Thank you both for believing that the two of us could do anything, and helping us make that possible. You've supported us through it all and even though we neglected the laundry, dinner, the kids, you guys…you both still manage to make us feel like we can conquer the world. We promise to make it up to you on a beach somewhere!

The first full-length novel from
USA TODAY **BESTSELLING AUTHOR**

ALEXA RILEY

A strong, possessive man finds the woman of his
dreams, and takes fate into his hands. He'll do
everything to make her his.

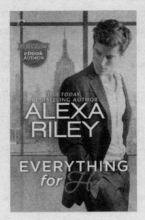

"Alexa Riley crafts a deliciously sexy…story, complete with
dark and manipulative undertones." —*Fresh Fiction*

Available now, wherever books and ebooks are sold!

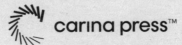

CarinaPress.com
Facebook.com/CarinaPress
Twitter.com/CarinaPress

CARAR4522

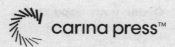

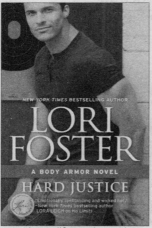